To Neil & Andrea,
'Fortunate Voyagers'
Lachie, 2. Dec 2021

> 'We are all travellers
> in the wilderness of this world,
> and the best that we find is an honest friend.
> He is a fortunate voyager who finds many.'
>
> – ROBERT LOUIS STEVENSON –

Epigraph

SIR PAUL McCARTNEY

When I was a young boy in Liverpool, my Auntie Dilys
gave me a copy of *Treasure Island* which I very much
enjoyed reading. Robert Louis Stevenson's style and
sense of adventure transported me to the land of
Long John Silver, Ben Gunn and 'Jim Lad'.
It was a great escape from the dark and dreary
British winter and I remember it
with fondness to this day.

FORTUNATE VOYAGER

A CELEBRATION OF ROBERT LOUIS STEVENSON

— LIMITED EDITION —

Commissioned by
The Robert Louis Stevenson Club
in Celebration of its Centenary

-m-
MERCHISTON PUBLISHING

— LIMITED EDITION —

First published in 2021 by Merchiston Publishing
10 Colinton Rd, Edinburgh, EH10 5DT
by MSc Publishing staff and students at Edinburgh Napier University
Avril Gray, David McCluskey,
Marina Domínguez Salgado, Lorn Fraser, Daniel Gilbert, Kylie Haggen, Grace Harley, Nina Joynson, Francesca Lombardo, Jack Lowe, Lauren McFarlane, Alastair Oates, Maria Rasinkangas, Hannah Scott, Frances Tappin

In collaboration with the RLS Club

Epigraph © Sir Paul McCartney, 2021
Celebrating a Centenary and *About RLS* © RLS Club, 2021
Introduction © Nicola Sturgeon, 2021

Individual pieces remain in the copyright of their respective authors © 2021:

Meet Nurse for a Poetic Child! © Dr Lachlan Munro; *Land of Counterpane* © Gillean Somerville-Arjat; *RLS and the Speculative Society of Edinburgh* © Professor David W.R. Purdie; *Neither Saint nor Sinner* © Jeremy Hodges; *Stevenson in Time* © Professor Barry Menikoff; *Ordinary Case of RLS and RLS* © Kevin MacNeil; *Remembering RLS* © Professor Adrian Poole; *The Mystery of the Velvet Coat* © Alanna Knight; *How I Came to Robert Louis Stevenson* © Ailene S. Hunter; *Stevenson the Humanitarian* © Peter Shaw Fraser; *RLS Took Me Hostage* © Stuart Campbell; *Growing up with the Name* © Professor Robert-Louis Abrahamson; *Encountering Robert Louis Stevenson* © Professor Joseph Farrell; *A Friend for Life* © James Robertson; *The Taste of Coffee and the Prose of Stevenson* © Professor Richard Dury; *Drink Deep of the Comforts of Shelter* © Rabbi Rita Leonard; *RLS and MS* © Alan Taylor; *Robert Louis Stevenson, Joseph Conrad and Ford Madox Ford: Playing the 'Sedulous Ape'* © Professor Linda Dryden; *My Desert Island Choice* © Val McDermid; *The First Book I Read* © Michael Morpurgo; *Reading 'Markheim'* © Professor Ian Campbell; *Stevenson and Dostoevsky* © Dr Tom Hubbard; *My Debt to Stevenson* © Ian Rankin; *In Search of Jekyll and Hyde* © Anthony O'Neill; *To Robert Louis Stevenson, a Thank You* © Lin Anderson; *Dramatising Stevenson for Radio* © Catherine Czerkawska; *The Hoose O'Shaws* © Isobel Reid; *Sing Me a Song of a Lad that is Gone* © David C. Clapham SSC; *Stevenson and Weir* © Sarah Purser; *Writing RLS* © John Purser; *An Unfinished Masterpiece* © Paul H. Scott; *Stevenson: the First Global Author* © Professor Penny Fielding; *Stevenson the Ubiquitous* © Ian Nimmo; *The Resident Curator* © Nicholas Rankin; *Re-reading Robert Louis Stevenson's South Sea Tales* © Jane Rogers; *Literature, Travels, Friends, and Life* © Kumiko Koiwa; *A Stevenson Haiku* © Nigel Planer; *Walking with RLS* © Gail Simmons; *Visiting the World in Stevenson's Way* © Christian Brochier; *Stevenson and James Watt in France* © Hervé Gournay; *From the Cévennes Diary and Poems, 2008* © Jim Bertram; *Brief Encounter* © David Reid; *Following Stevenson* © Lord Stewart; *Living with Louis* © Christopher Rush; *From An Inland Voyage Diary and Poems, 2011* © Jim Bertram; *Stevenson has a Home in Monterey* © Monica Hudson, Lindy Perez and Elizabeth Anderson; *Two Poems* © Elaine Parks; *RLS: Writer in Eternal Residence* © Professor Alan Riach; *From the North American Diary and Poems, 2013* © Jim Bertram; *Tusitala Still Matters to Samoans, after 130 Years* © James Winegar; *Lord, Teach Us the Lessons: Revisiting the Vailima Prayers* © Neil Adam; *A Beautiful Adventure* © John Shedden; *Robert Louis Stevenon is Still with Us* © Christian Brochier; *A Far Cry from Edinburgh* © Eileen Dunlop; *My Father and RLS: A Life in Parallel* © Magnus Linklater; *RLS – a Living Experience in my Upbringing and Adult World* © Dr Cathy Ratcliff; *For We are Very Lucky: Recollections of 17 Heriot Row* © John Macfie; *Yonder is Auldhame* © Cynthia Stephens; *Curating Stevenson* © Elaine Greig; *Not 'Watching the Detectives'* © Martin White; *RLS – Scotland's Greatest Writer?* © Craig Robertson

All contributions within this title are published under the Creative Commons
Attribution-NonCommercial-NoDerivative Works 3.0 Unported License

Cover Images © The National Galleries of Scotland & the British Library
Cover & Book Design © Merchiston Publishing
RLS Pencil Portrait *(opposite)* © Professor Linda Dryden

Generously supported by The Edward Clark Trust

ISBN: 978-1-911524-03-8

Printed by Bell & Bain Ltd, Glasgow, G46 7UQ
Typeset in Adobe Caslon Pro 10.5/13

'The most beautiful adventures are not those we go to seek'
– *Robert Louis Stevenson,* An Inland Voyage –

Drawing by Professor Linda Dryden

Celebrating a Centenary

THE ROBERT LOUIS STEVENSON CLUB was founded in 1920 with the aim of promoting interest in the life and works of one of the world's best-loved authors. Many were still living who had met and known Louis – pronounced 'Lewis', as all his friends called him – and one of the Club's first tasks was to pull together their memories into a book, *I Can Remember Robert Louis Stevenson*, edited by Rosaline Masson.

In 2020, the Club decided to mark its Centenary by drawing together contributions to an anthology from a wide variety of Stevenson lovers. This time it took a team of five – David Reid, Gillean Somerville-Arjat, Linda Dryden, Ian Nimmo and Jeremy Hodges – to complete the task, persuading some 60 contributors worldwide to give generously of their time and literary skills. They range from the First Minister of Scotland and a former Beatle to some of today's best writers of fiction, experts in the field of Stevenson Studies, and people from all walks of life who have been inspired by Stevenson the man and the wide variety of writing he has left us.

Stevenson was the most charismatic of authors, fortunate in finding friends everywhere as he roamed the globe, and many continue to fall in love with him today. The RLS Club has been delighted to share Louis as a friend with MSc Publishing staff and students at Edinburgh Napier University, whose expertise, enthusiasm and commitment have made this commemorative publication possible.

The Club continues to further interest in Stevenson and his works with a programme of lectures, readings, walks, visits at home and abroad, and participation in the annual RLS Day festivities in Edinburgh.

For more information visit http://robert-louis-stevenson.org/rls-club

About Robert Louis Stevenson

BORN IN EDINBURGH on 13 November 1850, Robert Louis Stevenson had a privileged childhood as the only son of doting parents, the lighthouse engineer Thomas Stevenson and his wife Margaret Isabella Balfour. Yet it was a childhood marred by illness that led to frequent confinements in bed, cared for by his nurse Alison Cunningham, known to her young charge as 'Cummy'. For many adults, childhood becomes a distant memory, but RLS never lost the ability to see life through the eyes of a child and to express it vividly in the poems that became *A Child's Garden of Verses*.

At 16, Stevenson matriculated at the University of Edinburgh to study subjects that would prepare him to follow in the footsteps of his father and grandfather as a lighthouse engineer. He had no great interest in engineering and frequently absented himself from lectures to roam the streets of Edinburgh and follow his own curriculum with a view to becoming an author. Eventually his parents accepted his choice of career but insisted he should study law to give him a profession to fall back on.

In all, Stevenson would spend eight years as a student, including an unplanned gap year when his confession that he no longer believed in the Christian religion led to traumatic rows with his parents and a nervous breakdown, resulting in his being 'ordered south' by a doctor to recuperate alone at Menton on the Riviera. Much though Stevenson loved Edinburgh, and would long for his home city in exile, he also spent some dark and unhappy times there, from which 'the Spec' – the university debating society he attended with his friend Charles Baxter offered some respite. Otherwise he sought release on walking tours away from Edinburgh, written up as stylish essays.

In 1876, Robert Louis Stevenson's interest in the new sport of canoeing led to a trip with his friend Sir Walter Simpson from Antwerp, through the canals and rivers of Belgium and France to the village of Grèz-sur-Loing on the edge of the Forest of Fontainebleau, where RLS met up with his artist friends and first encountered Fanny Osbourne, the American woman who would become his wife. The trip would be written up as Stevenson's first book, *An Inland Voyage*.

Every weir or lock along the route meant a 'portage' for Stevenson and Simpson, who had to haul their small but heavy wooden craft out of the water and carry them to the next stretch. At one such portage they had the chance to admire the engineering skills of James Watt at the Hachette lock house on the river Sambre by Maroilles in Northern France – where a new project celebrates the local connection with two Scottish geniuses, literary and mechanical.

In 1878, Fanny Osbourne's husband insisted on her return to California, leaving Stevenson bereft. Unable to face life without her in Edinburgh, he set off on his most ambitious hiking tour yet that would become *Travels with a Donkey in the Cévennes*. This pioneering travel book set the standard for generations of travel writers and is still an inspiration for the thousands who follow in his footsteps across the Cévennes today, with or without a donkey, staying along the way at various French hostelries 'sur le chemin de Robert Louis Stevenson'.

In 1879, apparently in response to a distressed message from Fanny Osbourne in California, Stevenson left Edinburgh suddenly without informing his parents of his intentions and at Greenock boarded the SS *Devonia*, bound for New York. From there he took an emigrant train across the Wild West and, in poor health, arrived in Monterey where Fanny was now living apart from her husband who remained in San Francisco. Getting a divorce proved a long and complicated business and Stevenson spent four months in Monterey, struggling to make ends meet while waiting for the day when Fanny would be free to marry. Today the town and the old adobe house where he stayed is home to the thriving Monterey Stevenson Club which keeps his memory alive.

On leaving Monterey, Stevenson spent time in San Francisco where he suffered his first chest haemorrhage. He was nursed back to health by Fanny and her sister and, following a 'marriage in extremis', was taken to convalesce on honeymoon in a disused miners' bunkhouse at the abandoned Silverado silver mine near St Helena.

Despite several close calls with 'Bluidy Jack', as Stevenson called the illness that plagued him with life-threatening haemorrhages, his marriage to Fanny lasted nearly 15 years. It was at times a turbulent relationship but never gave him cause to regret his choice of wife, and Fanny cared for him diligently though years of health-imposed exile, from Switzerland and the South of France to Bournemouth, Saranac in New York State and ultimately the South Seas. In Hawai'i he visited the leper colony of Molokai and learned of the selfless missionary work there by Father Damien, whom he later defended against slurs on the priest's character in a bitter open letter to the Rev Charles McEwen Hyde of Honolulu.

The Stevensons settled eventually in Samoa, where they made their last home in a wooden colonial mansion on an estate called Vailima, where RLS was working on his last great novel *Weir of Hermiston* when he suffered a stroke and died shortly after his 44th birthday. He and Fanny now share a grave 'under the wide and starry sky' on the summit of Mount Vaea.

Contents

Epigraph SIR PAUL MCCARTNEY	iii
Celebrating a Centenary	ix
About Robert Louis Stevenson	xi
Introduction NICOLA STURGEON FIRST MINISTER OF SCOTLAND	xxi

— THE MAN —

Meet Nurse for a Poetic Child! DR LACHLAN MUNRO	3
Land of Counterpane GILLEAN SOMERVILLE-ARJAT	9
RLS and the Speculative Society of Edinburgh PROFESSOR DAVID W.R. PURDIE	13
Neither Saint Nor Sinner JEREMY HODGES	18

Stevenson in Time PROFESSOR BARRY MENIKOFF	24
Ordinary Case of RLS and RLS KEVIN MACNEIL	29
Remembering RLS PROFESSOR ADRIAN POOLE	34
The Mystery of the Velvet Coat ALANNA KNIGHT	39
How I Came to Robert Louis Stevenson AILENE S. HUNTER	42
Stevenson the Humanitarian PETER SHAW FRASER	45
RLS Took Me Hostage STUART CAMPBELL	47
Growing up with the Name PROFESSOR ROBERT-LOUIS ABRAHAMSON	51
Encountering Robert Louis Stevenson PROFESSOR JOSEPH FARRELL	55

— THE WRITER —

A Friend for Life JAMES ROBERTSON	65
The Taste of Coffee and the Prose of Stevenson PROFESSOR RICHARD DURY	70
'Drink Deep of the Comforts of Shelter' RABBI RITA LEONARD	74

RLS and MS ALAN TAYLOR	77
Robert Louis Stevenson, Joseph Conrad and Ford Madox Ford: Playing the 'Sedulous Ape' PROFESSOR LINDA DRYDEN	82
My Desert Island Choice VAL MCDERMID	88
The First Book I Read MICHAEL MORPURGO	90
Reading 'Markheim' PROFESSOR IAN CAMPBELL	96
Stevenson and Dostoevsky DR TOM HUBBARD	102
My Debt to Stevenson IAN RANKIN	108
In Search of Jekyll and Hyde ANTHONY O'NEILL	110
To Robert Louis Stevenson, a Thank You LIN ANDERSON	113
Dramatising Stevenson for Radio CATHERINE CZERKAWSKA	115
The Hoose O'Shaws ISOBEL REID	120
Sing Me a Song of a Lad that is Gone DAVID C. CLAPHAM SSC	123
Stevenson and Weir SARAH PURSER	128

Writing RLS 132
JOHN PURSER

An Unfinished Masterpiece 136
PAUL H. SCOTT

Stevenson: the First Global Author 140
PROFESSOR PENNY FIELDING

Stevenson the Ubiquitous 145
IAN NIMMO

The Resident Curator 153
NICHOLAS RANKIN

Re-reading Robert Louis Stevenson's
South Sea Tales 159
JANE ROGERS

Literature, Travels, Friends, and Life 165
KUMIKO KOIWA

— THE TRAVELLER —

A Stevenson Haiku 171
NIGEL PLANER

Walking with RLS 172
GAIL SIMMONS

Visiting the World in Stevenson's Way 177
CHRISTIAN BROCHIER

Stevenson and James Watt in France 181
HERVÉ GOURNAY

From the Cévennes Diary and Poems, 2008 JIM BERTRAM	185
Brief Encounter DAVID REID	193
Following Stevenson LORD STEWART	197
Living with Louis CHRISTOPHER RUSH	204
From An Inland Voyage Diary and Poems, 2011 JIM BERTRAM	212
Stevenson has a Home in Monterey MONICA HUDSON, LINDY PEREZ & ELIZABETH ANDERSON	215
Two Poems ELAINE PARKS	219
RLS: Writer in Eternal Residence PROFESSOR ALAN RIACH	222
From the North American Diary and Poems, 2013 JIM BERTRAM	228
Tusitala Still Matters to Samoans, after 130 Years JAMES WINEGAR	231
Lord, Teach Us the Lessons: Revisiting the Vailima Prayers NEIL ADAM	237

A Beautiful Adventure 241
JOHN SHEDDEN

Robert Louis Stevenson is Still with Us 246
CHRISTIAN BROCHIER

— THE SCOT —

A Far Cry from Edinburgh 251
EILEEN DUNLOP

My Father and RLS: a Life in Parallel 257
MAGNUS LINKLATER

RLS: A Living Experience in My
Upbringing and Adult World 263
DR CATHY RATCLIFF

For We are Very Lucky:
Recollections of 17 Heriot Row 267
JOHN MACFIE

Yonder is Auldhame 275
CYNTHIA STEPHENS

Curating Stevenson 280
ELAINE GREIG

Not 'Watching the Detectives' 284
MARTIN WHITE

RLS: Scotland's Greatest Writer? 287
CRAIG ROBERTSON

Introduction

NICOLA STURGEON
FIRST MINISTER OF SCOTLAND

WHEN US SENATOR JOHN McCAIN died in August 2018, the final page of his memoir was widely circulated on social media. It was a moving piece of prose, in which he reflected on the end of his 'happy life lived in imperfect service to a country made of ideals'. One thing which struck me was that the lines chosen by McCain as an epilogue to his memoir were from Robert Louis Stevenson's 'Requiem':

Home is the sailor, home from sea,
And the hunter home from the hill.

It was an unexpected but very poignant reminder that the work of Robert Louis Stevenson still – more than a hundred years after his death – holds a place in the hearts of millions of people around the world.

There are good reasons for that. Stevenson was a master of a range of work – from children's verse to the psychological novel. He was also – like so many great writers – both rooted in the land of his birth, and truly internationalist in his outlook. He travelled far and wide around the world, and his works include modern versions of the *Arabian Nights* – but many of his greatest works are set in or inspired by Scotland.

My personal favourite of his works is *Strange Case of Dr Jekyll and Mr Hyde*, which I remember reading as a student. Although set in London, it is clearly influenced by Stevenson's Edinburgh background, and by historical figures such as William Brodie. It is both an insightful exploration of people's capacity for good and evil, and an absolutely gripping read. As a result, it highlights many of the qualities which have made Stevenson so revered by generations of readers.

Strange Case of Dr Jekyll and Mr Hyde is a novel with its roots in Scottish literary tradition – especially the work of James Hogg. However, it has also exerted a strong influence on many of Scotland's most prominent modern authors. Ian Rankin has spoken of Stevenson's influence on his decision to take up crime fiction. Many reviewers of Graeme Macrae Burnet's superb *His Bloody Project* compared it to Stevenson's work. Alasdair Gray and Val McDermid are among the many other contemporary novelists I admire who have praised Stevenson's work – in fact, Val McDermid has cited *Treasure Island* as the work she wishes she had written.

Even when I am not reading people who have been inspired by Stevenson, I get reminders of his legacy on a regular basis. The First Minister's residence in Edinburgh is a few hundred metres from the house on Heriot Row where Stevenson grew up. And outside the Scottish Parliament, at the foot of Edinburgh's Canongate, there is a wall which is engraved with quotations. One of those quotations is from Stevenson's *Songs of Travel*: 'Bright is the ring of words.' It appeals to me as a very simple summary of the joy and optimism which people can take from songs, poems and narratives. And it encapsulates the pleasure which Stevenson has brought to so many people across the world. His words have rung brightly for well over a century now – and they will continue to do so for as long as people love stories.

Nicola Sturgeon

Nicola Sturgeon studied law, worked as a solicitor, and became a Member of the Scottish Parliament in 1999. Since 2007 she has held several government positions, including Deputy First Minister of Scotland. She became SNP Leader and First Minister in November 2014. Nicola lives in Glasgow with her husband, Peter, and her hobby is reading.

— STEVENSON —
THE MAN

Meet Nurse for a Poetic Child!
DR LACHLAN MUNRO

'They may talk about heredity, but if I inherited any literary talent it was from Cummy. It was she who gave me the first feeling for literature'
– *'Cummy': The Nurse of Robert Louis Stevenson*, Lord Guthrie –

'She was more patient than I can suppose of an angel; hours together she would help console me in my paroxysms; and I remember with particular directness, how she would lift me out of bed, and take me, rolled in blankets, to the window, whence I might look forth into the blue night starred with street-lamps, and see where the gas still burned behind the windows of other sick rooms'.
– *Memoirs*, RLS –

'Alison was a very dear woman, very Scots, an innate Covenanter'.
– *I Can Remember Robert Louis Stevenson*, Walter Blaikie –

NO BOOK ON STEVENSON can be written without reference to Alison Cunningham, his childhood nurse, the woman known affectionately to all as 'Cummy'. Stevenson's mother, Margaret, who had a weak constitution that her son inherited, was prone to taking to her bed – ill-equipped to care for the fragile 'Lew'. Cummy, however, from in the mining village of Torryburn across the Forth, the only daughter among five brothers, was cut from tougher cloth. Born in 1822 on the upper floor at 53 Main Street, which still stands, Cummy worked as a dressmaker in

MEET NURSE FOR A POETIC CHILD!

Dunfermline, before moving to Edinburgh, aged 27, where she was nurse to young Walter Blaikie. In adulthood, Blaikie, who was related to Stevenson on his mother's side, became a distinguished art printer with the Edinburgh publishers T & A Constable, and was a close friend of 'Cummie's' more famous charge. Many years later, the 28 volume Edinburgh Edition of Stevenson's works was published under Blaikie's supervision.

Cummy was not Stevenson's first nurse – two had left, and another was found drinking gin in a pub with baby 'Lew' lying asleep on the bar. Cummy, however, took his precarious life into her charge when he was 18 months old and cooled his fevers, eased his hacking, exhausting coughs, his pneumonia, his insomnia, his stomach troubles, his deliriums, and assuaged his fears. She joined in his games, sang and whistled hymns and old Scots songs. She took him for jaunts in his perambulator around Edinburgh, and in the evening taught him how to read the easier passages from Fenimore Cooper and Ballantyne, and recounted the legends and lore of her native Fife. Above all, she encouraged him to write his own stories, giving him a love of words and their sounds. Although she believed that theatre was the work of the devil, her own performances were dramatic, reading the works of others as a poet would scarcely dare to read his own, gloating on the rhythm, dwelling with delight on the assonances and alliterations.

Cummy could be warm, loving, and full of fun, but she also put the fear of God into 'her laddie', fuelling his nightmares as well as calming them. His parents were both devout, but just below Cummy's motherly exterior burned a fierce, tough-minded Calvinist. Her antecedents were New Licht Anti-Burghers, uncompromising in matters of faith, and Stevenson in his essay 'Nuits Blanches' would write: 'That I was eminently religious, there can be no doubt. I had an extreme terror of Hell, implanted in me, I suppose, by my good nurse, which used to haunt me terribly on stormy nights.'

Cummy recorded that she had read the Bible to the young Stevenson three or four times, and to reinforce his religious orthodoxy she drummed the Shorter Catechism into him, and told him tales of the Covenanters, and Scotland's brutal Killing Times. His mother recorded with great satisfaction the frequency of his church-going, and before he was three, his favourite game was 'making a church'.

Cummy proudly recorded one such church visit in her diary:

> Lew came home from the English Church in a great way, because, he said, the minister was preaching against Presbyterianism. No wonder he was angry! 'What,' said Lew with some warmth, 'an English clergyman preaching against a Church for which our forefathers have bled and died! How dare he!' So dear Lew did not go back to the church in the afternoon.'

There is little doubt that Cummy's tales of religion, heroism, sacrifice, and superstition influenced his vulnerable and fertile mind in the longer term, for both good and ill. Stevenson himself thought this influence was considerable, as have his many biographers. One such, Stephen Gwynn, believed it was these Covenanting stories, and Cummy's reading of Presbyterian tracts that gave Stevenson his distinctive voice:

> When in *Kidnapped* and *Catriona* and *The Master of Ballantrae* Stevenson had to recount dramatic happenings through the imagined person of a serious-minded Scot, the speech which he chose, the words and the turn of phrase, the whole idiom of the mind, took colour from those far-off readings. His ear was attuned from the first to the solemn and long-drawn cadences of 17th-century Scottish prose.

Meet Nurse for a Poetic Child!

Stevenson himself wrote in his 'Rosa Quo Locorum':

> The Lord is gone up with a shout, and God with the sound of a trumpet' – memorial version, I know not where to find the text – rings still in my ear from my first childhood, and perhaps with something of my nurse's accent.

The result of such an extreme upbringing can go either way, and as often as not, a steady course of Bible study in childhood can remove any trace of religious belief in the adult, but with Stevenson it went further, and he became drawn to sin rather than dissuaded by it. In his 'Memoirs of Himself', he recalled Cummy's sometimes negative effects on his childhood:

> The idea of sin… far from repelling, soon exerts an attraction on young minds… until the child grows to think nothing more glorious than to be struck dead in the very act of some surprising wickedness… And generally, the principal effect of this false, common doctrine of sin, is to put a point on lust.

What Cummy thought of these words is not recorded. Stevenson would eventually rebel against everything he had been brought up to worship and respect, but he could not escape entirely, and Cummy's influence was more than offset by the debt he owed her for his survival and his art. He wrote to her in 1873:

> If you should happen to think that you might have had a child of your own, and that it was hard you should have spent so many years taking care of someone else's prodigal, just think this: you have been for a great deal in my life; you have made much that there is in me, just as surely as if you had conceived me; and there are sons who are more ungrateful to their mothers than I am to you. For I am not ungrateful,

my dear Cummy, and it is with a very sincere emotion that
I write myself Your little boy.

No greater thanks could have been paid than his dedication to Cummy of his most beloved work, *A Child's Garden of Verses*, which also contains this poem:

For the long nights you lay awake
And watched for my unworthy sake:
For your most comfortable hand
That led me through the uneven land:
For all the story-books you read:
For all the pains you comforted:

For all you pitied, all you bore,
In sad and happy days of yore:–
My second Mother, my first Wife
The angel in my infant life –
From the sick child, now well and old,
Take, nurse, the little book you hold!

And grant it, Heaven, that all who read
May find as dear a nurse at need,
And every child who lists my rhyme,
In the bright, fireside, nursery clime,
May hear it in as kind a voice
As made my childish days rejoice!

Stevenson, however, paid Cummy a more subtle literary compliment in his adventure story *Kidnapped*. The young serving girl who rescues David Balfour and Alan Breck and takes them across the Forth was named Alison Hastie, after Cummy's mother, whose grave can be found at Old Crombie Kirk near Torryburn. Though Alison remained anonymous in *Kidnapped*, in due course she was named in its sequel, *Catriona*, where it transpires that she has become a nurse in the House of Shaws, bringing up Stevenson's imaginary forebears. On July 16, 1886, Stevenson wrote this dedication to her:

> My dear Cummy, Herewith goes my new book in which you will find some places that you know: I hope you like it: I do. The name of the girl at Limekilns (as will appear if the sequel is ever written) was Hastie, and I conceive she was an ancestress of yours; as David was no doubt some kind of relative of mine.

Cummy was treated generously by the Stevenson family, outliving 'her laddie' by almost 20 years and becoming a celebrity in her own right and even visited by Stevenson enthusiasts, including the Duchess of Sutherland. She lived to the ripe old age of 91 on the pension the family gave her, and Stevenson, while he lived, kept in touch and gave her gifts of all kinds, including autographed first editions of his works.

Dr Lachlan Munro is a political and literary historian. His love of Stevenson was kindled by his fascination with the historical reality of *Kidnapped* and his walking of the route from Mull to Edinburgh. This culminated in his book *The Scenery of Dreams: The True Story of Robert Louis Stevenson's 'Kidnapped'* (2018).

Land of Counterpane
GILLEAN SOMERVILLE-ARJAT

THE 1950s seem very far away now. A bleak post-WWII decade that began with blitzed ruins, ration cards, a Labour government, new directions in the state of the nation's health and education, and attendance at Sunday school. It also included steam engines, power cuts and stay-at-home mums. It occupies a time roughly equidistant between the death of Robert Louis Stevenson in 1894 and the triumphs and terrors of our digital age whose technology would have been a matter of pure science fiction in his.

I was seven years old, lying, unusually, in my parents' bed, aware of daylight outside, but the room dark, the curtains drawn as if someone had died, my parents talking in low murmurs. Every so often my mother would appear beside me, lay a hand on my forehead and check my temperature. Something was wrong. I don't remember being in pain, just a sense of slipping in and out of fevered dreams. I had appendicitis, but our local GP had dismissed my mother's diagnosis – she was a fully qualified doctor though not practising at the time – and complications had set in. She must have persuaded him eventually because an ambulance did come and two men stretchered me down our narrow staircase, raising me high round an awkward turn, then outside into a cold, cloudy day and on to Falkirk Royal Infirmary.

I was in a children's ward for several weeks. Each day a timetable of set routines, interrupted by sudden alarms and excursions as new emergencies were hustled in. Nurses tended us, wearing not scrubs but starched uniforms with white pinafores and caps and black stockings with seams. Hospital was a serious and disciplined business. Every so often, Matron, revered like royalty, ponderous in black, with a cape that swung like a nun's scapular, topped with a white ruched cap that Queen Victoria or Stevenson's mother might have worn as widows, graced us with her distinctive presence. There were painful stitches and embarrassing bedpans, but also treats, such as sweets after meals, which we were actually instructed to eat, and comics which I was not normally allowed. My parents initially couldn't enter the ward, but only wave at me through the porthole windows in the swing doors at one end. Eventually they let my mother in as a special favour because of her MB ChB qualifications. My father's doctorate, a PhD in English pulpit oratory, allowed him to sneak in under the radar, no questions asked. He was the 'properer' doctor of the two, he always maintained: a view hotly contested, of course, over many family meals. Come on. Who was more useful to have around when you fell ill?

Home for a prolonged convalescence, back in my own bed, I had lessons to catch up on. As my father was a headmaster, however long I was absent from school, my education must not be allowed to fall behind. When my parents decided I was up to speed I was given a book of bible stories with full colour illustrations – I remember a cutaway plan of Noah's Ark and a turbaned Belshazzar rising from his feast, wide-eyed with fear at the sight of 'MENE, MENE, TEKEL UPHARSIN' beamed on to his Babylonian palace walls.

But I was also given a copy of *A Child's Garden of Verses*. I didn't have toy soldiers or boats like Stevenson, nor did I go in for dolls, but the hills and glens of my crumpled quilt jiggled and shoogled with stuffed animals, storybooks, colouring books and pencils. So, despite the sums and the spellings, '… *all my toys beside me lay / To keep me happy all the day…*'

Because of frequent unscheduled power cuts, we always had a supply of candles and round metal Willie Winkie-style candle-holders with question-mark handles. Climbing the stairs to bed by candlelight the flickering flames threw great looming shadows where anything ready to terrify a child's imagination might lurk, as in 'North-West Passage':

All round the house is the jet-black night:
It stares through the window-pane;
It crawls in the corners, hiding from the light,
And it moves with the moving flame.

Summer meant holidays, travelling north by steam train high above the Hawes Inn at South Queensferry across the Forth Rail Bridge, which Stevenson never saw, perhaps for a day of donkey rides, sandcastles, paddling and ice-cream on the beach at Aberdour or Burntisland, or farther on to Inverness and the moorland hills around Loch Ness where my mother grew up. Stevenson captures the beating rhythm of these old trains:

Faster than fairies, faster than witches,
Bridges and houses, hedges and ditches;
And charging along like troops in a battle,
All through the meadows horses and cattle: …
And ever again, in the wink of an eye,
Painted stations whistle by.

Children rarely want to go to bed when their parents require. 'Escape at Bedtime' captures the atmosphere of winter nights with cloudless frosty skies, moon and stars visible. Racing free out into the garden, leaving behind the lights and the warmth of the house, is a moment of exhilaration:

*The lights from the parlour and kitchen shone out
Through the blinds and the windows and bars;
And high overhead and all moving about,
There were thousands of millions of stars.*

How do the poems stack up all these years later? They may not attract the attention of literary theorists much, but they're still in print in a whole variety of formats long after they were first published in 1885. Despite the fact that Stevenson grew up during the jingoistic days of the British Empire, the poems don't feel as dated as much as you might expect. With their jaunty rhythms and seemingly effortless simplicity, the deservedly famous poems like 'The Lamplighter', 'My Shadow', 'Keepsake Mill', 'The Land of Story Books', 'Armies in the Fire', 'North-West Passage' still resonate. Stevenson's ability to inhabit the egotism of childhood, infused with the ironic awareness of adulthood, removes them from mawkish sentimentality. There's the wonder of new sensations and experiences, the sadness of partings, his evocation of the wind at night like a highwayman galloping, the surprising memory of his aunt's long skirts trundling along the floor, the noisy mills by the Water of Leith, the dreams of travel to distant, exotic lands where other children live.

Maybe it takes someone of my age to appreciate where Stevenson is coming from in these poems, but I challenge anyone who has ever fallen under their spell not to renew that acquaintance with a prickle of pleasure and a wry nod of recognition.

After careers in English teaching and university administration, Gillean Somerville-Arjat has now retired. She has published a collection of short fiction, *Uncle George and the Cacti and Other Stories*, available from Amazon, and writes a fortnightly column and occasional articles for the online *Scottish Review*.

RLS and the Speculative Society of Edinburgh
(Hereinafter 'The Spec')

PROFESSOR DAVID W.R. PURDIE

'I DO THINK that the Spec is about the only good thing in Edinburgh.' Thus wrote Robert Louis Stevenson to a fellow member of the Speculative Society in 1873. Independent-minded, articulate and a natural debater, RLS was prime Spec material. His accolade to the Spec was deeply felt – and the regard was mutual.

In the Autumn term of 1867, the 17-year-old Stevenson matriculated at Edinburgh University and two years later was elected to the Spec. He was to have studied engineering under Professor Fleeming Jenkin but, to his father's grief, he had little interest in the subject. Key friendships were formed at this time with fellow student members of the Society such as Charles Baxter who would become his lawyer, man of business and dedicatee of *Kidnapped*. Another was Sir Walter Simpson, son of the famous obstetrician Sir James Young Simpson. Rather more senior was Professor Jenkin, in whose family's amateur dramatics RLS took a lively part.

The Spec was founded in 1764 by six undergraduates headed by William Creech, later to be the publisher of Robert Burns and Lord Provost of Edinburgh. Its purpose, unchanged to this day, was to foster the art and craft of debating and to promote excellence in English composition. Stevenson was twice elected a president of the Spec (1872–73 and 1873–74) and in his 'Memories and Portraits' he left us this vivid description:

> The Speculative Society is a body of some antiquity, and has counted among its members Walter Scott, Henry Brougham, Francis Jeffrey, Benjamin Constant and many a legal and local celebrity besides. It has its rooms in the oldest buildings of the University of Edinburgh. There is a hall, Turkey-carpeted, hung with pictures and looking, when lighted up at night by fire and candle, like some goodly dining-room and a passage-like library, walled with books in wire cages. Betwixt the two runs a corridor with a fireplace, benches and prints of famous old Spec men whose young successors can warm themselves, loaf, read and, in defiance of the Senatus-consults, smoke.

In 1895 the Spec acquired from Charles Baxter WS the original manuscript of the 'Valedictory Address' which RLS sent to the Society in 1873. It was found among his papers at Vailima and is now one of the most treasured possessions of our Spec Library at Old College. There could be no better witness of his relationship with the Society than RLS himself. Thus:

> Gentlemen, it is about five years ago since I made both my first appearance and speech in this Hall. It seemed very gloomy and my fellow Members struck me as aged, formal and impressive. I felt uneasy at their familiarity with each other, and at the curious aggregation which drew them together into little groups and coteries, leaving me excluded and alone. When anyone spoke to me, it was more almsgiving than conversation. I felt the loneliness of a boy's first day at school.

The Interval over, I made a speech in a state of nervous exaltation impossible to describe.

A thick, white vapour seemed to fill the room to the level of my eyes, submerging the Secretary, the Librarian, and the ruck of other Members; but I could see the President towering above on his raised platform, gloomy and awful. After the meeting, the same aggregate groups met for the walk homeward, again leaving me out. My electricity seemed negative. I ended my night by walking home alone, in the blackness of despondency. How I should have laughed had anyone stopped me on the Bridges and told me that I would spend in that Society some of the happiest hours of my life and find friends among those very members now so forbiddingly polite!

I look back upon these good times with no regrets. I think all of you will find it so when you leave this Hall for the last time, shutting the door upon three years of happy life. Your retrospect will leave with you and who can tell how interesting these reminiscences may become?

Lord Jeffrey, you remember, chronicles Walter Scott sitting at the Secretary's table, a great woollen nightcap drawn snugly over his ears and apologising in quaint terms for the strange figure he presents to the Society. It must have seemed a slight matter to Jeffrey at the time, but it later transpired that our then Secretary with his 'portentous machine' (the nightcap) drawn over his ears, would become one of Scotland's greatest men. His very fame created interest over this little occurrence, as do his ill-written and ill-spelled Minutes conserved in our Library.

Who knows, gentlemen, with what future Scotts or Jeffreys we may have been sharing this meeting-hall? About what great man shall we have curious anecdotes to tell over our dining-tables and write to his biographers in a shaky, octogenarian hand? We shall have many stories of fellow

Members who did not come to the surface in after-life, but went straight to the bottom, 'whose war-vessels sank in the sea...' if you will let me quote Walt Whitman.

Yes, if here we should have some budding Scott, or a new Shakespeare we shall all, gentlemen, have a hand in the finished article! Certain thoughts of ours, or at least our way of thinking, will have taken hold upon his mind. Some repartee, some happy word, will have fallen upon the 'good soil' of his genius, to then bring forth an hundredfold. We shall all have had a hand, I repeat, at making that Shakespeare or that Scott.

Few men have been more profoundly influenced by the Society than Stevenson himself. The three years of his 'Ordinary Membership' was *the* critical time of his life. Those student years when he was reckoned an idler and yet was busy learning how to write. And write he did for the Spec itself, each of the 30 Ordinary Members being required to deliver three essays to the Society. Great care is required for these since on delivery each becomes the subject of a critical debate and a vote as to whether the essay be added to the Spec's Archives, or to the flames; a fire being kept burning hungrily in the Hall's grate!

The Address quoted above was to have been read by its author on the evening of 25 March, 1873. The minutes of that date record: 'Mr Charles Baxter then read Mr Stevenson's valedictory address, Mr Stevenson being unable to attend through illness.'

The manuscript itself is endorsed with a characteristic note:

I am strictly on my back & have not turned on either side since yesterday morning. Very jolly, however.

– RLS

Prescient indeed was that address. The hand that wrote it was not destined to become that of a 'shaky octogenarian', far from it. But unknown to his Spec colleagues, they were indeed in the company of 'a budding Scott', one whose works will ever remain a jewel in the crown of our Literature.

Professor David Purdie's association with RLS began with *Treasure Island* and was renewed when he joined the Speculative Society at Edinburgh University and found his manuscript letters to 'the Spec'. He is an Honorary Fellow of the Institute for Advanced Studies in the Humanities, where Stevenson's work remains a frequent subject of scholarly research.

Neither Saint Nor Sinner
JEREMY HODGES

ROBERT LOUIS STEVENSON was no saint, despite narrowly escaping beatification in a wave of posthumous adulation sweeping his home city of Edinburgh. A packed public meeting chaired by Lord Rosebery led to the revered writer's installation in effigy at St Giles Cathedral, a bas relief by Augustus Saint-Gaudens shorn of its original hedonistic verses in favour of a prayer, and the characteristic Stevenson cigarette replaced with a pen in the frail fingers of a saintly, bed-bound invalid. Similar small substitutions had been made in Louis's letters by his fastidious editor Sidney Colvin, while the more rumbustious W.E. Henley raged at the 'seraph in chocolate' and 'barley sugar effigy' portrayed in the authorised biography of his one-time friend. So what was the truth about Scotland's best-loved author?

As a journalist commissioned by *The Sunday Times* to come up with an 'exclusive' to mark the 1994 centenary of Stevenson's death, I found plenty of unsolved mysteries in the life of a man who exuded charisma. Louis inspired love and loyalty in almost all who met him, male or female, in person or through his writings where they felt they had found a friend. Those wide-set, lamp-like eyes seemed to look directly into your heart as he took a warm interest in your life and confided in you about his own. Yet like many people possessed of charm, the real Louis behind the persona could be maddeningly elusive. Emerging from underneath Colvin's blue pencil, his letters are full of cryptic comments and allusions, inviting you to read between the lines. So where was I to begin?

My knowledge of Stevenson was minimal, beyond the unforgettable experience of reading *Treasure Island* and a nodding acquaintance with *A Child's Garden of Verses*. Before coming to live north of the border I was not even aware – God forgive me – that Stevenson was Scottish. I had not read *Kidnapped*, nor its sequel *Catriona* – and therein lay the first puzzle. Various RLS biographies made passing reference to the story, or myth, of Kate Drummond – a girl Louis allegedly met in an Edinburgh brothel but was forced to abandon after his parents refused to countenance him marrying a prostitute. This seemed lurid enough for a Sunday paper read, but was there any truth in it?

The young lovers allegedly met in or around a brothel in Leith Street, where Louis made friends with the girls while bunking off his university lectures, circa 1872. In 1871 there had been a Census, so I began scrolling through reels of microfilm in search of Drummonds in that particular Leith Street tenement. I found one Catherine Drummond of the right age, born in Crieff, while her mother's people lived in Prestonpans. At this point I opened a copy of *Catriona* – and discovered its heroine was a Miss Catriona Drummond, hailing from the Braes of Balquhidder near Crieff and subsequently following her father to the Battle of Prestonpans. So far, so circumstantial. But the name of the real girl who rescued her father James Mor from Edinburgh Castle was not Catriona but Maili, or May – so why did Stevenson change it to the Gaelic version of Kate? Was the novel somehow the story of his own love affair, disguised in period costume? Perversely, I scoured his literary masterpiece for biographical clues.

What I lacked was any confirmation from Louis that he was forced to give up an affair – until, among letters written at the time, I found his confession that he had once received a string of letters from a girl who struggled to find money for a postage stamp. He left them unanswered, hoping they would stop. It distressed him to recall that she had spent money on fancy paper with a flower motif. In *Catriona*, after a lovers' tiff, Miss Drummond throws a flower out of the window. Later David Balfour retrieves it and restores their love. Might this be Louis trying to make things right in fiction that had gone badly wrong in real life?

My speculations proved nothing but made for a good read. And they had given me a taste for finding out all I could about this complex character who was clearly a biographer's dream. So began my long obsession with 'Louis', as I was soon calling him in dinner table conversations with my family. Some 25 years and four books later, they are still having to live with him.

Recent biographers had put the emphasis on Louis's later years in the South Seas – more colourful but less revealing than his formative years in his home city, about which little had been written for decades. So I decided to concentrate on the 'lamplit, vicious fairy land' of Edinburgh, where he roamed the streets reliving the city's rich past, neglected his studies in favour of teaching himself to write, got drunk, frequented brothels, lost his religion – and had the most traumatic falling-out with his devout parents, leading to a nervous breakdown.

On the way I met his closest friends – his madcap artist cousin Bob, whose wild and entertaining wit apparently surpassed that of Oscar Wilde but was never written down; the level-headed lawyer Charles Baxter, whose bombproof constitution and wicked sense of humour survived years of hard drinking until broken by the death of his first wife; the respectable baronet Sir Walter Simpson who had a secret teenage mistress and a daughter born out of wedlock; and the gifted but doomed Walter Ferrier, whose fate Louis felt he might easily have suffered himself. This golden youth from a literary family drank himself to death at 33, while his poor, paralysed mother thanked God his squalid demise had not been witnessed by his late, esteemed father – a professor of philosophy who caught syphilis from a

London prostitute and died of it in his fifties, having apparently and unwittingly infected his wife.

Syphilis is never a welcome topic, in polite Edinburgh drawing-rooms or elsewhere. Even today, there are those who don't like to think their favourite childhood stories and poems were written by a man who suffered from it. Much though I admire and love Stevenson, I would not want to meet him after telling the world the secret he confided in a letter marked 'Private' to Baxter: 'The doctor has just told me that I have succeeded in playing the devil with myself to a singular degree…' Yet the knowledge that he would die early, perhaps paralysed or insane, stayed with him for 22 years until he was killed by a stroke – one of the many possible outcomes of syphilis. It was an almost inevitable result of the Bohemian lifestyle which Victorian Edinburgh drove him to lead before marriage. While Louis in exile loved and longed for his home city, there were times when it made him angry, frustrated and desperately unhappy, and the consequences should not be swept under the carpet.

Marriage made any previous affairs a closed book – certainly none are detailed in the biography approved by his wife. Yet my growing curiosity uncovered several others, including apparently a proposal of marriage to Flora Masson, the fair-haired, highly intelligent daughter of the professor of English at Edinburgh university. Either Louis changed his mind after meeting Fanny Osbourne or Flora turned him down, but her name lives on in *The Misadventures of John Nicholson* and also as the heroine of *St. Ives*. And to the end she retained fond memories of Louis, recalled most vividly in her contribution to *I Can Remember Robert Louis Stevenson*.

Various other young ladies, real or imagined, flit through the Stevenson apocrypha, from Mary H the prostitute, whose love he never suspected until she confessed it many years later, to a mystery woman from Aberdeen who allegedly bore him a son. Certainly there were strange goings-on in his life that required him to go into hiding in Henley's lodgings, shortly before the *Inland Voyage* journey that led him to his future wife. Such shadowy females are perhaps most properly disparaged and discounted by other biographers, although for journalistic purposes I've had fun with them all.

But I found the real woman largely airbrushed out of the story was Katharine de Mattos, sister of cousin Bob. She and Louis had a brief, childhood romance during a family holiday in the Borders, and I think she carried a candle for him to the end. Katharine had a disastrous marriage to a philandering atheist, from which Louis rescued her by taking her away secretly to France when he went on his *Travels with a Donkey* – a fact she put on record in *I Can Remember Robert Louis Stevenson*. Later, she helped Fanny rescue Louis from a near-fatal haemorrhage in an Exeter hotel, and as he recovered at home in Bournemouth she helped create *Strange Case of Dr Jekyll and Mr Hyde*, which he dedicated to her.

There are numerous theories about the original inspiration for *Jekyll and Hyde*, but I was surprised to find nobody had hit upon Eugene Chantrelle, a French teacher in Edinburgh with whom Louis was friendly before Chantrelle was hanged for the murder of his wife. At the trial, Stevenson was stunned to learn that his one-time acquaintance was a debauched, alcoholic serial killer and rapist, outwardly respectable like Henry Jekyll but inwardly wicked as Edward Hyde, two personalities in one body and to my mind the obvious unlovely inspiration for Stevenson's gothic horror tale. Chantrelle made Louis realise that while we are not all serial killers we can all have a dark side to our personality.

Certainly Katharine saw the Hyde side of her cousin when her relationship with him and his wife changed dramatically. From being Fanny's best friend, Katharine suddenly found she had become her worst enemy in a row over a 'stolen' short story which also destroyed Louis's friendship with Henley. The bitter and hysterical verbal bludgeoning Katharine received in a letter from her cousin is a sad reminder that on occasion he could be less than charming and kind.

Yet in my search for exclusives – if you cannot come up with something new in a biography, don't bother – have I also been unkind and unfair to a man who did not always hold all the good cards in life but played a poor hand well? In dwelling on the faults that made him human, not a saint in a cathedral, have I been guilty of ungentlemanly conduct? If so, I can only hope Louis might forgive me. As he once observed: 'If you are so sensibly pained by the misconduct of your subject, and so paternally delighted with his virtues, you will always be an excellent gentleman, but a somewhat questionable biographer'.

For all his faults, Robert Louis Stevenson was one of the most courageous and charismatic characters this world has seen. He has inspired countless readers, around the world and from all walks of life, with a breath-taking array of writing that touches the heart as well as the imagination. For that, and for the pleasure of his company these past 25 years, I owe him a great debt of thanks.

Jeremy Hodges is a retired journalist and author of the RLS biography *Lamplit, Vicious Fairy Land* (downloadable free from robert-louis-stevenson.org), *Stevenson's Paris* (Amazon Kindle) and *Mrs Jekyll & Cousin Hyde* (Luath, 2017). He edits the Robert Louis Stevenson Club newsletter and co-ordinates the annual RLS Day celebrations.

Stevenson in Time

PROFESSOR BARRY MENIKOFF

TIME DEVASTATES LITERATURE. It is an unforgiving master, degrading the good and the beautiful along with the bad and the ugly. Voices that once sounded big start to dim, and after enough years, go mute altogether. Although that may sound harsh, it is the nature of scribbling, which is part of the larger churning of culture and civilisation. But this is not a common view.

Guardians of mental high life would have us believe that we preserve only the best of what was thought and said, classics that have stood the test of time – one of those phrases whose sound now rings tinny. Are we so sure that all those scratchings of which we know nothing and which are entombed in old libraries, do not rise to the level of art? Is the record from Chaucer forward, chronicled in the histories of English language writing, the final word? Possibly it was through the eighteenth century, although even that is doubtful, but as we get closer to our own age it is far less certain. There is simply too much writing to read, and winnowing it is complicated almost beyond measure. External factors creep into our selection process, and we begin charting the ebb and flow of writers' standing in the world. *Voilà!* Reputation is all.

In 1894, the year of Stevenson's death, Dr Oliver Wendell Holmes died in Cambridge, Massachusetts, although at a considerably more advanced age. He was a monumental figure in letters, yet hardly anyone today knows his name, except to confuse it with the Supreme Court justice who was his son. Stevenson revered *The Autocrat of the Breakfast-Table* and densely annotated his copy – it was the reason the new *Atlantic* magazine succeeded. Now, nobody reads it.

When Herman Melville died, he was a civil servant in lower Manhattan who received an obituary for two books about the South Seas he had written half a century earlier – works that the Scottish traveller refers to in his own Pacific journal. Yet it was a mere fluke that somebody in the Jazz Age unburied him. And who *really* reads Henry James, apart from a remnant that refuses to concede to the popular rages of the day?

If I were to jump into the twentieth century, I could compile lists of worthies whose work lives in a nether world that few know of and even fewer care to enter. There is simply not enough room at the top, and so a hierarchy needs to be created, say Joyce, Woolf, Hemingway and Faulkner. But the principle remains: those presumed best are crowned. Looking back, Austen is Queen, Dickens King, but Thackeray has already slipped and George Meredith is nowhere to be found. Kipling? How many know he was the first English language recipient of the Nobel? Even Stockholm medallists are not immune from the inexorability of time and culture.

An old proverb has it that 'life is short, art long'. I would tweak it to 'life is short, art chancy'. So, we turn to Stevenson, a poster boy for that pithy saying. 'RLS IS DEAD' read on the sandwich boards in London, was imprinted on the mind of a small boy, Walter de la Mare, who a quarter of a century later, vividly recalled them in a talk on the writer at a newlyformed club in Edinburgh. The obits confirmed that Stevenson was an international star, known simply by his initials. But a closer look peels back some of the dazzle. He had one great bestseller in his life, *Jekyll and Hyde*, a pulp fiction thriller. It made him famous. But from the start he was always a writer's writer, and that meant he was the darling of Grub Street more than the general public.

His Pacific writing had indifferent success, when it was not a failure altogether, and it was only *David Balfour* – known in the UK as *Catriona* – that restored his standing in his final phase. But he was RLS, no matter what he wrote; and by the time he died, his life had already outsold his books, as Henry James said in a more oblique way. It would continue to do so in the twentieth century, as biographies piled on one after another. As for the writing, it went into a tailspin by World War I, even though collected editions continued to be printed. A recovery had to wait until near the end of the twentieth century, when Stevenson could be read anew by a generation untied to stale custom. Does this prove Matthew Arnold's axiom that we should read the best that was thought and said and that the vagabond in the velvet coat can take his rightful place alongside Austen et al? I suspect not.

For Stevenson is an anomaly, an irregularity, in English language literature, a name with wider recognition among people who do not read, yet barely known by those who do. He permeates the general culture, all the while staying invisible to its consciousness. He is on every tourist's ride through The Pirates of the Caribbean at Disneyland, on the tongue of every speaker who uses 'Jekyll and Hyde' as a shorthand for split personality, and in everybody who hums along with Gene Kelly, clueless that 'singing in the rain' comes from a verse in *A Child's Garden of Verses* – not to mention the untold sayings that rank him alongside Samuel Johnson in the league of most-quoted authors. Nonetheless, step inside a bookstore in America, and maybe six to ten inches of a ruler will cover his name, as opposed to John Steinbeck, who could take up half a shelf. For, with the exception of *Treasure Island* and *Kidnapped*, which cling to their sobriquet as boys' books, and the ubiquitous *Jekyll and Hyde*, Stevenson has not deeply penetrated the broadest literary culture. Despite the effusions of luminaries such as Borges, Nabokov and Calvino, that is not likely to change.

Still he lives on. For those who find him, his appeal is so kaleidoscopic that he might be called a chameleon author, as he takes on different guises for his diverse readers: the child who wants to go up in the swing again, or the young person who thrills to a talking parrot and one-legged pirate; the scholar who engages with an existential philosopher in essays and a fabulist in short tales; the nationalist who follows in exacting detail the fictional chronicle of his country's past; the lover who sees in Uma and Wiltshire the sweetness of bare skin, in David and Catriona the tenderness of romance; and the poet who senses notes in a verse-maker's simplicity that strike a depth of feeling too easily overlooked, yet once heard never forgotten (*Sing me a song of a lad that has gone / Glad did I live and gladly die*). For Stevenson, poetry was bred in the bone, it sang in his prose, and it was never far from sadness. He caught it early in the loneliness on the links of a Scottish coast, and he heard it late in the strain of the island blackbird, 'and the ceaseless requiem of the surf'. Art is memory, wrote Cyril Connolly, and memory is the recollection of lost desire, the valiant but vain effort to bring back the sensation of splendour in the hour. All else is sorrow.

Favoured by the gods, Stevenson was not meant to grow old, no matter how profound, if melancholy, his vision. Intellectual and antiquarian, a classicist at heart but a modernist in temper, his vying, if not quite contradictory, qualities have made his readers partisans, for the poetry, the essays, the novels or the South Seas tales. Yet, he hovers over it all. As a man, he was an artist, peerless in style, and forever dateless. But as an artist, he never ceased to be a man, committed to his family and friends, to that vast enterprise called Vailima, even at the expense of his life. Yet he never complained, choosing instead to deliver prayers for all, imploring the gods for patience while he and all around him strove for courage and grace to bear up and to go on. Stevenson collapsed at 44, in the middle of preparing a luncheon salad, after having made some morning pages of prose. Time wore down the rock that was the indomitable writer in his living days, but it was never completely dislodged. For those who know where to look, its unbroken majesty continues to offer the consolation of philosophy, and innumerable pleasures of the imagination.

1 Robert Louis Stevenson, *In The South Seas* (New York: Charles Scribner & Sons, 1896), p.88.

Born and bred in Brooklyn, Barry Menikoff found himself landed on an island in the Pacific, where he first read Stevenson. The jocular signature scrawled by RLS on letters home, 'The Exile of Samoa', seemed strangely prophetic. Following him in deep libraries, and living amid the blue coral and green palms, has, he says, been a great adventure.

Ordinary Case of RLS and RLS
KEVIN MACNEIL

What if RLS had not rebelled against his family to marry
Fanny Osbourne and embark on a globetrotting voyage to become
a best-selling author based in Samoa? What if he had married
one of the ladies of the night he knew in Edinburgh and
knuckled down to being a lighthouse engineer in Scotland?
Here a present-day Scots author imagines what would happen
if these two potential versions of RLS met…

THERE ONCE LIVED in Edinburgh's affluent New Town a man called Robert Louis Stevenson. He was born into a family of eminent engineers whose accomplishments included numerous 'impossible' lighthouses. Robert Louis Stevenson's father, Thomas, wished for him to be a lighthouse engineer, to continue the family's noble tradition. RLS, however, was an imaginative, romantic young man; he secretly yearned to be a writer.

As he approached adulthood, RLS deviated from his parents' Presbyterian world-view. He enthused in a poem:

I love night in the city,
The lighted streets and the swinging gait of harlots.'

The burgeoning Bohemian met, and fell in love with, a woman of the night named Mary. 'We had much to talk about,' Stevenson was heard to say, 'and found that we had been dear friends without knowing it.'

So much in love was RLS that he proposed to marry this soulmate of his. It was with enormous difficulty that the young man persuaded his mother and father that a woman of ill-repute might make a worthy bride. His appeal to his parents' Christian propensity towards forgiveness and redemption, coupled with Mary's natural charm, convinced them that the marriage was acceptable: the great and necessary disappointment therein being that, if he were to have his parents' blessing, RLS must give up his literary ambitions and follow his father's upstanding vocation.

Stevenson thus sacrificed his preferred talents and studied engineering at the University of Edinburgh. Three days after graduating, he married Mary, and Thomas bought for the couple a cottage in Colinton. And there RLS and Mary lived more or less contentedly with their two children, a boy and a girl.

He, however, could not forget his true ambition and often wondered about the direction his life might have taken had he disobeyed his father and lived a more artistic existence. By now, he had designed a number of 'impossible' lighthouses of his own and, while these received public and professional acclaim, he saw in them only the impossible books he could have written in their stead.

'But darling,' said Mary, 'your lighthouses save lives – and they shall outlive all of us. You ought to be proud of them, as I am and as your parents are.'

'Aye,' replied Stevenson with a thin smile.

At night, RLS retreated into dreams as vivid as his daily reality; pirates, brownies and bodysnatchers visited him.

When he was able, he escaped his responsibilities and sat by a gravestone in Greyfriars Kirkyard, saturated in melancholy, leafing through a novel by Henry James, panging with jealousy. Sometimes he pictured the life he could – should – have had, and he squirmed with restlessness. He saw himself adventuring in Europe and America and in – the most exotic place he could imagine – Samoa. What on Earth, he asked himself, could life in Samoa actually be like? Imagine!

Time passed with a dual nature: sometimes quickly, sometimes slowly. Stevenson's melancholy deepened and he grew frail and jaundiced. At length, he could no longer suppress his dissatisfaction and he confessed to his wife that he felt unhappy with his life. Shocked, Mary shared this information with her parents-in-law. They agreed that since the children were now fully grown, they should arrange for RLS to make a journey to Samoa, accompanied by Mary, that RLS might regain his vitality.

The Stevensons' voyage was a difficult one. Sea-sick but excited, they endeavoured to relive their courting days. And when they landed at Samoa, what a transformation took place in RLS! His face brightened with wonder. Wide-eyed, he exclaimed: 'Why, I have had the most curious sensation, almost as though I have been here before!'

'Naturally, darling,' said Mary, 'you have dreamed of Samoa so often and so yearningly that you are half-convinced you have previously visited.'

They settled into a rented home along with a retinue of servants, and so began a bemused surrender to the semi-familiar. One of the servants told them of a popular man known as the Teller of Tales, whom they might visit, for he had a wealth of fantastic stories and had originally come from a distant land where they spoke English like the Stevensons did.

RLS was unsure. He was feeling inspired to write and was uncertain about meeting a fellow writer who seemed to be prominent and successful – and possibly a compatriot at that. The more he heard about the Teller of Tales, though, the more intrigued he grew. It was said, for example, that the Teller of Tales knew many famous authors such as Henry James.

Encouraged by Mary, he resolved to visit this tale teller. Arrangements were made and facilitated by their respective servants. The day arrived and, as they approached the storyteller's house, RLS fell silent.

'Don't be so anxious, dear,' said Mary.

A woman opened the door to them – not a servant, but clearly the lady of the house. 'Good afternoon – welcome,' she said in an American accent. 'We have been so looking forward to making your acquaintance.'

RLS stared at the most beautiful woman he had ever seen. He was quite literally unable to move. He could not even blink. She gave him a strange look, her lips unconsciously parting.

Mary frowned.

'Do... do come in,' the American woman said, but as she did so, Stevenson blanched and his stare intensified further. For the man now moving from the inner darkness towards them – surely the Teller of Tales – looked so similar to him as to be like a brother, perhaps even a twin. This doppelgänger stared at Mary, and it was as though a look of the most charged love passed between them. Then he turned to RLS. In every way, the two men matched each other. Even their mannerisms were uncannily similar. At the same moment, as if recognising something, they both made to speak.

'I can hardly tell...' said the Teller of Tales.

'... which is really me,' said Stevenson.

And at a stroke, both men as one – mirror-perfect – fell down dead.

The Teller of Tales is remembered for his stories, which have lived on in printed and oral form. RLS is commemorated by a number of impressive lighthouses, which have saved countless lives. On RLS's gravestone and on Mary's gravestone alike, one can read Stevenson's only publicly available literary work:

Life – what is life? Upon a moorland bare
To see love coming and see love depart.

Kevin MacNeil

Born and raised in the Outer Hebrides, Kevin MacNeil is a Scottish novelist, poet, playwright and screenwriter. He has won several literary prizes, and was shortlisted for the Saltire Fiction of the Year Award. He edited *Robert Louis Stevenson: An Anthology*, by Jorge Luis Borges and Adolfo Bioy Casares, and lectures in Creative Writing at Stirling University.

Remembering RLS

PROFESSOR ADRIAN POOLE

FROM AS EARLY as I can remember, I have known the family tale of our distant relationship with RLS. The connection is through my maternal grandmother, and her kinship with the Balfours of Pilrig. My childhood and adolescence in Edinburgh brought plenty of reminders. One of the partners of the law firm on Queen Street, to which both my (maternal) grandfather and father belonged, even lived for a time in the Stevenson house on Heriot Row. The Balfour grandmother and her sister all lived with their families a short walk away in Doune Terrace. Some relative had a precious key to the Heriot Row Gardens that allowed me to play there.

But I never properly appreciated Stevenson the writer until very much later in life. I must have read *Treasure Island* and *Kidnapped* early on, though quite possibly in their *Classics Illustrated* versions. But I fear that they made far less of an impression than everything by John Buchan and other fiction fed to boys of a certain social class in the 1950s, by W.E. Johns and G.A. Henty and P.C. Wren and 'Sapper' (H.C. McNeil), all now helplessly exposed as the functionaries of a shameful 'imperialism', in due course to be superseded by Arthur Conan Doyle, Leslie Charteris, Mickey Spillane, and – irresistible to teenagers in the 1960s – Ian Fleming.

It was only when I advanced towards an academic career with a PhD on the melancholy late nineteenth-century realist writer George Gissing that I began to notice Stevenson (so much more fun). Not that Stevenson was a subject for much academic study or scholarship in the 1970s: he was still too 'popular', still suffering from the modernist backlash of the early twentieth century. Eventually it was one of the heroes of the modernists, Henry James, who put me properly on to Stevenson. I was intrigued by the relationship between them, secured mainly in Bournemouth, where James would love to sit conversing with 'the seductive Louis', as he called him. It was a surprising friendship, given the different kinds of fiction they wrote, but a heartening one, not least for the way it stretched across the Atlantic, and in due course the globe, to the younger man's last years in Samoa.

In fact, I have only come to a true appreciation for Stevenson in the last 20 years or so, at a more advanced age than he himself ever reached. Here I must add a further personal connection. In 1997 or 1998 – we argue about the year – I met the woman who would become my wife. She came from California. We met in Edinburgh. She wielded no pistols, as Fanny Osbourne did, but she carried something of that intrepid woman's aura. Not only did she seem to know everything about Stevenson, she actually knew the (to me) far-flung places associated with him on the west coast of America: San Francisco and Oakland, Monterey, Carmel, the Napa Valley. In due course we would drive up 'the Silverado trail' and through the RLS State Park, visit the RLS museum in St Helena, and the RLS house in Monterey. I would marvel at some of the furniture that had surveyed the journey from Heriot Row to Samoa and back to Monterey – along with the many ornaments and objects and photos culled along the way. But the moment that truly clinched things was when she mentioned that she had actually travelled (alone) to Vailima, Stevenson's house in Samoa. This was the woman for me.

Since then I have done a fair amount of work on Stevenson,

editing *The Master of Ballantrae* for Penguin Classics, writing on him for the *Cambridge Companion to English Novelists*, giving talks and contributing essays on the significance to his writing of 'memory' and 'style'. But he has also prompted reflection on my personal past and ancestry, including the world of late-Victorian Edinburgh in which Stevenson grew up.

There was a colourful figure in his young manhood who caught my attention: Fleeming Jenkin, Professor of Engineering and keen amateur actor and producer, a wonderful bridge for the young RLS between the arts and the sciences. I realised that there was a significant connection to Jenkin's world through the maternal grandfather I've already mentioned, the lawyer in Queen Street, Douglas Dickson, or to be more exact through *his* father, James Douglas Hamilton Dickson (1849–1931). This great-grandfather began life in Glasgow, developed into a talented mathematician and engineer, worked with William Thomson (later Lord Kelvin) on the transatlantic cable, and moved in the same circles as Fleeming Jenkin. He married an Edinburgh girl and ended up as a don in Cambridge – where the son was born who would return to Edinburgh and marry into the Balfour family. I still have the jeroboam of wine (empty) with which the Fellows of Peterhouse celebrated the permission given for this great-grandfather to marry (October 29, 1881), the first such event under the late-Victorian change of statutes that made such a novelty possible. To the best of my knowledge, he is the only member of the family to make it into the *Oxford Dictionary of National Biography*.

I too have ended up as a Cambridge don, not in Peterhouse but in the College of which Stevenson's close friend Sidney Colvin was a Fellow. I like to think of Stevenson working on *Travels with a Donkey* in Colvin's rooms in Trinity across the court from my own, shortly after his return from the Cévennes. I enthuse about Stevenson to as many students and colleagues and friends as I can, but I fear that the range of his works familiar to readers at large has in recent years shrunk. The later Stevenson of the Pacific Islands attracts a good deal of attention from academics with interests in colonial and post-colonial writing. But the old favourites, *Treasure Island* and *A Child's Garden of Verses*, have receded from general currency, and so too have the Scottish novels, *Kidnapped* and *The Master of Ballantrae*. Of course, the one thing that everyone knows is *Strange Case of Dr Jekyll and Mr Hyde*, not least because it frequently figures as a prescribed school-text but also because it has attained the very rare status of a modern myth. As often as I go to Edinburgh nowadays I try to find time to admire the magnificent memorial to RLS in St Giles Cathedral by the American sculptor Augustus Saint-Gaudens. A couple of years ago I found myself listening to a young couple trying to remember who Stevenson was until one of them came up with *Jekyll and Hyde*.

To be personal once more, I find Stevenson very good for special occasions. At our wedding I read the great prayer that Saint-Gaudens includes on his bas-relief, beginning 'Give us grace and strength to forbear and to persevere', and ending 'and in all changes of fortune, and down to the gates of death, loyal and loving to one another'. More recently, at a celebratory event for my retirement I was called on to read something. I chose two short passages of Stevenson's, one from the start of his underrated book *Edinburgh: Picturesque Notes*, about leaning over the bridge which joins the New Town and the Old, 'that windiest spot, or high altar, in this northern temple of the winds', and watching the trains 'vanishing into the tunnel on a voyage to brighter skies'; the other from the end of *Across the Plains* about arriving at dawn on the other side of the world, where 'the city of San Francisco, and the bay of gold and corn, were lit from end to end with summer daylight'.

It seemed an appropriate way to honour two places and experiences that have played such a significant role in both our lives. I have much for which to thank Robert Louis Stevenson.

Adrian Poole is Emeritus Professor of English Literature at the University of Cambridge, and a Fellow of Trinity College. He has written on Charles Dickens, George Eliot, Thomas Hardy, Robert Louis Stevenson, and Henry James. He edited the *Cambridge Companion to English Novelists* (2009), for which he wrote the chapter on Stevenson.

The Mystery of the Velvet Coat
ALANNA KNIGHT

ROBERT LOUIS STEVENSON entered my life by way of my son's school project when, to my surprise, I learned that *Treasure Island* had been written just 40 miles away in Braemar. My husband, instructed to bring a biography from Aberdeen University's library, staggered in under a yard-high load of books: 'And when you've finished these, there's the same again.'

Biographies led me to read everything Stevenson had written, enchanted by his ease and perfect use of language that as a new author I knew I could never achieve. John Cairney shared my hero-worship and wanted a play, *The Private Life of RLS*, duly premiered, with John Shedden and Rose McBain in the main roles.

A black cravat was urgently needed for Stevenson's father. Panic! As stage manager and wardrobe mistress, I remembered black-out curtain material from WW2 in the cabin trunk once owned by my sea captain great-grandfather. Curiously ploughing further into the depths of discarded Victoriana, items carefully wrapped in brown paper, a good shake and a chunk of black velvet emerged as a once-elegant smoking jacket. Much the worse for incarceration, a steam iron and determination revealed that it had once adorned a slim man of middle height, an ideal stage costume for RLS. Dashing to the theatre with my trophies,

I found it fitted John so well that he shivered: 'Could have been made for me'.

Play over, a modest success, I phoned mother and told her about the amazing coincidence. My excitement was greeted with silence. She knew all the trunk's contents before it came to me and she firmly denied all knowledge of any such garment. Desperately, I described it again in detail, narrow shoulders, braided bits. 'Never would have fitted any of our men, all over six foot, built like barn doors,' she laughed.

Exasperated, I put down the phone. A sudden thought. Wasn't Stevenson's Edinburgh nickname Velvet Coat? Somewhere among the biographies I remembered his 1887 Bournemouth portrait. And there he was, wearing the identical jacket John Cairney now claimed as perfect for his solo presentation *Mr RLS*. When he took it back to Glasgow for a new lining, his surprised tailor declared it 'gey auld, Mr Cairney, made in the last century'. The mystery remains, how and where did it come from?

The Passionate Kindness was my book of the play, followed by a radio adaptation of *Across the Plains* which led to various other projects, literary events and the eventual plan of *The Robert Louis Stevenson Treasury*, to be a comprehensive account of his life, the people, places and printed word. It was a mammoth task and before the computer age, involving many notebooks and constant trips from Aberdeen to Edinburgh's National Library.

On one such visit, the librarian about to retire led me into the archives to inspect a box of photographic slides of the Stevenson family. Blowing off the dust of almost a century, the writing almost illegible, spidery and brown with age, I knew I held gold in my hands. They had been taken by Lloyd Osbourne, Stevenson's stepson on their travels in the South Seas, and I was faced with solving my first Edinburgh mystery – identifying the places and Stevenson's appropriate quotation.

After RLS' *In the South Seas* was published in 1896, my next three-book contract for historical novels awaited in Aberdeen.

But fate had another card to play. 'And now,' as Stevenson said in his preface to *Treasure Island*, 'admire the finger of predestination…' Staying in a friend's house in the handsome Georgian area of Edinburgh's south side, one day I watched a tall, distinguished-looking man in a deerstalker hat and Inverness cape, a stranger, walking along the crescent, looking up at the windows.

Why, he could be a Victorian detective, I thought. My agent, the late great Giles Gordon, agreed. And so the Inspector Faro series came to life, set in no place more appropriate than Edinburgh of the 1870s, a city I knew better than any other after walking the paths and touching the stones with Stevenson's guidance for the past 15 years.

Edinburgh has been my home now for 30 years and, armed by the occasional query from overseas or a panel request, Stevenson has a habit of popping up when least expected. With this latest anthology request, he seems reluctant to end our association.

Born in Tyneside of Scots Irish parentage, Alanna Knight MBE was a historical novelist and crime writer with more than 70 books to her name. Her publications spanned stage and radio plays, novels, travels at home and abroad, and *The Robert Louis Stevenson Treasury* (1985). She died in December 2020, aged 97.

How I Came to Robert Louis Stevenson
AILENE S. HUNTER

MY MOTHER loved to sing and to recite poetry. Among my earliest memories are Mummy singing 'Shadow March' to me when I was having my bath and reciting 'The Lamplighter' which reminded her of the 'Leerie' who lit the gas lamps on the common stair of the Glasgow tenement where she grew up. So it was probably not surprising that when we had to go to John Smith's bookshop in St Vincent Street to choose the book I would receive as Second Prize in my class, aged just eight, that we chose *A Child's Garden of Verses*. Like RLS, in summer I had to 'go to bed by day' and so woke too early, and would enjoy 'the pleasant land of counterpane' (with dolls rather than soldiers) or read my book until it was time to get up. My name was Ailene Stevenson Cunningham and my father's name was Robert so the author and his dedicatee, Alison Cunningham, sounded like members of the family. I identified with the only child in the poems, unused to having to share with siblings, who, when grown up, would 'tell the other girls and boys not to meddle with my toys'. I still love those poems.

Later, although they were boys, I identified with the characters of Jim Hawkins and David Balfour in their adventures. *Kidnapped* was one of only two books which made me cry as a teenager. (The other was *Jane Eyre* when Jane had to leave Mr

Rochester.) I was so sad when David and Alan Breck parted on Corstorphine Hill and was so happy to see them reunited in *Catriona*.

In my mid-teens, I read *Voyage to Windward* by J.C. Furnas on the recommendation of Miss Cockburn, my English teacher, and discovered that the story of Stevenson's life was just as fascinating as the stories he wrote. Over subsequent years I read and collected the stories, essays, novels and letters of the man who had become my favourite author. He never seemed like a nineteenth-century writer. Compared to someone like Sir Walter Scott, Stevenson's style seemed very modern.

Many years later, I discovered there was a Robert Louis Stevenson Club, so I joined. Then, recently widowed and looking for new interests, I saw them advertise a 're-enactment of the "Duel by Bagpipe" at Balquhidder from *Kidnapped*'. How could you re-enact a fictional event? It sounded mad, so I thought I would go along. I was a bit nervous about meeting the Club members (as a Glaswegian, I feared they would be 'snooty Edinburgh people') but found them good company and very friendly and greatly enjoyed the 'Duel' – accompanied by Athole Brose! – and the ceilidh that followed. It was great to find there were others as enthusiastic about RLS as I was. I became a regular at Club events and formed strong friendships with many of my fellow members. I have been honoured to serve on the Club Committee, and have enjoyed illuminating discussions at the Book Club and participated in Robert Louis Stevenson Day readings, as well as enjoying many talks and walks in Edinburgh and elsewhere.

Over the years I have travelled with the Club to California (twice) and Eastern USA. I have walked the Cévennes and followed the *Inland Voyage*. I have visited Appin, Erraid, Ballantrae, Bristol and London, and from Heriot Row to Monterey, and the Napa Valley and Saranac Lake to Grez-sur-Loing, I have discovered a worldwide network of Stevenson enthusiasts all devoted to 'our' Robert Louis Stevenson.

Travelling with the RLS Club opened doors that would not have been accessible otherwise. One such was our visit to the wonderful Beinecke Collection at Yale University where hands-on study of a manuscript of 'The Vagabond' led to a little bit of research. The printed version of 'The Vagabond' in *Songs of Travel* says it is 'To an Air of Schubert' and with help from Richard Thesiger-Pratt, then Director of Music at Glasgow Cathedral, and the Club's Newsletter Editor, Jeremy Hodges, we showed that this was likely to be 'Mut' ('Courage') – number 22 of the song cycle *Winterreise*. I was so delighted that Richard was able to sing this alongside other settings of RLS Poems, including the more usually heard Vaughan Williams *Songs of Travel* performed by his colleague Dominic Barberi when I had the great pleasure of hosting an RLS Club meeting at Glasgow Cathedral where, with Elizabeth Baird, we also showed RLS had West of Scotland connections as well as Edinburgh ones!

I strongly believe that literary societies reflect the personality of the writer they honour. I always feel RLS would have fitted so well in the company of the Club which bears his name that we should have a spare chair for him at our meetings, or when we go for an Italian lunch afterwards.

Thanks to my mother, my teacher and so many dear friends among the RLS devotees, and above all to Stevenson himself, my life has been greatly enriched.

Born and still based in Glasgow, Ailene S. Hunter is an active member of the Robert Louis Stevenson Club. Since retiring from her job as an NHS Clinical Biochemist she has been a Volunteer Guide in Glasgow Cathedral and supports various musical organisations.

Stevenson the Humanitarian
PETER SHAW FRASER

STEVENSON'S REPUTATION as a writer has had its ups and downs and there are many, myself included, whose admiration for the man, at times, overshadows the written word. He himself is very clearly revealed in the earlier published works – *An Inland Voyage*, *Travels with a Donkey* – and many of the articles and essays. All of these are almost a diary of his disarming lateral thinking, and even more so in the lyrical experience of the Fontainebleau Forest days – the youthful, light-hearted years which one would have been happy to share.

After the publication of *Strange Case of Dr Jekyll and Mr Hyde*, my admiration for Stevenson enters a darker mood – that of the mature Stevenson, battling courageously with illness and stressful responsibilities concurrent with an enormous written output of fiction, where the self is less evident in created characters and situations.

But for me, the most memorable of all his combined virtues of physical and moral courage are to be seen in the open letter to the Rev Dr Hyde of Honolulu in defence of the priest, Father Damien, whom Hyde had in Stevenson's view vilified. This is set against the background of Stevenson's own visits to the infamous leper colony of Molokai in the Hawaiian archipelago, where Damien had ministered to people generally regarded as untouchables. In the letter, published as a pamphlet in 1890, the shafts of Stevenson's controlled fury strike home time after time in some of the most powerful prose ever written, ending with an astonishing paragraph which would almost make the heart turn and bring one to tears:

> Is it growing at all clear to you what a picture you have drawn of your own heart? I will try yet once again to make it clearer. You had a father: suppose this tale were about him, and some informant brought it to you, proof in hand. I am not making too high an estimate of your emotional nature when I suppose you would regret the circumstance? That you would feel the tale of frailty the more keenly since it shamed the author of your days? And that the last thing you would do would be to publish it in the religious press? Well, the man who tried to do what Damien did is my father, and the father of the man in the Apia bar, and the father of all who love goodness; and he was your father, too, if God had given you the grace to see it.

Aberdeenshire-born Peter Shaw Fraser FRSA obtained a Diploma at the Glasgow School of Art and a Scholarship to study Design and Crafts. He spent 15 years working with psychiatric patients, qualifying as an occupational therapist. He produced designs in wood and lacquer, published books on puppetry with Batsford, and exhibited in Aberdeen, Chichester, Washington and Tasmania.

RLS Took Me Hostage
STUART CAMPBELL

STEVENSON took me hostage half a century ago, when life was full of possibility and 'I was young and easy under the apple boughs' (he hates it when I quote other writers), and I was clearly destined to become a famous writer. Teaching English was only a temporary aberration. All I had to do was read the Great Works of world literature and, by a process of literary osmosis, absorb their talent through my pores. I started with the Russians, then the French, then the Japanese (for some odd reason), followed by the English and finally, I am ashamed to admit, the Scots. Stevenson was last on my list. He forgave me, but the price he extracted was my soul. I recently spoke to someone who remembered me from that time and he, to my acute embarrassment, reminded me that I went through a period of dressing like Stevenson.

A parallel obsession from that bygone era was second-hand books. It was not enough to have read every word RLS wrote, I had to physically possess every volume that bore his name. Only during the years spent working with a mental health charity did I realise that I could be sectioned under the terms of The Mental Health (Care and Treatment) (Scotland) Act 2003. Yes, dear reader, I am a hoarder. That is why I own 62 different editions of *Treasure Island* – (available for exhibitions or purchase), eight complete sets of his collected works (every UK and American first edition), alongside critical works, bibliographies and anything else written by his wife, step-children, uncles, grandfather and family pet minder (*RLS and his Sine Qua Non* by Adelaide Boodle). I mustn't forget the drawing executed by RLS, purchased with a small legacy, a letter that he wrote inviting pals to join him and Fanny for a Christmas meal, and several volumes inscribed by him, and by others, including Princess Ka'iulani, W.E. Henley, and Katharine de Mattos. I also own Lloyd Osbourne's spectacles, but that is a sadness too far.

I foolishly thought that Stevenson might release me from this bondage if I were to make him some small sacrifice, a peace offering if you will. An opportunity presented itself some 20 years ago when I was an English Adviser for the Lothian Region. I received a phone call from the BBC, who wanted someone to help them produce a teaching pack aimed at making Stevenson's work accessible to a wide range of school kids. After a surreal discussion with the BBC's own 'paper engineer', it was decided to house the resource in a DIY cardboard treasure chest, which would be known as *Dead Man's Chest*. The pupil materials would be contained in a marbled slip case, and the whole thing was to be accompanied by an edited version of the Omnibus programme about his life. I had no feedback about the impact of *Dead Man's Chest* in the classroom until, on a difficult afternoon in the office, I received a welcome phone call from an English teacher in Hull who wanted to thank me personally for the materials that had rendered his class comatose. For me that was enough, but Stevenson obviously felt the ransom was insufficient.

The next opportunity to placate him was also heralded by a phone call. A representative from a worthy philanthropic literary society in London was seeking advice on how best to honour the anniversary of Stevenson's death. By chance I had been reading *In the South Seas* and was struck by Stevenson's wish to reassure the young students drinking in Rutherford's bar in Edinburgh that everything would work out for the best. It seemed such a kind thought to have from thousands of miles away. Accordingly, I suggested that they might want to nail his thoughts to the wall by erecting a plaque outside of the bar. I heard nothing more but in due course the plaque appeared.

> There was nothing visible but the southern stars, and the steersman out there by the binnacle lamp; (…) The night was as warm as milk; and all of a sudden, I had a vision of – Drummond Street. It came to me in a flash of lightning; I simply returned… and into the past. And when I remembered all that I hoped and feared as I pickled about Rutherford's in the rain and the east wind; how I feared I should make a mere shipwreck and yet timidly hoped not; how I feared I should never have a friend, far less a wife, and yet passionately hoped I might; how I hoped (if I did not take to drink) I should possibly write one little book (…) I should like the incident set upon a brass plate at the corner of that dreary thoroughfare, for all students to read, poor devils, when their hearts are down.
> – *RLS Letter to Charles Baxter* (1888)

There was never any acknowledgement of my contribution, but it still pleases me whenever I walk past the corner of Drummond Street.

But still he wouldn't let me go. Family holidays were skewed to include detours to various Stevenson haunts. We might not otherwise have chosen to visit Monterey, Grez-sur-Loing, or indeed the sea caves outside of Wick where he met with some local savages (consistently poor reports on TripAdvisor).

By way of a final attempt at exorcism, I produced an anthology of his love poetry, *RLS in Love*. The idea emerged after I read several unfinished poetic vignettes in *Unpublished Manuscripts*. These – often bleak – verses led me to look more closely at the poems Stevenson wrote to the various women in his life, and ultimately to the conclusion that he was indeed a love poet of substance. Surely now he would get off my back. But no.

More recently, I thought he would be pleased to see the two novels and two travelogues that I have written nestling on the shelf beneath his first editions.

'Look!' I shouted when he put in an unexpected appearance the other day. 'I'm a writer as well. Isn't that what you wanted? Will you release me? You've made your point. I've paid my debt.'

'Look at your titles,' he said toying with a cigarette as he did when posing for the Sargent portrait.

'What?'

'*Boswell's Bus Pass* and *Daniel Defoe's Railway Journey*. You must be joking!'

'Yes, but my last novel featured a shipwreck. What more can you want? Now, will you please let me go?'

'No,' he said.

Stuart Campbell is the author of a novel, *John McPake and the Sea Beggars*, and three tales of hot air balloons, *The Aeronaut's Guide to Rapture*. A new novel, *The Reek of Sulphur*, is due out in 2021. He works as a Mental Health trainer in Glasgow and is currently completing Stevenson's unfinished novel, *The Great North Road*.

Growing up with the Name
PROFESSOR ROBERT-LOUIS ABRAHAMSON

'WERE YOU REALLY named after Robert Louis Stevenson?' I get asked this all the time, and the answer is, 'Well, sort of'. My grandmother's half-brother Louis had died shortly before I was born, and my parents felt an obligation to name their first child after him. But my mother had also promised her grandmother, Rebecca, to name her first child after her. The child was a boy, and they had to find a name beginning with R. The way they told me the story, it was either Robert or Richard, and my father said, 'Robert Louis Abrahamson, Robert Louis Stevenson: that sounds good.' And there I was.

I cannot remember being told about Stevenson when I was young, but I treasured my little illustrated copy of *A Child's Garden of Verses* because I knew I had a connection with the man whose name was on the cover. And I must have identified myself with Stevenson early on, because I remember being perhaps nine years old and looking into an anthology of British poetry to see how much Stevenson they had included. There was only one poem ('Requiem', of course), and I was outraged. This had nothing to do with literature, but simply ego-identification.

In my teens I read the fiction everyone reads: *Treasure Island*, *Kidnapped*, *Jekyll and Hyde* and, attracted by a dashing picture on the cover of James Durie stepping out of a boat, *The Master of Ballantrae*. When I was 16, I came across the 1901 Scribner's 20-volume edition of Stevenson's *Works*, most volumes never having been opened, for only $17 for the whole set. That was more money than I had with me, and I had to borrow a few dollars, but now I was on my way to collecting the one author I had to have on my shelves.

I can still remember the moment when I shifted from an attachment to Stevenson just because we shared the same name, to a genuine affinity for him (I had by this time affected a hyphen between the two names, as a slight way of differentiating us). The school library had just acquired a copy of Stevenson's selected writings, which the librarian let me sign out before it had even been catalogued. I was sitting on the bus going home and turned (as one does) to the shortest pieces first, which happened to be the *Prayers Written at Vailima*. 'Purge out of every heart the lurking grudge…'. The prayer immediately resonated with something in me, and I remember vividly thinking that there really was something other than our name that connected us. I was moved by his compassionate acceptance of human frailty (though I couldn't have put it like that at the time).

At Amherst College in the late 60s, no one had anything to say about Stevenson. I wrote an essay in my first year about the opening pages of *New Arabian Nights*, astounding my tutor, who, having been educated in the late 1920s, came from the generation that rejected all things Stevensonian. But when I went to the University of Edinburgh to study Scottish Literature, I was surprised to find Stevenson still very much a presence both in the English Department and on the streets. One day I went into Macdonald's Tobacconist on George IV Bridge (the sign is still hanging there) and sweet old Miss Macdonald said to me, 'You mind me of Robert Louis Stevenson'. I told her my name, and every time I would go into the shop after that, she would hand me a sheet of her own poetry, written in lavender ink: 'I thought you might like to look at this.' And in that small shop on Buccleuch

Street, an outpost of Thin's, selling mostly classical literature, the man one day learned my name. 'You know, when you first came in, I said to Miss Johnston here, didn't I? ['Oh, aye,' she said] that you looked like Robert Louis Stevenson.' And then he took me to the back room, away from the chaste ears of Miss Johnston, to tell me an off-colour anecdote Moray Maclaren had once told him about Stevenson.

All of this worked just to confirm my identification with Stevenson on the basis of my name (and perhaps also my looks, or the way I dressed, which is another story). When Ian Campbell asked me to submit an essay for the Robert Louis Stevenson prize, I declined. I was too ashamed to admit to him that I had such a proprietary interest in Stevenson that I would need to come in first place, but I knew I didn't have the ability to write first-place material.

In fact, this proprietary feeling kept me from getting involved in any academic work on the man or his writings until 2002, when I was finally able to give a paper on Stevenson at one of the early RLS conferences. That was my shift to a more distanced, but no less passionate, engagement with the man and his writings. This more academic approach has culminated in my editing the essays for the New Edinburgh Edition of Stevenson's *Works* – no ego-identification there anymore, but (I hope) critical and scholarly attention to the writing.

But the questions still continue: 'Were you really named after Robert Louis Stevenson?' And I answer, 'Well, sort of', and then add that I can think of no one better to share a name with. And after all these years of having Stevenson as a sort of older brother and as an academic focus, I have never tired of the man or the writings, but only gone deeper in my appreciation and gratitude.

Growing up with the Name

Robert-Louis Abrahamson, Emeritus Professor, University of Maryland, now living in England, attended Amherst College and Edinburgh University before earning his PhD in Scottish literature from Rutgers University. He has always felt an affinity to his namesake. He edited the critical edition of *Virginibus Puerisque* for Edinburgh University Press and is co-editing *Familiar Studies of Men and Books*.

Encountering Robert Louis Stevenson
PROFESSOR JOSEPH FARRELL

THERE IS SOMETHING decidedly Stevensonian, perhaps the Stevenson of *New Arabian Nights*, in the invitation to describe in 2021 remembering, or actually meeting, Robert Louis Stevenson. It is tempting to invent some form of Gothic or fantastic encounter, perhaps in an unmarked doorway in the Old Town opening onto a mysterious club, or in the Napa Valley in a spot shrouded by a Californian mist, or in the woods around Vailima where he grew annoyed with himself for falling prey to atavistic fears aroused by unaccountable keening wails or strange cries from somewhere in the thick foliage, but I will leave that task to a more inventive spirit.

The reality of my first awareness of RLS was more workaday. There are encounters with some books or some writers where a reader can remember precisely the place and time of first reading, or even re-create the excitement and state of mind when the book or author changed one's very sense of the known world. My own list of such encounters would include sitting in my grandmother's house reading *A Christmas Carol* and forming the belief, which I have never rejected, that the cosmos was wider than what was visible and tangible, and that ghosts could exist but that they torment themselves more than people they haunt; I can re-create the state of mind in which I read G.K. Chesterton's *The Napoleon of Notting*

Hill, and was struck by the way he integrated fantasy and politics and used those dissimilar twins to fashion both a wide philosophy and a manifesto for small nations; and later the excitement of sitting in an unkempt library in Rome reading Petrarch's *Sonnets*, and gaining an insight into how emotional turmoil could enrich as it unbalanced even the most brilliant minds.

But Robert Louis Stevenson? Making his acquaintance does not have for me any such crispness, for there was never a time he was not a presence in my consciousness, or at least I can recall no such time. I was born and brought up in a housing estate in Motherwell, and although as boys we had other interests and games, Stevenson was part of the talk and play of our daily lives. It is not that we were all avid readers, although some of us were, and my father ensured that the municipal library was part of the mental as well as physical geography of the town, but Stevenson's work was then conveyed by other media as well as the printed page. The BBC would broadcast adaptations of his work on children's TV, the comics we swapped and circulated included not only the *Dandy* and *Beano* but also a series named *Illustrated Classics* which first brought us into contact with such works as *The Black Arrow* and *Kidnapped* as well as with *Ivanhoe* or *Tale of Two Cities*. In addition, there was pantomime where productions of *Treasure Island* were often on stage for the family's annual visit to the theatre. I will never forget the sheer terror induced in the audience in Rutherglen Rep when an actor playing the old sea-dog broke off from chanting, '15 men on the dead man's chest', to tell Jim Hawkins to look out for 'the seafaring man with one leg'. We juvenile sophisticates knew exactly what that one-legged man was up to, but were still reduced to a state of dread by the words spoken by the character on stage.

Graham Greene wrote that the mild pleasure he would anticipate as an adult on hearing that a new novel by E.M. Foster was about to be published was a feeble shadow of the sheer exhilaration he felt as a boy when on the library shelves he came across an unread adventure story by, for instance, G.H. Henty, and every book-lover will sympathise. Greene could have added that his delight in childish things, as St Paul had it, would fade to be replaced by more mature tastes. The writer whose works I devoured in my youth was John Buchan. At the age of 16, I contracted TB and ended up in a hospital near Aberdeen. On admission, I had one book with me, *The Power House*, but the hospital had been a fully-fledged sanatorium and had a room for teenagers suffering from adolescent tuberculosis. It was well stocked with books, including the complete works of Buchan in those little single editions Nelson published and that Dickson McCunn would have appreciated, had he not been a character in some of them. I turned to the flap on the back cover and read down, one by one, completing the set days before I was declared cured.

I continue to think of John Buchan with affection and gratitude but I could not bring him with me, unlike Stevenson, into adulthood. For RLS, the decisive change was the discovery of the interpretation of him offered by G.K. Chesterton, whose book on Stevenson I still consider supreme among the many works written on him.[1] Before the publication of that work, Chesterton dedicated *The Man who was Thursday* to Edmund Clerihew Bentley, his friend who gave his name to the idiosyncratic poetic form, the clerihew. The dedication was in the form of a long poem, not merely a declaration of friendship, but an account of how through reading Stevenson the two had moved from the nihilism of their youth to the discovery of positive values and the adoption of a more generous outlook on life. The poem opens with the lines:

A cloud was on the minds of men
And wailing went the weather,
Yea, a sick cloud upon the soul
When we were boys together.
Science announced nonentity
And art admired decay.

He proceeds to say that '*some giants laboured in that cloud / to lift it from the world.*' One such giant was Walt Whitman, but the other was Stevenson. Chesterton continues:

Truth out of Tusitala spoke
And pleasure out of pain.
Yes, cool and clear and sudden as
A bird sings in the grey,
Dunedin to Samoa spoke
And darkness unto day.[2]

These lines were a shock. Was this really the writer whose adventure stories had thrilled us, whose account of the duel between the Master and his brother or of the siege on the round house we had acted out, or whose description of David Balfour and Alan Breck Stewart's journey through the heather we had retraced on maps?

It was, but G.K. Chesterton opened new vistas when, in addition to the joy and thrills we had found in the novels, he offered if not exactly a philosophy at least a hierarchy of moral and aesthetic values. 'It seems to me', Chesterton wrote, 'that there is a moral to the art of Stevenson... and that it is one that will have a real bearing on the future of European culture'.[3] He added that Stevenson's work required to be seen 'in relation to the history of the whole European mind and mood,' at a time when 'there was thrown across all the earth and sky the gigantic shadow of Schopenhauer.'[4] Perhaps he went too far when he said that the voyage of the Hispaniola in *Treasure Island* was a protest against the darkness implicit in the thought of Schopenhauer, but the wider point is that he made Stevenson a cavalier against pessimism, cosmic pessimism, philosophical pessimism not merely a gloomy disposition of the mind or heart. In a polemical essay on some critic who compared Edgar Allan Poe and RLS and even suggested that Stevenson was 'only an inferior imitator of Poe',

G.K. Chesterton clarified the gulf of vision and values between the two writers by offering a poetic analysis of the duel between the brothers in *The Master of Ballantrae*, where 'the starlight seems as hard as the steel and the candle-flames as steady as the swords', and went on to conclude that 'death in Stevenson is brighter than life in Poe'.

For Chesterton, RLS was more than a teller of tales, not that there was anything wrong with that. Years later I discovered the international esteem in which Stevenson was held at a time when his stock was low in British academies. I read in Italo Calvino that 'in *Treasure Island* and *Kidnapped* the poetry – and it is seriously good poetry – is all of a piece with a pedagogic spirit';[5] I found the Sicilian writer Leonardo Sciascia writing of the joy he found in Stevenson, and quoting in one of his novels J.L. Borges's description of *Treasure Island* as 'the nearest to happiness it is possible to attain'.[6] G.K. Chesterton's image of Stevenson and his more demanding approach were not totally extravagant. One of Stevenson's most quoted lines comes in a letter to Sidney Colvin: 'I believe in the ultimate decency of things.'[7] That statement, put in simple terms but expressing an outlook and attitude of defiance to those who preached blackness and despair, sets him against not only fin de siècle decadence but against nihilism, cynicism and cults of might and power. More especially in his later work, he sought to provide some form of philosophical underpinning, causing him to dismiss his own *St Ives* for having 'no philosophic pith under the yarn'.[8] He dramatised a struggle over ideas of justice, especially justice denied, in *Kidnapped*, *Catriona* and more overtly in *Weir of Hermiston*, and everywhere he proclaims the value of a quest for happiness, personal as well social.

There was for me one last episode in the encounter with Robert Louis Stevenson, and this occurred in a land which, to quote G.K. Chesterton again, 'Stevenson was more inclined to describe as the Islands of the Blest.' I had been invited to Melbourne University as Visiting Professor, and my wife and I decided to take advantage of the Easter break to travel to Samoa. We had a struggle to persuade the young woman in the travel agency to sell us the appropriate tickets, since she recommended Fiji, where she said the beaches were superior. When we explained we wanted to visit the island where Robert Louis Stevenson had spent his last years, she was bemused and asked who this Robert Louis Stevenson was. Being a modern girl, she Googled him and came up with the information that he was author of *Treasure Island*, which gave us authorisation to go.

Samoa changed RLS and he changed Samoa, or at least helped it remain what it wished to be, in the sense that he did what he could to defend the people, their culture and way of life from the depredations of imperialism. However ludicrous and unjustified it may be, his reputation is now under threat from a new angle, from the post-colonial school of criticism which would package all white men and white writers who write of other lands in the one exploitative category, but when he came face to face in Samoa with the reality of imperialism, RLS cried from the very centre of his being that this was not decent. He wrote outraged letters to *The Times* denouncing incidents of the misuse of power, sided with the chief Mata'afa, whom he saw as the best equipped to defend the interests of his islands against intruders, declared his love for Samoa, stated he wished to be buried there, and called on the Samoans to be more active and industrious to guarantee their own survival when it was under threat. In his late creative work, he divided his inventive energy between Samoa and Scotland, drawing parallels between the history and folklore of the two nations, treating in his novels social themes which were common to both. In Samoa, Robert Louis Stevenson revealed himself not only as a good writer, but as a good man.

1 G.K. Chesterton, *Robert Louis Stevenson*, (London, Hodder and Stoughton, 1927).

2 G.K. Chesterton, *The Man Who Was Thursday: A Nightmare*, (London, House of Stratus, 2001) (first edition, 1908).

3 G.K. Chesterton, *Robert Louis Stevenson*, cit, p.30.

4 Ibid, p.90.

5 Italo Calvino, *Letters 1941-85*, translation by Martin McLaughlin, introduction by Michael Wood, (Princeton & Oxford, Princeton University Press, 2013).

6 Leonardo Sciascia, translation by Joseph Farrell, *The Knight and Death*, (London, Granta Press, 2003).

7 *The Letters of Robert Louis Stevenson*, volume 8, edited by Bradford A. Booth and Ernest Mehew (New Haven & London, Yale University Press).

8 *The Letters of Robert Louis Stevenson*, volume 8, cit., p310.

Joseph Farrell is Emeritus Professor of Italian at the University of Strathclyde. He has also been a theatre reviewer, translator of novels and plays, editor of several volumes on literary topics and author of books on varied subjects including *Robert Louis Stevenson in Samoa* (McLehose, 2017).

— STEVENSON —
THE WRITER

A Friend for Life

JAMES ROBERTSON

NEAR THE START of his 1888 essay, *On Some Technical Elements of Style in Literature*, Robert Louis Stevenson warns 'that well-known character, the general reader' that 'I am here embarked upon a most distasteful business: taking down the picture from the wall and looking on the back; and, like the inquiring child, pulling the musical cart to pieces.'

One of the many things I like about Stevenson is his openness regarding the difficulties of writing, coupled with his keeping such difficulties in perspective. In fact, any writer who accepts that we – writers, that is – fail as often as we succeed, and that if we are out of favour with the world it isn't necessarily the world's fault, is likely to find a sympathetic companion in Stevenson. His cry (not in this essay, but in a letter of 1883 to his cousin Bob), 'There is but one art – to omit! O if I knew how to omit, I would ask no other knowledge,' must strike a chord with anybody who is serious about writing as well as they can.

A good deal of what is in 'Technical Elements of Style' has not aged well – Stevenson is *too* technical, *too* prescriptive – but I think I understand him when he writes that:

> [T]he true business of the literary artist is to plait or weave his meaning, involving it round itself so that each sentence,

by successive phrases, shall first come into a kind of knot, and then, after a moment of suspended meaning, solve and clear itself.

This comes in a section on what he calls 'The Web' – 'a web at once sensuous and logical, an elegant and pregnant texture: that is style, that is the foundation of the art of literature.' He goes on to discuss rhythm, the use of different consonant sounds, repetition and so on – in both prose and poetry, but particularly the former. In considering all this, Stevenson does exactly what he said he would do and pulls the musical cart to pieces. He thus demonstrates how much he cares about his craft; for, whether consciously or subconsciously, by instinct or training, all good writers work with these elements all the time.

Stevenson was a Victorian and could not help but have one foot planted firmly in the nineteenth century, but the other was stretching towards the twentieth century and, if he had lived another 10 or 15 years, he would have straddled the ages and the cultural shift between them. Times and terms change. What he calls 'the Web' or 'style', I would call – certainly as far as fiction is concerned – 'voice'. To me, getting the voice is the trickiest part of the whole business of writing a short story or novel. The hard question is not, 'where do you get your ideas from?' It is, 'how do you translate those ideas into something which 'that well-known character, the general reader' can believe; better still, so that they forget that believing is even an issue?' And the only way to do that is through voice.

Fiction is a contract between writer and reader: whatever the writer has written, however brilliant their creation may be, it is dormant and *beyond* belief until a reader opens it and starts to make something of the squiggles and dots and lines of print. Voice is the key that unlocks this process. Novels are meetings of two imaginations in a world made entirely of paper and ink, and it is not surprising that sometimes the meetings go badly. But when they go well, then you become intimate friends, possibly for life.

Stevenson completely understood this. In another essay, 'Letter to a Young Gentleman who Proposes to Embrace a Career of Art', which has lasted much better, he writes about the hard graft of being a practitioner of any art, how art consists as much of toil as of pleasure, and how little the public cares about anything except the end-product, and not even that if the work should fail:

> Under the shadow of this cold thought, alone in his studio, the artist must preserve from day to day his constancy to the ideal. It is this which makes his life noble; it is by this that the practice of his craft strengthens and matures his character…

But then Stevenson adds two warnings:

> First, if you are to continue to be a law to yourself, you must beware of the first signs of laziness. This idealism in honesty can only be supported by perpetual effort; the standard is easily lowered, the artist who says 'It will do' is on the downward path; three or four pot-boilers are enough at times (above all at wrong times) to falsify a talent… This is the danger on the one side; there is no less upon the other. The consciousness of how much the artist is (and must be) a law to himself, debauches the small heads. Perceiving recondite merits very hard to attain, making or swallowing artistic formulae, or perhaps falling in love with some particular proficiency of his own, many artists forget the end of all art: to please.

This might seem like advice handed down from on high, but it isn't: Stevenson is writing from experience, aware that he himself has veered between the two dangers, has come close to falsifying his own talent. He is being completely honest and, while we might balk (at first glance) at the notion that the end of all art is to please, even the writer who claims not to give a damn about reviews or book sales or popularity wants the quality of their work to be admired by *somebody*.

Nor does Stevenson offer the compensation of being recognised by posterity. Enoch Powell wrote that all political careers end in failure, because that is the nature of politics and of human affairs. Stevenson describes 'the necessary end' of writers thus:

> We all pledge ourselves to be able to continue to delight. And the day will come to each, and even to the most admired, when the ardour shall have declined and the cunning shall be lost, and he shall sit by his deserted booth ashamed... [Then] he must lie exposed to the gibes of the wreckers of the press, who earn a little bitter bread by the condemnation of trash which they have not read, and the praise of excellence which they cannot understand.

The outlook, then, appears bleak. But, when one considers the range and quality of what Stevenson produced in his 20 years as a published author, the weather improves considerably. Poet, essayist, travel writer, novelist, writer of short stories and fables, he was not restricted by genre, by age of readership or by geographical or time settings. Some of his very best fiction ('The Beach of Falesá' and *The Ebb-Tide*) is set in the South Seas, far from the Scotland that shaped him; yet it was also there that he re-imagined his homeland and wrote what might have become one of the greatest of Scottish novels, the unfinished *Weir of Hermiston*. There is always something new to be found in his work, even, or especially, in the most familiar tales such as *Strange Case of Dr Jekyll and Mr Hyde*, *The Bottle Imp*, *Kidnapped* or *Treasure Island*, all of which stand up to repeated readings.

For that, I know I am not alone in being grateful. I reread Stevenson more than I reread any other author. He is light of touch, yet wise; entertaining, yet thoughtful. You can feel in the way he puts sentences together that life – that thing for which he once said books were a mighty bloodless substitute – excites and intrigues him, and that he wants as much of it as he can get.

He didn't get nearly enough, but his books are bursting with it. It's an odd thing but I began seriously to devour Stevenson about 44 years ago, in my teens. So, I have been reading him for as long as he lived. That's quite a set of gifts from one writer to another, born over 100 years later. Thank you.

James Robertson is a poet, translator and writer of fiction. His novels include *Joseph Knight*, *The Testament of Gideon Mack*, *And the Land Lay Still* and *To Be Continued*. He is also a co-founder and editor of the Scots language imprint Itchy Coo.

The Taste of Coffee and the Prose of Stevenson

PROFESSOR RICHARD DURY

IN A FAMOUS TEXT, the Argentinian writer Jorge Luis Borges lists the things he likes, and ends the list with '*el sabor del café y la prosa de Stevenson*'[1]. That juxtaposition suggests a savoured pleasure, experienced as we read. In a similar vein, Arthur Symons compared reading Stevenson to a stimulating experience of impressions and discoveries: 'To read him is to be forever setting out on a fresh journey... Anything may happen, or nothing; the air is full of the gaiety of possible chances.'[2] And Henry James said, with unusual simplicity: 'It is a delight to read him.'[3]

There are, of course, other pleasures in reading Stevenson – those explored in literary criticism or in conversations about a book with others: the pleasure of interpretation, characterising, analysis and perceiving links. But these come *after* reading and involve generalising from scattered clues. In contrast, the savoured pleasure resides in sentences and their unfolding, an experience more like listening to music.

Let's look at a sentence from *Travels with a Donkey*: 'The great affair is to move; to feel the needs and hitches of our life more nearly; to come down off this featherbed of civilisation, and find the globe granite underfoot and strewn with cutting flints.' Here, as we read, we are aware of the rhythm of the three-part sentence divided by Stevenson's typical semicolons, of the way the second and third part are increasingly long, and of the repeated parallel structures holding it all together. A high point for me is the way in the last part we cannot help feeling the deliberate pause we have to make before 'granite' (expecting an adjective like 'hard' and finding a noun), while at the same time the pause and hesitation imitates what it is describing: the careful footstep of the walker. And intertwined form and meaning enter into our consciousness at other points, too: 'needs and hitches' sums up the limitations on our will in a strikingly concise formula, and the unexpected choice of 'globe' (linked by alliteration to 'granite') reminds us of our material condition. There is in this small space, as in a Beatles song, a lot going on.

We experience, here too, an excitement, a heightened awareness as we observe an impressive performance. A contemporary commented on Stevenson's 'absurd felicity of expression which leaves us in doubt whether to laugh or cry aloud with pleasure'. We enjoy, for example, the way Stevenson plays with words and momentarily deceives us. He occasionally uses a word with two possible meanings, such as in the Dedication of *Familiar Studies* to his father 'by whose devices the great sea lights in every quarter of the world now shine more brightly', where 'devices' can mean both 'stratagems' and 'mechanical equipment'. In the 1884 'Fontainebleau' essay, he comments on how we would like to leave some presence behind in scenes that have given delight. He says, 'we would leave, if but in gratitude, a pillar and a legend', where 'legend' plausibly means both 'inscription' and 'story'. The reader feels a playful relationship with the game-playing author, and is left wondering if the word has one meaning or the other or both together, and whether that last is possible.

Another playful move by Stevenson that makes us aware of the reading experience is when he cheekily wraps up a challenging statement in a 'presupposition', a part of the sentence that is presented as 'common ground'. Near the beginning of 'An

Apology for Idlers', for example, he writes (assuming the voice of the debater): 'It is admitted that the presence of people who refuse to enter in the great handicap race for sixpenny pieces, is at once an insult and a disenchantment for those who do'. Here our familiar world of work and career is passed off as 'the great handicap race for sixpenny pieces' and we are divided between not quite catching what is going on ('What was that?') and, seeing the point, in doubt whether to laugh or cry. We feel involved in playful cheekiness elsewhere, too: in the campish excess of *New Arabian Nights*, for example, or that passage in 'A Chapter on Dreams' that no reader forgets where Stevenson winkingly pretends to tell an anecdote about 'a friend' and then pretends that he needs to reveal that it was all about him.

Italo Calvino repeatedly praised Stevenson's 'lightness', a quality which refers in part to a world-view of serene acceptance, but also to Stevenson's language, its lack of heavy syntactical structures. This, too, is experienced as we read. In the sentence from *Travels with a Donkey* above, there are no subordinate clauses, and this is typical of his juxtaposing style (as further shown in his use of semicolons). Rather than a relative clause, Stevenson often prefers an epithet before the noun that captures the phenomenon with impressive concision. Thus, *In the South Seas* contains a reference, not to 'the darkness, which was beginning to lighten' but to 'the attenuating darkness' of the unknown shores they were approaching. He says: 'Slowly they began to take shape in the attenuating darkness.' And in *The Master of Ballantrae* we find not 'cold that made breathing difficult' but 'a stifling cold'.

Sometimes the epithet is a playful challenge to the reader to search for meaning, as when (in *Edinburgh Picturesque Notes*) he says that young advocates are obliged to waste time in Parliament House: 'Here, by a ferocious custom, idle youths must promenade from ten till two.' The custom, we may suppose, is oppressive, even aggressive or irrational, but impossible to oppose. *In the South Seas* contains a reference to an atoll 'lying coiled like a serpent, tail to mouth, in the outrageous ocean', where the reader is left to 'translate' the penultimate word with reference to the context: violent, enormous, shocking, but also perhaps 'raging outside'.

And to end, here is another sentence that gives me pleasure. It is from *Prince Otto*:

> At a quarter before six on the following morning Doctor Gotthold was already at his desk in the library; and with a small cup of black coffee at his elbow, and an eye occasionally wandering to the busts and the long array of many-coloured books, was quietly reviewing the labours of the day before.

This is an example of Stevenson's 'lightness': in the space of one sentence of simple syntax we learn that Gotthold is a diligent employee of the Palace, an early riser, an orderly person, someone who savours simple pleasures, and is at ease with himself and his surroundings. At the same time we learn that the library is a long room, a pleasant space, and with a planned rather than an accumulated décor. Brilliant.

1 In the prose poem 'Borges y yo', El hacedor (1960).

2 Arthur Symons, 'Robert Louis Stevenson', *Studies in Prose and Verse* (London: Dent, 1904).

3 Henry James, 'Robert Louis Stevenson' (1888) in *Henry James and Robert Louis Stevenson. A Record of Friendship and Criticism*, ed. Janet Adam Smith (London: Rupert Hart-Davis, 1948).

Richard Dury, now retired after teaching for many years at the University of Bergamo in Italy, continues to collaborate with the RLS Website which he founded in 1996, and to compile a twice-yearly RLS Newsletter. He is a General Editor of the new Edinburgh Edition of Stevenson's works.

'Drink Deep of the Comforts of Shelter'
RABBI RITA LEONARD

WHEN FACING the most violent of life's storms, Stevenson finds me, and I suspect you, too. 'Drink deep of the comforts of shelter' – this poetical string of words fell off a shelf before me in the May of 2018 on a trembling mountain atop Hawai'i's most active volcano. There my library, darkly lit and laden with the spirit of Louis, is home to orphans – books long ago infused with the tobacco of, dare I say, manly former owners, trusted friends though ghostly they may be to we who loved them. In unison, the living and the dead, they rest in reclusion strangely together. So it was at the beginning of months of earthly violence by fire, ash, and nearly 800 quivers a day of varying magnitudes that I was steadied, and remained so, by those seven words of Stevenson's.

Edgar Allan Poe's *Annabel Lee*, a poem I'd taken to memory between desperate breaths, had taught me well how words do lift one out of the realm of physical woe; for I had been a 'suitcase kid', often water-boarded and, yes, kidnapped for ransom by a demonic stepfather. In truth, poetry serves as a potent distraction in moments of peril. Even as the world is being rearranged, the blood of the earth is running wild beneath one's feet. Even when human blood pounds the brain severely, whatever in the absolute one's higher soul craves to unearth, it does – so reliable are the favorite passages popping into our minds… or right off our shelves!

I believe each of us carries within us a dominant seventh chord, needful of resolution. The volcanic awakening of Kilauea, accompanied by Stevenson's knowingness of what every living thing requires – shelter and the comfort of it – unleashed my dominant seventh chord. The buried wounds that ever sought their tonic brought me into a surreal calm-in-the-storm. It snapped open the brass latches of my 'blue valise' – that unseen place where, stowed away, slept what was stolen away from my mother, my crippled uncle and me. The sibling's greed, our lost inheritance, 'the cruelest lies often told in silence!', as Stevenson put it, became visible. Evidence, the truest compass, revealed letters, coordinating dates, numbers and the undeniable embedded DNA which explains why I weep rivers upon hearing bagpipes, have trained Border Collies in America and written music to many Stevenson poems, well before I learned he was a Scot.

Stevenson's genius consistently provides unparalleled security. He embraces the Hunchback and the Hyde within us all. Just as when reading 'she girds me in my sailor's coat and starts me in the dark', we are comforted into dreams beyond this broken world by the beating of his immortal heart. O, where would we be without Louis but lost?

'Bring her in to the coast!' my foster uncle shouted out to me as he pointed up to the night sky before going for his shut-eye below deck. I was only nine years old. Ever since then, whether in tropical rainforest or amongst the pine trees of the Adirondacks, the distant stars remain faithful allies, enchanting me homewards as does the Stevensonian chord towards whatever is in need of resolution. Of all the poets, I confess, he alone is my north star.

Living under the spell of the visceral-unknown in the places I do, where to survive one must conquer all manner of fear to justify every breath, feels right to me. I rely upon history and my invisibles, whose books I keep safe for them. I call the unseen in with every heartbeat – Louis and his father Thomas, especially Thomas, when the snow is deep and one cannot pry open the doors of my home in wintry-brutal Saranac – just the same as I do on the volcano when unforeseen earthquakes rumble throughout the house. Content am I to be ever in need of such valiant warriors and challenges. Poetry itself is my armour, has saved me from the abyss, just as a father might have, untiringly.

In Saranac, I find my spirit ever in defence of our Louis. On bitter cold nights when walking my dogs, sometimes we pass the house where Custer's wife accused Stevenson of muting his female characters. I hear her voice haunt the town, it brings my blood to the boil; for writers of music know how silence is at the very least as powerful as sound. Louis gave the sheer reflection of injustice, the very, very little voice, to Alison in 'A Winter's Tale', as *The Master of Ballantrae* is subtitled. Heading homewards, he never fails to nudge and quicken our pace over the treacherous black ice; for across the street from my house is Dr Trudeau's laboratory in the Historic Saranac Lake building. Never forget that Stevenson despised going in there, a place of utter dread to him! Repulsed by science, revived by romance, it was Trudeau's ghoulish experiments in jars that sent Stevenson a-running back up to Baker's, his 'hatbox on the hill', in rebellion there to sip wine and smoke cigarettes by the fireside. To welcome Stevenson into my home, to honour him, I always keep my curtains tightly closed.

There is an old Jewish legend that tells how when a great being dies his soul bursts into a myriad particles, yearning to attach themselves to kindly babies about to be born. As these infants grow, their lives brush against each other, thus intensifying the deceased's gifts, predestined to repair what is broken in the world. So be it with us!

President of the Stevenson Society of America, Rabbi Rita Leonard is founder of the Congregation Or YisroEil and The Robert Louis Stevenson Tea Room Gardens & Children's Museum in Hawai'i. She is a liturgical composer, gardener, trainer of Border Collies and miniaturist who cultivates the rarest of teas atop Hawaii's Mauna Kea, the most active volcano on earth.

RLS & MS

ALAN TAYLOR

IN *The Prime of Miss Jean Brodie*, Muriel Spark's critically acclaimed and internationally popular bestselling novel, the eponymous teacher leads her young charges – 'the *crème de la crème*' – on a circuitous walk through Edinburgh's Old Town. As they go, one of the girls, Sandy Stranger, is thinking not of what Miss Brodie is telling them but of a fantasy liaison with Alan Breck, the romantic hero of Robert Louis Stevenson's *Kidnapped*: 'Miss Sandy Stranger requests the pleasure of Mr Alan Breck's company at dinner on Tuesday the 6th of January at 8 o'clock.'

Sandy, like her creator, is a girl who lives as much in her imagination as she does in the real world. Alan Breck, she dreams, will arrive at a house in a lonely harbour on the Fife coast of which she has 'by devious means become the mistress'. He will be wearing full Highland dress and Sandy, her imagination now running at full tilt, sees herself and Alan 'swept away' in sexual intercourse.

> She saw the picture of it happening in her mind, and Sandy could not stand for this spoiling. She argued with herself, surely people have time to *think*, they have to stop to think while they are taking their clothes off, and if they stop to think, how can they be swept away?

I have often wondered what it would be like to invite, not Alan Breck or Sandy Stranger to dinner, but Stevenson and Spark. It would surely be fun. In my mind's eye, I see them gathering in some warm spot, in Samoa, say, or Tuscany. They are sitting outdoors, enjoying the warmth of a late summer's evening. A few glasses of wine have been taken and they are both in flirtatious mood. What, as one eavesdrops, are the topics of conversation? Are they talking about writing? Perhaps. Or their long estrangement from their native heath? Or, more probably, about their upbringing in Edinburgh, in the place that RLS believed – with some reason – was cruel to those such as himself who kept poor health and which Spark felt could never understand her. Both were not just Scottish by formation, as Spark liked to reiterate, they were Edinburgh by formation. Its people, its history, religion, politics, setting, architecture, language, weather and its sense of itself had all combined to make them who they were. No matter how far they travelled from it they could not escape that.

Stevenson died in 1894, almost of a quarter of a century before Spark was born. Nevertheless, as she was wont to say, the city had changed comparatively little from his time to hers. Certainly, it felt more like a big, provincial town than a compact, capital city, and it was physically much the same. One small but significant change was that lamp-lighters – leeries – now used long poles rather than climb ladders to turn on the lamp-light. Spark recalled:

> Like Stevenson, I used to wait at the window to witness this performance, and a few years later, when I came to possess *A Child's Garden of Verses*, I felt a close affinity with our long-dead Edinburgh writer, on the basis of more than one shared experience. The Braid Hills, the Blackford Hill and Pond, the Pentland Hills of Stevenson's poems, his 'hills of home' were mine, too.

Spark grew up in a first-floor flat in a tenement on the south side of the city, within sight of Bruntsfield Links. Her family, the Cambergs, were in part Jewish and, while not exactly on the breadline, they were hardly well-to-do. Occasionally, for example, they took in lodgers to make ends meet. In contrast, Stevenson was brought up in the New Town to which the bourgeoisie had decamped to escape the degradation and debauchery in the Royal Mile and environs. His family were from the city's Brahmin class and enjoyed the privileges and perks that came with it. If Stevenson passed through Bruntsfield, which he must have done often, it was while en route to the village of Swanston and the Pentland Hills. As Sandy muses in *The Prime*, echoing no doubt the thoughts of Spark, 'there were other people's Edinburghs quite different from hers, and with which she held only the names of districts and streets and monuments in common'. Indeed, until Miss Brodie takes the girls on their famous walk, none of the girls had ever properly been exposed to the reek of the Old Town.

Often, when reading *The Prime*, especially the passage in which Brodie's set are taken on their famous walk, I have thought of RLS. Like him, Spark knows intuitively how to move her characters from A to B without sounding like a voice on satnav. It comes naturally to her as it did to him. One thinks of Alan Breck and David Balfour racing through the hills with the reader trailing in their wake. We are in much the same situation with Jean Brodie and her impressionable 'set'. We are followers and go where they go, intrigued to learn where they will end up.

Spark knew the work of Stevenson intimately and shared his ambivalence toward Edinburgh where piety and primness collide with prurience and promiscuity. This is exemplified in the story of the notorious Deacon Brodie who by day led a life of conspicuous probity, a cabinet maker who numbered among his clients well-known and respectable figures. By night, though, he changed character and became a daring thief who would rob the very people he had earlier been pleased to serve. Hanged in 1788 before a mob of around 40,000, Brodie appeared to epitomise Edinburgh's Janus-face and Stevenson fictionalised him in *Strange Case of Dr Jekyll and Mr Hyde*. For her part, Spark borrowed Brodie's name and gave it to her best-known character. Or so it is often supposed. But in her autobiography, *Curriculum Vitae* (1992) which, among other things, offers a vivid portrait in Edinburgh in the years immediately after World War, I she remarked:

> I do not know exactly why I chose the name Miss Brodie. But I learned recently that Charlotte Rule, that young American woman who taught me to read when I was three, had been a Miss Brodie and a school teacher before her marriage. Could I have heard this fact and recorded it unconsciously?

No mention is made of Deacon Brodie, which is curious. Had Spark forgotten about him?

Spark's best friend at her school – James Gillespie's, the model of the Marcia Blaine School in *The Prime* – was called Frances Niven. They remained in touch long after their school days were over, and would meet when Spark visited Edinburgh. Frances was Spark's introduction to the New Town. She often used to go to play with her in her family home at 10 Howard Place, which is exactly next door to No 8 where Stevenson was born. 'It was our delight,' Spark wrote, 'to slip through the hedge dividing the two gardens to Robert Louis Stevenson's territory, although in reality he had been little more than two years old when his parents moved house'.

Throughout her long life – she died in 2006, aged 88 – she remained a fan of Stevenson. Like her, he wrote prose that sings like the best poetry. Like her, too, his sentences are peculiarly, hypnotically Scottish. In a sense, he was her mentor. By leaving Scotland he showed that one was no less Scottish. He, like her, had itchy feet and wanted to see what the world had to offer beyond the pewter skies, snell winds and buttoned-up coats of the place he – and she – never failed to regard as home.

In 1989, Spark returned to Edinburgh, which she did quite regularly, usually without fanfare. The occasion was the unveiling in Princes Street Gardens of a memorial to RLS made by Ian Hamilton Finlay and commissioned by the Robert Louis Stevenson Club. 'Stevenson,' she said, 'was superb at his craft. It had the particular persuasiveness of the just and haughty Edinburgh temper.' She was particularly impressed by the simplicity of the inscription: 'RLS – A MAN OF LETTERS 1850–1894.' It seemed somehow to suit the man. Not for him or her the likes of the Scott Monument. Her own grave, in a walled cemetery just outside the somnambulant village of Oliveto in the Val di Chiana in Tuscany, is similarly without ostentation. On the headstone is a line from one of her own poems and, immediately beneath her name, one word: 'Poeta'.

Alan Taylor has been a journalist for nigh on four decades. He was deputy editor of *The Scotsman* and managing editor of Scotsman Publications. His most recent books are *Glasgow: The Autobiography* and *Appointment in Arezzo: A Friendship with Muriel Spark*. He was also series editor of the centenary edition of Spark's novels.

Robert Louis Stevenson, Joseph Conrad and Ford Madox Ford: Playing the 'Sedulous Ape'

PROFESSOR LINDA DRYDEN

LIKE MOST PEOPLE I knew the story of *Jekyll and Hyde* (1886) long before I read the book. It is one of those tales that have entered into the mythology of our cultural lives, and has become a referent for all issues to do with binary notions of good and evil. I would contend that no one can read the book for the first time without already knowing the central mystery of Hyde's true identity: such is the power of Stevenson's imagination in that remarkable book. *Treasure Island* (1883) is similarly ubiquitous in our culture. It has spawned theme parks, movies, adventure holidays, and even influenced geography: there is a small atoll off the coast of Fiji that is called 'Treasure Island'. It is thus the case that Stevenson remains a hugely influential figure more than 120 years after his death.

For those of us who admire and respect Stevenson it therefore comes as quite a surprise that he is still often regarded as a lightweight author, often seen as a children's writer. When I began my PhD on Joseph Conrad 25 years ago, I was tasked with reading Stevenson alongside Rider Haggard, G.A. Henty and W.H.G. Kingston as examples of the kind of imperial literature for boys against which Conrad was writing in his Malay fiction. To be fair, my supervisor never under-rated Stevenson and pointed out to me that *Treasure Island* was a far darker and more ambiguous tale than its cultural legacy suggests. I thus came to Stevenson through the circuitous route of thinking about Conrad and his relationship with the fiction of romance and adventure.

In subsequent years I have come to read Stevenson with increasing respect and admiration. While researching my recent monograph, *Joseph Conrad and H.G. Wells: The Fin de Siècle Literary Scene*, I found it was absolutely vital that I referenced Stevenson, such was his influence on both Conrad and Wells. Yet despite this influence, both authors tended to belittle Stevenson. Wells, in an otherwise appreciative article, 'The Lost Stevenson', for the *Saturday Review* on 13 June 1896, mourns the loss 'of all that Stevenson might have been had not the Scott tradition laid hold of him'[1]. Here Wells is denigrating the Scottish romance tradition, which he regards as debased and superficial. Wells felt that Stevenson was lacking in the qualities that would have made him great: he 'had imagination; he had insight, a fine ear, a sense of and an ambition for style, and a persistent industry'. But Wells states that Stevenson 'lacked that saving obstinacy, that inflexible self-conceit that is, perhaps, the essence of originality' (*Literary Criticism* 102). It is a harsh judgment.

Conrad was equally dismissive of Stevenson's legacy, famously declaring: 'I am no sort of airy R.L. Stevenson who considered his art a prostitute and the artist as no better than one. I dare say he was punctual – but I don't envy him.'[2] In fact, as I have proven in *Joseph Conrad and H.G. Wells*, despite Conrad's declared disdain, he was deeply indebted to Stevenson, both in terms of content and style. It is generally accepted by literary critics that Conrad's novel, *Victory: An Island Tale* (1915), is influenced by *The Ebb-Tide* (1894): and I have discovered that when they collaborated on their deeply flawed novel, *Romance*

(1901), Conrad and Ford Madox Ford, took their lead from *Treasure Island*. Ford had begun the novel and went to Conrad with the fledgling manuscript to persuade him to help with the story. When Ford began reading the manuscript he claims that 'Conrad had expected to hear a reading by the finest stylist in England of a work, far flung in popularity as *Treasure Island*...'[3]. Thus, from the very beginning of the collaborative venture, Stevenson was in the minds of both authors.

However, Conrad persisted in dismissing Stevenson. In 1928, reflecting on Conrad's career after his death in 1924, Ernest Dawson registered dismay at his remarks about Stevenson: 'Another time he was criticizing a story deliberately written in the *New Arabian Nights* vein, and said: "Ah yes, I daresay it is very good of its kind; I don't know my Stevenson at all well, but... *ought to do much better than that*" which seemed to me almost blasphemy'[4]. Nevertheless, it was Stevenson to whom Conrad and Ford turned when revising *Romance*, hoping to emulate the popularity of *Treasure Island*. Indeed, when *Romance* was eventually published the reviewer for *The Sketch* on 4 November 1903 claimed that 'The adventures of the hero are presented so vividly that recollections of R.L. Stevenson come to the reader again and again.'[5]

In fact, a comparison between the openings of *Romance* and *Treasure Island* reveals some startling similarities that prove that Conrad and Ford were actually copying the structure and trying to evoke the atmosphere of Stevenson's tale. The first page of *Romance* exemplifies the atmospheric build-up that Conrad and Ford were seeking:

> I remember the chilly smell of the typical West Indian store, the indescribable smell of damp gloom, of locos, of pimento, of olive oil, of new sugar, of new rum; the glassy double sheen of Ramon's great spectacles, the piercing eyes in the mahogany face while the tap, tap, tap of a cane on the flags

went on behind the inner door; the click of the latch; the stream of light. The door, petulantly thrust inwards, struck against some barrels. I remember the rattling of the bolts on that door, and the tall figure that appeared there, snuff-box in hand.[6]

The opening of *Treasure Island* provided the template for Conrad and Ford's introductory paragraphs, but it has a significantly different pace:

I remember him as if it were yesterday, as he came plodding to the inn door, his sea-chest following behind him in a hand-barrow; a tall, strong, heavy, nut-brown man; his tarry pigtail falling over the shoulders of his soiled blue coat; his hands ragged and scarred, with black broken nails; and the sabre cut across one cheek, a dirty, livid white. I remember him looking round the cove and whistling to himself as he did so, and then breaking out in that old sea-song that he sang so often afterwards – 'Fifteen men on a dead man's chest, Yo-ho-ho and a bottle of rum!' – in the high, old tottering voice that seemed to have been tuned and broken at the capstan bars.[7]

The passages are strikingly similar, not just in the invocation of memory and nostalgia to initiate the narrative, but in the deliberate use of 'I remember' to begin two sentences in each passage. Then there are the detailed descriptions of the two central characters, built up through a series of related clauses. There can be little doubt that Conrad and Ford had pored over the opening pages of *Treasure Island* and, to borrow from Stevenson, tried their hand at playing 'the sedulous ape'. However, their attempt at emulating Stevenson fell flat and *Romance* was neither a critical nor a commercial success. This was largely because they lacked Stevenson's mastery of the adventure romance genre.

Treasure Island is a stunningly successful adventure story, heavily tinged with ambiguity and moral dubiety. Stevenson produced a story that captivates children and adults alike with its swashbuckling action, its charismatic anti-hero Long John Silver, and its conflicted boy-hero Jim Hawkins. It is a masterpiece of its kind and it is little wonder that Conrad and Ford, however begrudgingly, turned to this extraordinary story in the hope of replicating its success. That they failed in their venture is only further proof of the artistic and narrative virtuosity of Stevenson's art. His unique talents have ensured that his works endure to this day and will continue to inspire generations of readers and writers who have been captivated by *Treasure Island*, *Jekyll and Hyde* and so many other tales that flowed from the pen of the great Tusitala.

1 Parrinder, Patrick and Robert Philmus, eds. *H. G. Wells: Literary Criticism*. Sussex: Harvester, 1980.

2 Conrad, Joseph. *The Collected Letters of Joseph Conrad, Volume 2: 1898-1902*. Eds. Frederick R. Karl and Laurence Davies. Cambridge: Cambridge UP, 1988.

3 Ford, Ford Madox. *Joseph Conrad: A Personal Remembrance*. London: Duckworth & Co., 1924.

4 Dawson, Ernest. 'Some Recollections of Joseph Conrad,' *Fortnightly Review* (August 1928).

5 Peters, John, G. ed. *Contemporary Reviews, The Cambridge Edition of the Works of Joseph Conrad, Volume 2: Typhoon to Under Western Eyes*. Cambridge: Cambridge University Press, 2012.

6 Conrad, Joseph and Ford Madox Hueffer. *Romance: A Novel*. London: Thomas Nelson and Sons, n.d.

7 Stevenson, Robert Louis. *Treasure Island*. London: Cassell & Company, Limited, 1883, p.1. The passages above concerning the comparison between *Romance* and *Treasure Island* are taken directly from *Joseph Conrad and H. G. Wells: The Fin de Siècle Literary Scene*. Basingstoke: Palgrave, 2015.

Professor Linda Dryden

Linda Dryden is Professor of English Literature at Edinburgh Napier University and has published monographs on Conrad, Wells, and the Gothic and an edited book on Conrad and Stevenson. Linda created and manages the Robert Louis Stevenson website (www.robert-louis-stevenson.org), and is co-founder of RLS Day with Edinburgh UNESCO City of Literature Trust.

My Desert Island Choice
VAL McDERMID

WHEN I WAS A GUEST on Desert Island Discs, the book I chose to accompany the complete works of Shakespeare and the Bible was a book that technically doesn't exist (not least because it would be too heavy to lift) but which was acceptable in the fantastical world of the Radio Four programme. I asked for the collected works of Robert Louis Stevenson.

Why, with all the world's literature at my disposal, did I choose this?

The answer is simple. I could think of no other writer whose work encompasses such a range of subject matter and style. From *Strange Case of Dr Jekyll and Mr Hyde* to *The Master of Ballantrae*, from *Travels with a Donkey in the Cévennes* to *A Child's Garden of Verses*, Stevenson has something to speak to whatever state of mind I might find myself in on my desert island.

If I had to narrow down my choice to one book, it would be *Treasure Island*. I first encountered it when I was eight or nine years old, in the form we now call a graphic novel, but was called a comic back then. I was entranced by the story and the characters. I eventually tracked the book down in the library and fell in love with it. It remains, for me, the book that has everything. Tremendous story, packed with excitement, surprises, and reversals of fortune. Great characters – everybody knows Long John

Silver, Jim Hawkins and Ben Gunn with his longing for cheese (an entirely credible desire, in my view). Vivid settings, wonderful writing and, almost best of all, an open ending that let me imagine my own further adventures. Scarcely a year goes by when I don't either re-read or listen again to *Treasure Island*.

Stevenson is, I think, one of Scotland's most remarkable writers.

Val McDermid is a bestselling crime writer, playwright and broadcaster. She has published more than 40 books, been translated into more than 40 languages and won many awards. Her work has been adapted for TV and radio. She is a Fellow of the Royal Society of Literature and of the Royal Society of Edinburgh.

The First Book I Read
MICHAEL MORPURGO

BEETHOVEN'S *Fifth Symphony*, Van Gogh's *Sunflowers*, Shakespeare's *Hamlet*, Dickens's *Great Expectations*, Michelangelo's *David*. All so iconic they are simply an integral part of our cultural DNA. We grow up with them. We grow old with them. About all of them so much has been said or written that there would seem to be little more to add. Familiarity has not bred contempt, far from it. They are as familiar as family, always with us, never forgotten; taken for granted sometimes perhaps, but beloved all the same.

All of us have a book we first read when we were young that we hold as dear to our hearts as these great works. For me this is Robert Louis Stevenson's *Treasure Island*. It was the first story that set my heart racing, the first step on the road that drew me to literature and music and art. So my response to this book is wholly unobjective. This introduction is in a way a declaration of love and thanks, of admiration for a great writer and a great book that changed my life, and that of many others, I suspect.

Until I read *Treasure Island* I was not remotely interested in reading books for myself. My parents had done all they could to foster in me a love of stories and of poetry. My mother used to read to my brother Pieter and me every night at bedtime. She was an actress and had the most wonderful reading voice. She could make the words of poems sing and dance. She could bring stories to life, make them real to us, and exciting and funny. She could play all the characters: Captain Hook in *Peter Pan and Wendy*, Toad in *The Wind in the Willows*, the crocodile in Kipling's 'The Elephant's Child'. She seemed to love reading them as much as Pieter and I loved listening. She left us thinking about them in the dark, dreaming about them. Those bedtime readings were the best of childhood to me.

There were, it seemed to me then, almost no walls in the house, just books. Bookcases lined every wall. My stepfather wrote them, and published them; my grandfather wrote them too. And everyone read them, admired them and loved them, except me. For me they were too thick, too long, the print crowded on to the pages. They were also, so my stepfather said, 'important', 'good for me', would 'help me with my school work'. At eight or nine, I was expected to read through great tomes, like *Oliver Twist* or *Jane Eyre*, to be always enthusiastic, and knowledgeable too, if and when I was asked questions about them, as inevitably happened. I found a way round this by reading the classics in comic books called Classics Illustrated. To me they were crib sheets, but I also found that in this form I liked them. The only proper books I ever read were by Enid Blyton, and I loved those because the plots moved as fast as they did in comic books. The fact that Enid Blyton was banned at home and at school only made them more tempting and fascinating to me. All other books I shunned. Instead I played rugby, cricket, conkers and jacks, and went cycling. I could do without books.

At home they had at least tried to inculcate in me a love of stories and books. My mother certainly sowed the seeds. Other efforts may have been clumsy, but they had done their best as they saw it. At school, however, it seemed that all stories and poems were simply used for testing, be it for neatness of handwriting, or comprehension, or spelling. I came rather quickly to associate words and books with fear and failure.

Then one day, aged about ten, I happened to come across the Classics Illustrated edition of *Treasure Island* – having previously rejected several times the musty, dusty, closely printed edition we had at home. But this wasn't the first time I had come across the name of Robert Louis Stevenson. I first heard of Stevenson, and *Treasure Island* come to that, through a card game we used to play at home, called 'Author'. It was a sort of literary 'Happy Families', the author's name being the 'family' name, the author's book titles being the four members you had to collect to make a 'Happy Family', Mr, Mrs, Miss and Master. It's how I first learned, for instance, that Nathaniel Hawthorne wrote *The Scarlet Letter*, that Charles Dickens wrote not only *David Copperfield* but also *A Christmas Carol*, that Thackeray's middle name was Makepeace, and most importantly that Robert Louis Stevenson wrote *Strange Case of Dr Jekyll and Mr Hyde*, *Kidnapped*, *Catriona* and *Treasure Island*.

I think it was because I liked the quietly contemplative look on Stevenson's face, and perhaps because of the intriguing title of *Treasure Island*, that, when we were playing 'Author', I particularly wanted to collect the Stevenson 'Happy Family' cards before anyone else got them. The other authors I cared much less about – though I still wanted to collect them before anyone else. I never rated Dickens, who looked to me on his picture like a tired bloodhound with a beard. No, Robert Louis Stevenson was the one for me; he was my kind of man. He liked pirates and treasure. I liked pirates and treasure. So one day I sat and read *Treasure Island*, the full, musty and dusty, closely printed text. I read it in one sitting, and I loved it. I did not know it at the time, of course, but this was for me the beginning of a long voyage, the journey of my books and stories, a journey I'm still on.

When, much later on – by this time I was a teacher – I had read all his extraordinary books, travel books, children's stories, dark novels, as well as his poetry, and I had read something of his life too – of his adventures and travels, his fame, his last island home and his tragic early death – there stirred up in me a longing to follow in his footsteps, to go where my dreams led me as he had, to write my stories, to dare all, even to die young if I had to. That was many years ago, and I have grown out of that last romantic aspiration. However, the excitement I found in his stories and my admiration for Stevenson have stayed with me all my life. He became and remains my chief mentor.

So what exactly is the magic of Stevenson's genius as a writer and a storyteller? For a story to resonate, to captivate, the reader must believe absolutely in the characters and their relationships, in the place and time in which the story happens. The unfolding of the plot must also be entirely credible, not contrived, growing organically out of circumstance, out of the characters.

With a deft dab of description, with a turn of phrase or a tone of voice, Robert Louis Stevenson brings everyone in *Treasure Island* to life: Jim Hawkins, Long John Silver, Dr Livesey, Ben Gunn and the rest. Each and every one is both plausible and complex. Through Jim's wide eyes – I was Jim when I first read this book, saw all of it, lived it, through him – we see the Jekyll and Hyde in Long John Silver. Like Jim, we are at first entertained and entranced by Silver, then appalled and entranced again. The thread of the story is seamless because no one is pulling the strings except the characters themselves; the author just goes along with them, or so it seems. It takes life so convincingly. We believe at once in poor Ben Gunn, live with Jim as he overhears murderous conspiracy while hidden in the barrel of apples on board the Hispaniola, and as he endures danger and fear with his friends behind the stockade on Treasure Island.

As for place, I know the Admiral Benbow inn, where the book begins, as well as I do my own village pub. I can picture every nook and cranny of it. I know the Hispaniola as well as if I'd sailed on her – from the exact location of the barrel of apples in which Jim hides, to how the sails are set and how the lantern swings below in the cabin, how she creaks and groans at sea or riding at anchor.

And *Treasure Island* I know like I know the island of Bryher in the Isles of Scilly, where I've spent my summer holidays for over thirty years. (I'm sure *Treasure Island* is why I go there.) Jim Hawkins has taken me to Treasure Island and shown me the lie of the land, the marshy groves, the stockade on the hill. I know the entire coastline as Jim takes the helm of the Hispaniola, and single-handedly sails the ship. All utterly incredible, but made credible.

Then there's the plot itself. From the first time we hear the eerie refrain, 'Fifteen men on the dead man's chest – / Yo-ho-ho, and a bottle of rum', and then learn of the mysterious 'black spot', we are hooked. And once hooked, Stevenson never lets us go. He takes us on a giddy journey of twists and turns of fate, through hope to horror and despair, and back to hope again; all of it unexpected, all of it thrilling. He pulls no punches – there is violence and blood. There are no cardboard cut-out pirates – these are cut-throat pirates. We see man's greed for gold in the raw. We see men murdered, watch them die, hear their cries. We live the adventure with Jim, are terrified with him, and all the while we are urging him on, willing him to watch out, to win through somehow.

Whether he does or not, I won't tell you. Read the book. If you haven't already, you have a treat in store. If you've read it before, and think perhaps that once is enough, then begin it again. It will surprise you. I've just reread it for the umpteenth time in my life and was enthralled, as I was all those years ago when I was a young boy, when it changed my life.

It was because of Stevenson and *Treasure Island* that I first picked up a pen and thought I could write, and first dared to tell a story out loud to a class of expectant and highly critical children. It is no accident that islands still fascinate me, that so many of my stories take place on imagined islands, as in *Kensuke's Kingdom*, or on the Scilly Isles themselves: *Why the Whales Came*, *The Wreck of the Zanzibar*, and most recently *Listen to the Moon*. No accident that sea-voyages feature so strongly and so often in my stories – in

Alone on a Wide, Wide Sea, for instance – as they do in Stevenson's. But I have steered clear of pirates and treasure. Safer for mariners, and for writers too. That's his territory, his story.

Which is why I do have one thing that I hold against Stevenson: he wrote *Treasure Island* and I didn't. (I'll forgive him though.) It's the one book above all others I should have loved to have written myself. But I suppose it's just as well because, although I hope I might have told the tale well enough, Stevenson told it wonderfully, beautifully, poetically. For Robert Louis Stevenson wasn't just a fine storyteller, he was one of our greatest writers, and, to my mind, *Treasure Island* is the most masterly of all his masterpieces.

Sir Michael Morpurgo is one of Britain's best loved writers for children, who has written more than 130 books including *The Butterfly Lion*, *Kensuke's Kingdom*, *Why the Whales Came*, *Private Peaceful*, *Shadow*, and *War Horse*, adapted for a hit stage production and film. His Farms for City Children charity, founded with his wife Clare, has benefited more than 70,000 children.

Reading 'Markheim'

PROFESSOR IAN CAMPBELL

STEVENSON was a man of many talents. For fiction of adventure, of the high seas, of the history of his country, he is rightly remembered as a master craftsman. But many of his stories are short masterpieces of their kind. This discussion is of *Markheim*, in which Stevenson imagines a Christmas Day murder in a pawnbroker's house, committed for money but interrupted by a ghostly visitant with every appearance of Satan, who fences with words as Markheim contemplates what he has done – and what more he might do if he follows Satan's advice and murders the returning maidservant, rifles the dead pawnbroker's house, and takes enough money to pay his debts and find security.

Like *Dr Jekyll and Mr Hyde*, this story may have the outward appearance of a shilling shocker, but faces the reader with profound questions. Like much fiction which finds room for a satanic visitor, *Markheim* uses skilful writing to suggest the presence of an otherworldly intelligence with supernatural powers, and the same writing powerfully suggests a brooding menace which makes *Markheim* a classic.

Brief, beautifully controlled, it moves from the murder to the confrontation and debate to a climax so original – so open to multiple readings – that the reader is left without the comforting knowledge of good and evil which might have been suggested.

This is a shocker which leaves its barb in the memory long after it is finished.

Chief among Stevenson's battery of effects is his use of silence and light. The murder itself is over very quickly and early in the story: Stevenson's technique dwells on Markheim's overstretched nerves after the deed, the many clocks in the pawnbroker's – 'some score of small voices in that shop' and outside 'the passage of a lad's feet, heavily running on the pavement' – and then the chiming of the clocks, 'so many tongues in that dumb chamber', ironically marking the hour of three in the afternoon (Christmas it may be, but with a dead body in the room the hour of Jesus's death would not have escaped the readers' notice).

Light, too, is skilfully manipulated by an author who knew how to evoke Markheim's over-strained observation of the shop and its dead occupant, where:

> The candle stood on the counter, its flame solemnly wagging in a draught; and by that inconsiderable movement the whole room was filled with noiseless bustle and kept heaving like a sea; the tall shadows nodding, the gross blots of darkness swelling and dwindling as with respiration, the faces of the portraits and the china gods changing and wavering like images in water. The inner door stood ajar, and peered into that league of shadows with a long slit of daylight like a pointing finger.

That long slit of daylight follows him waveringly through the house as he mounts the stairs, trying to ignore the ticking and chiming clocks, till he finds himself upstairs and locks the door safely behind him. Then, foraging for money upstairs, Markheim is startled by the sound of a step which 'mounted the stair slowly and steadily, and presently a hand was laid upon the knob, and the lock clicked, and the door opened'. He knows himself alone in the house, but when a face looks round the opened door his strained vision (in the wavering light) is of a blurred face: 'at times he thought he bore a likeness to himself; and always, like a lump of living terror, there lay in his bosom the conviction that this thing was not of the earth and not of God.'

If the visitant is indeed of another world, then the blurred face and the poor visibility are perfect details; so, too, is the idea that the satanic being looks like its victim (an idea Hogg played with splendidly in the *Confessions*). The core of the story follows: the devil (to call him so) cornering Markheim into a confession that his life has hit rock bottom with murder and theft, that his stock exchange gambling has ruined him – that he might as well kill the maidservant (on her way home now, as the supernatural visitor knows) and finish the job, robbing the house at his leisure.

And this is where *Markheim* becomes much more than a shilling shocker. Desperately, trying to find a place where he can exist as a moral being, Markheim tries to convince the devil he is at the start of a new and purer life, leaving gambling and previous sins behind him: 'I begin to see myself all changed, these hands the agents of good, this heart at peace.' But inexorably the devil contradicts him, looking at the list of Markheim's recent sins: 'Content yourself with what you are, for you will never change; and the words of your part on this stage are irrevocably written down.'

Then the maidservant rings the bell, and he urges Markheim to commit one more murder to make himself master of everything in the house. But at the same moment, Stevenson allows Markheim to make the most telling statement in the whole narrative: 'If I be condemned to evil acts… there is still one door of freedom open – I can cease from action.' And so he does, opening the door to the maidservant and admitting to the murder as his only way out of a life he sees as an endless maze of evil. He accepts (and the reader is nudged into accepting) the idea that he is not a free moral agent; he is what he is. It is a splendidly managed climax to a brief but telling confrontation between good (fallible good) and evil: if we are not free agents, Markheim sees this as the only way out.

Were the story to end there, it would be a small masterpiece of supernatural fiction. But in Stevenson's hands it becomes something altogether more. As Markheim goes slowly downstairs to open the door and confront the maidservant, 'the features of the visitor began to undergo a wonderful and lovely change: they brightened and softened with a tender triumph, and, even as they brightened, faded and dislimned. But Markheim did not pause to watch or understand the transformation.'

The reader is caught short. There are two possible readings: either the devil is playing tricks (changing appearance to try to stop Markheim from killing himself) or the whole scene was a visit from an angel in disguise leading Markheim to self-knowledge and realisation of his wasted life. If the first, Markheim did not stop to notice the change. If the second, Stevenson confronts his readers with something quite disturbing.

Granted that a supernatural agent of good may come to this earth to guide or help a human at a moment of crisis – as literature tells us often – why does Markheim walk away before the transformation? Why did he not think of allowing the transformed visitor to dissuade him from believing that he had no chance of changing to a morally sound existence? And – more troubling still – why does an angel wait till murder is done before intervening in Markheim's journey to self-knowledge? Was the life of a pawnbroker so worthless, to be tossed aside on the way to Markheim's self-illumination? On Christmas Day, surely a feast of new life and rebirth, is this how to read *Markheim*?

The dilemma is of a piece with the crucial moment in *Dr Jekyll and Mr Hyde* where Jekyll the scientist first takes the transforming drug, undergoes the pain of transformation, and feels an overwhelming urge to see the outcome for himself:

I determined, flushed as I was with hope and triumph, to venture in my new shape as far as to my bedroom. I crossed the yard, wherein the constellations looked down upon me, I could have thought, with wonder, the first creature of that sort that their unsleeping vigilance had yet disclosed to them; I stole through the corridors, a stranger in my own house; and coming to my room, I saw for the first time the appearance of Edward Hyde... Even as good shone upon the countenance of the one, evil was written broadly and plainly on the face of the other. Evil besides (which I must still believe to be the lethal side of man) had left on that body an imprint of deformity and decay. And yet when I looked upon that ugly idol in the glass, I was conscious of no repugnance, rather of a leap of welcome. This, too, was myself. It seemed natural and human. In my eyes it bore a livelier image of the spirit, it seemed more express and single, than the imperfect and divided countenance I had been hitherto accustomed to call mine.

Jekyll, like Markheim, is brought face to face with his true identity in the crucial moment of Stevenson's tale: and in acknowledging the true nature of his identity – 'this, too, was Myself' – he establishes in Stevenson's hands the challenge to ready-made notions of right and wrong which make this, too, much more than a shilling shocker. Stevenson was quite capable of writing about pure evil – the black spot, Shuan and the dirty pannikin, the dark climb up the staircase in the House of Shaws – but in *Dr Jekyll*, as in *Markheim*, he goes beyond the notion of pure evil to a realisation of the essential complexity of human nature, the irrelevance of shallow or ready-made moral positions, the challenge of moral decisions facing the conscious individual. Jekyll takes control of his newly enlarged life, and (as he admits) fatally enjoys his new freedom till it is too late to change course. Markheim takes control of his destiny, too, and makes his own decision to end it.

What Stevenson does not – will not – do is give authorial sanction or approval to what his characters do in that crucial moment. The authorial voice is quite silent as to the fate of the dead pawnbroker; the authorial voice is deliberately silent about the details of Hyde's life, as well as Jekyll's after the experiment. The vacuum remains to be filled by the reader's imaginative engagement with the text. Stevenson is doing far more than titillating the reader with a shilling shocker: he brings his characters face to face with a knowledge and a choice which (in the stories) destroys them, and gives the reader the opportunity to engage with a moral debate that far exceeds what the shilling shocker could offer.

Ian Campbell retired in 2009 from the University of Edinburgh, where he remains Emeritus Professor of Scottish and Victorian Literature. He has taught in the USA, Canada, Japan and China, and remains active as a senior editor of the Duke-Edinburgh edition of the Carlyle Letters. His *Selected Short Stories of RL Stevenson* is published by Kennedy & Boyd.

Stevenson and Dostoevsky
DR TOM HUBBARD

> If it were only possible… for every one of us to describe all his secret thoughts, without hesitating to disclose what he is afraid to tell and would not on any account tell other people, what he is afraid to tell his best friends, what, indeed, he is even at times afraid to confess to himself, the world would be filled with such a stench that we should all be suffocated. That's why, I may observe in parenthesis, our social proprieties and conventions are so good. They have a profound value, I won't say for morality, but simply for self-preservation, for comfort, which, of course, is even more, since morality is really that same comfort, that is, it's invented simply for the sake of comfort.

THAT UTTERANCE, by the demonically cynical Prince Valkovsky in Fyodor Dostoevsky's *The Insulted and the Injured* (1861), anticipates Sigmund Freud's division of the human psyche into id, ego, and superego. The latter's landmark book, *The Interpretation of Dreams*, was published in 1900. Stevenson's *Strange Case of Dr Jekyll and Mr Hyde* appeared at around the mid-point (1886) between these works by Dostoevsky and Freud. The Scot shares with the Russian and the Austrian a preoccupation with dreams and the workings of the unconscious mind.

Dostoevsky's best-known novel is *Crime and Punishment* (1866). In attempting to explain its protagonist Raskolnikov, that most humane of murderers, his loyal friend and fellow-student

Razumikhin remarks: 'Really, it is as if he had two separate personalities, each dominating him alternately.' In 1886, the year of *Jekyll and Hyde*, Stevenson claimed that *Crime and Punishment* was 'easily the greatest book I have read in ten years… Henry James could not finish it: all I can say is, it nearly finished me.' He also records his reading of *The Insulted and the Injured*.

In the preceding paragraph of this letter to J.A. Symonds, Stevenson refers to his own *Jekyll and Hyde* and to 'that damned old business of the war in the members'. His short story, *Markheim*, dates from 1884, anticipating these remarks in the tale's similarity to both *Crime and Punishment* and *Jekyll and Hyde*. With its scenario of a shabby-genteel quasi-intellectual who murders a mean-spirited antiques dealer and is subsequently confronted by a strange being – the apparent embodiment of his conscience – the story reads like a scaled-down version of Dostoevsky's novel: the solo piano version of a Russian symphony.

However, comparative discussion of Stevenson and Dostoevsky has tended to focus on *Jekyll and Hyde* and an earlier (and shorter) work by the Russian, *The Double* (1846). Its main character is an unprepossessing minor clerk called Golyadkin. *Goli* is Russian for 'naked', and our hero boasts of always being open, of not going in for intrigues like his colleagues in the office. Self-righteously, he claims not to wear a mask – but perhaps he does after all? At St Petersburg's Fontanka Embankment he appears, ominously, to meet his double. This person – if separate person he be, rather than a psychological projection – ingratiates himself with the 'original' Golyadkin, whom we come to know as Golyadkin Senior, the double being designated as Golyadkin Junior. The latter goes on to worm his way into the affections of everyone else by turning up at Golyadkin Senior's office, where he toadies to the bosses and resorts to the ambitious scheming which Golyadkin Senior would deny.

Is Junior what Senior would secretly wish to become, though he wouldn't admit it, least of all to himself? Dostoevsky keeps us guessing. Golyadkin Senior, who fantasises about his boss's beautiful daughter, becomes jealous of Junior who finds favour with the lady. Senior is a sexually frustrated minion trapped in the lowest echelons of the Tsarist regime's bureaucracy. Stevenson's Jekyll is also repressed by the strict superegos of the time, but he's an eminent medic and assures himself that he has an escape route via science, that magic of the nineteenth century. Golyadkin Senior lacks such status and know-how.

Moreover, we are not as privy to Jekyll's soul as we are to the 'original' Golyadkin. The former's 'confessional' statement is stiff and reticent in tone, more hypocritical than Hippocratic. In contrast to this too-premeditated document, we witness Golyadkin's disintegrating psyche as all too 'nakedly' apparent: we follow the fervent zigzags of his moods as they happen. Golyadkin Senior visits a doctor, who eventually consigns him to the asylum; Jekyll *is* the doctor, and that makes his story all the more chilling (for all the snow that falls constantly on Golyadkin's St Petersburg...)

Stevenson and Dostoevsky shared a literary pedigree in the genre of Gothic, with more than a nod to Edgar Allan Poe on whom they both wrote essays. Indeed, we can situate the Scot and the Russian at points in the trajectory from Gothic to surrealism. In *The Double*, as Golyadkin Senior is being transported to the madhouse, from his carriage window 'to right and left was the blackness of forests; it was remote and empty. Suddenly his heart stood still: two fiery eyes were looking at him in the darkness, and these two eyes shone with a sinister, diabolical joy.' On Stevenson's side, there is the memorably weird account, in *Jekyll and Hyde*, of the murder of Sir Danvers Carew MP, with Hyde 'hailing down a storm of blows, under which the bones were audibly shattered and the body jumped upon the roadway'.

The two writers were clearly obsessed with the irrational, so it is not surprising that certain of their fictional outcomes are based on seemingly blind chance, on random occurrences that cannot be explained in terms of conscious design by calculating men and gods. Both Stevenson and Dostoevsky made the most of the tensions in what we now euphemistically call gaming, of indeterminacy, played out for high stakes. In Dostoevsky, it is the roulette wheel which is the centre of the action in another short novel, *The Gambler* (1866); Stevenson's counterpart is a deck of cards in 'Story of the Young Man with the Cream Tarts', that first sinister section of the Suicide Club sequence in *New Arabian Nights*.

When faced with an extreme situation, James Durie, the Master of Ballantrae, similarly trusts to chance: he decides his next move by the toss of a coin: 'I know no better way… to express my scorn of human reason.' In this respect, he's kin to the anti-hero of Dostoevsky's *Notes from the Underground* (1864), who snarls at the perceived smugness of nineteenth-century scientific-technological progressivism: that 'Establishment', as it were, insists that two times two must always equal four, but the Underground Man is charmed by the notion that sometimes two times two could make five. In our own time when Enlightenment values are under attack, we might be forgiven for feeling queasy at such a defence of false facts, at such a petulant reliance on the arbitrary and the unexamined.

As representative figures go, a more resonant and indeed abiding example could be found in the Russian *skitalets*, the wanderer; here's a phenomenon which has a Scottish equivalent in the form of the *Scotus vagans*, the *stravaiger*, the thinking person ill at ease in his immediate and constricting environment:

> In the remote heart of his motherland he is in exile, not at home. (…) Later, when he roams, seized with anguish for his own land, in foreign countries and among strangers, as an unquestionably clever and sincere man he feels even more a stranger to himself. True, he, too, loves his country, but he

does not trust it. Of course, he has heard about its ideals but he has no faith in them. He merely believes in an utter impossibility of any kind of work in his native land, and he looks upon the few – now as heretofore – who believe in this possibility with a sad smile.

– Dostoevsky, *The Diary of a Writer* (1873)

The Master of Ballantrae is of this ilk. There's a tragic high point of what, in my view, is Stevenson's greatest novel, and it comes during the Master's frank confession to that dry old stick Mr Mackellar. He recounts the several instances of his 'unmerited cast-backs'. The coins, as it were, have not always spun well for him. However, with what melancholy grandeur he articulates it all!

> Three times I have had my hand upon the highest station: and I am not yet three-and-forty. I know the world as few men know it when they come to die – Court and camp, the East and the West; I know where to go, I see a thousand openings. I am now at the height of my resources, sound of health, of inordinate ambition. Well, all this I resign; I care not if I die, and the world never hear of me; I care only for one thing, and that I will have. Mind yourself; lest, when the roof falls, you, too, should be crushed under the ruins.

The *skitalets/stravaiger* is a feature of many cultures, of their folk traditions and legends; one thinks of the Wandering Jew and the Flying Dutchman. Jungian analysis would have us regard such examples as eternal archetypes. Surely, though, we ought to consider the hard material forces which cause these figures to be constantly on the move – economic, social, political, military, medical. Dostoevsky, notoriously, was hopeless with money, and a sick man: he fled from one spa town to another, in the Germany he professed to despise.

Stevenson's poor health caused him, ultimately, to settle at about the furthest possible point from his native Scotland.

[This article is based partly on a lecture given as part of my course on European literature from 1848 to 1918 at Glasgow University's Department of Adult and Continuing Education in the autumn term of 1992.]

Tom Hubbard was the first Librarian of the Scottish Poetry Library, and has worked extensively in academic posts in Europe and the USA. He is author of ten books of fiction, poetry and non-fiction, and editor or co-editor of other works. His most recent book is *The Devil and Michael Scot* (Grace Note, 2020). He is retired, sort of.

My Debt to Stevenson
IAN RANKIN

I DOUBT I would be a crime writer were it not for Robert Louis Stevenson. I'd always wanted to be a writer. At high school, I'd focused on poetry and song lyrics, and during my undergraduate days at the University of Edinburgh I moved to the short story. By the time I was 24, and beginning my PhD, I was ready to try a novel. But what sort of novel?

The subject of my PhD was Muriel Spark, author of that brilliant Edinburgh novel *The Prime of Miss Jean Brodie*. Edinburgh, however, had changed since Miss Brodie's day, and I wanted to reflect that. Additionally, Miss Brodie had taken me to *Dr Jekyll and Mr Hyde*. Brodie tells us she is descended from Deacon William Brodie, and Deacon Brodie – gentleman by day, thief by night – may well have influenced Stevenson's book.

In reading *Jekyll and Hyde*, two things struck me. One was that it felt a very Edinburgh story, yet frustratingly Stevenson had chosen to set his tale in far-distant London. Second, the book acts as a discussion of good and evil, about why we human beings choose to do terrible things sometimes. This moral conundrum is at the heart of all crime fiction, and I decided that I would write a crime novel set in contemporary Edinburgh, which would allow me to explore the city while also updating some of the ideas in Stevenson's book. In that first Inspector Rebus novel, *Knots and*

Crosses, we readers are meant to suspect that the hero may also be the villain. At the end, however, it is Rebus's 'alter ego' or one-time blood brother who turns out to have been the Hyde figure. Not that readers or reviewers noticed my intention. Frustrated by this, I wrote a second Rebus novel, again using *Jekyll and Hyde* as my template, and this time I even played with the name Hyde in titling the book *Hide and Seek*.

Along the way I had become a fan of Stevenson the man as well as Stevenson the writer. His life and adventures were extraordinary, his range as a writer breathtaking. His non-fiction, children's verse, and adventure stories are remarkable, his style pellucid, his eye and ear sharp. But while I read all his work with immense pleasure, I keep returning to *Dr Jekyll and Mr Hyde*. Within its pages lie the roots of Inspector Rebus and my own literary career. So thank you for that, RLS, Tusitala – teller of tales.

Ian Rankin OBE DL FRSE FRSL is the multimillion-copy worldwide bestseller of more than 30 novels and creator of John Rebus. His books have been translated into 36 languages and have been adapted for radio, the stage and the screen. His latest Rebus novel is *A Song for the Dark Times* (Orion).

In Search of Jekyll and Hyde
ANTHONY O'NEILL

IN 1972, my primary school in St Kilda (the Melbourne suburb in Australia, not the Scottish archipelago), opened a library on the top floor of the Gothic church building next door. It survived only a year before going up in flames – charred pages drifted around the schoolyard for days afterwards – but while it lasted it represented, for those of us of a bookish nature, a veritable portal to a world of wonders. Alongside my friend Anthony Chin, now a respectable Melbourne doctor, I regularly bounded up the rickety stairs to embark on my next literary adventure.

Years later, the only book I specifically remember borrowing from that ill-fated vault is RLS's *Strange Case of Dr Jekyll and Mr Hyde*. Owing, I imagine, to its sinister trappings, this title had not been included in the Dean & Son Classics I was already collecting from the local supermarket, so its presence in the school library, complete with lurid illustrations, represented something of a coup. With an added dose of wickedness.

Suffice to say I devoured it. It remains a mystery to me today how an eight-year-old navigated some of RLS's ornate prose, such as that which decorates the opening paragraphs – 'embarrassed in discourse, backward in sentiment', 'the high pressure of spirits involved in their misdeeds', 'the two men put the greatest store by these excursions', 'I incline to Cain's heresy'. Nevertheless, I was so enthralled by the horror and the textures (and RLS was a master of textures) that I implored my mother to get me a copy of my own.

Since classic titles were not as freely available in Australian bookstores as they are today, I vividly remember my exhausted mother complaining that she'd had to 'walk the streets of Melbourne' before she located a copy. And this, to my dismay, turned out to be the heavily compromised 'Retold by John Kennett' edition. I now joke that the original *Jekyll and Hyde* is so short that the abridged edition is somehow longer.

Notwithstanding my initial misgivings, it was a volume that quickly became one of my most prized possessions – odd to say, I was intoxicated even by its *fragrance* – and it remains on my shelves today, alongside four magnificently unabridged editions. The story meanwhile took deep root in my consciousness and inspired *The Lamplighter* – my 2003 attempt to imagine a 'lost' book written by an imaginary Robert Louis Stevenson-Arthur Conan Doyle hybrid – and, in large part, my eventual move to Edinburgh, where I now reside not far from RLS's childhood homes and the site where *Jekyll and Hyde* (the fragrant John Kennett version) was printed.

Even more directly, it resulted in my 2017 novel *Dr Jekyll & Mr Seek*, a presumptuous follow-up to the original tale – though I prefer to think that RLS was generous enough to write a prequel. In attempting to harmonise my own style and themes I was forced to deconstruct the original masterwork so thoroughly that I fear I'll never be able to enjoy it again – ashamed, principally, by my inability to match Stevenson's superbly measured prose and effortless erudition.

On the plus side, I did find an opportunity to thank, very belatedly, the lady who contributed so much to my obsession. So while RLS dedicated the book to his beloved cousin Katharine de Mattos, who played a crucial role in the genesis of the original story, I was able to dedicate my own humble offering to my late mother, who 'walked the streets of Melbourne looking for *Dr Jekyll and Mr Hyde*'.

A fitting tribute, I hope, to parents everywhere who walk an extra mile to instill in their children a love of reading. And to RLS, of course.

Anthony O'Neill is a novelist, born in Melbourne, Australia, the son of a policeman and a stenographer. He has lived for some years in his adopted city, Edinburgh. His books include *The Devil Upstairs*, *Dr Jekyll & Mr Seek*, *The Lamplighter*, *The Dark Side*, *The Empire of Eternity*, *Scheherazade*, and *The Unscratchables*.

To Robert Louis Stevenson, a Thank You

LIN ANDERSON

AS A YOUNG and avid reader in the 1960s, I spent a great deal of time at my local library. Back then you were only allowed to borrow two books at a time, both quickly read. I particularly loved adventure books, so Robert Louis Stevenson came high up on my list of good reads. I didn't care that the heroes of *Kidnapped* and *Treasure Island* were boys. In fact, I don't remember giving that a second thought.

A story is a character in action, and Stevenson's novels are full of great characters who have wonderful adventures. But they are much more than that. Special favourites such as *Treasure Island* and *Strange Case of Dr Jekyll and Mr Hyde*, taught me the art of a brilliantly concise narrative that paints an immediate visual image with cinematic intensity. Just what I wanted to achieve in my own writing, for which I can only thank their author.

As a writer of crime fiction, I find that the idea for each of my books arrives as a powerful visual scene in my head. I have no idea how the story will unfold, but I know that the adventure is about to begin. Stevenson taught me how a writer might capture a reader and hold them there, turning the pages, living the story as much as reading it. And all of this achieved with the minimum of words.

To Robert Louis Stevenson, a Thank You

As for *Strange Case of Dr Jekyll and Mr Hyde*, this amazing short form book is a psychological study of the duality of humankind, a crime thriller and a horror story all told in fewer than 90 pages. This book has influenced many of the current crop of Scottish crime writers, including myself.

It wasn't until after I became a writer that I discovered Stevenson's own story, and realised that whatever fictional adventures Stevenson created, none could surpass the adventure and the love story that was his own life.

Lin Anderson is a Scottish novelist and screenwriter best known for her bestselling series featuring forensic scientist Dr Rhona MacLeod, with *Follow the Dead* and *Paths of the Dead* both shortlisted for the McIlvanney Scottish Crime Book of the Year award. Lin is co-founder of the Bloody Scotland international crime writing festival.

Dramatising Stevenson for Radio
CATHERINE CZERKAWSKA

I FIRST ENCOUNTERED Robert Louis Stevenson when I was very young and confined to bed for what seemed like half the winter. Living in an area beset by industrial pollution, I was a seriously asthmatic child, and since treatments were fairly ineffective back in the 1950s, I was more often at home than at school. My father, who liked to browse second-hand book shops, bought me a copy of *A Child's Garden of Verses*. They were perhaps the first poems with which I could identify, especially 'The Land of Counterpane' and 'The Lamplighter', a poem that still gives me a pang of nostalgia for that twilight time, and the child I once was, peering out of a window into a darkening street, even though our small house in industrial Leeds had little else in common with Stevenson's Edinburgh. There were still a few gas lamps in Holbeck, though.

A few years later, I moved to Ayrshire with my family, and later still, I studied at Edinburgh University, growing familiar with the city, growing to love it. Then, as a young playwright, living and working in Scotland, I was commissioned to dramatise *Kidnapped* and its sequel, *Catriona*, for BBC Radio 4, for the Classic Serial slot. This was in 10 hour-long episodes, something that, sadly, would never happen now. Hardly anybody is ever given so much 'elbow room', no matter how well-loved the novels in question, and such big productions are very much the exception rather than the rule they once were. Ten hours of radio drama with a stellar cast involved some 600 pages of script and took up more than a year of my life. The production had David Rintoul as David Balfour, Paul Young as Alan Breck, Gerda Stevenson as Catriona and an extraordinarily wonderful Rikki Fulton as Uncle Ebenezer. Marilyn Imrie directed, and the production took place over many weeks. At one point the director pinned up a quote from *Kidnapped* in the studio, quoting David's description of his time imprisoned below deck on the ship: 'Day and night were alike in that ill-smelling cavern.' Radio studios can be claustrophobic at the best of times. All the same, I enjoyed the books more and more as I worked on them, marvelling at the genius of the man who had written them.

Catriona is the sequel to *Kidnapped*, but there are many years of Stevenson's life, and a good deal of growing maturity and sophistication between the two novels. Among much else, *Catriona* is about the relationship between the narrator of *Kidnapped*, David Balfour, and the eponymous Catriona, the feisty granddaughter of outlaw Rob Roy MacGregor and daughter of James McGregor Drummond, Rob Roy's eldest son. The novel contains one of the best and most honest descriptions of youthful sexual frustration I have ever come across. The growing affection and desire between the two young people is beautifully and bravely depicted in all its true physicality as well as its romance. It occurred to me while I was working on it that it must have seemed quite shocking when the novel was first published. Later, I also dramatised *Treasure Island* for BBC Radio 4, another thrilling adventure story, but if I were forced to choose a single Stevenson novel to take to my desert island, I think it would have to be *Kidnapped*. I loved it then, and I love and admire it now.

This is, for me, the ultimate Scottish novel, a powerful story with believable characters, speaking in dialogue which, all these years later, still practically sings off the page: a gift for any dramatist. *Kidnapped* is narrated by David Balfour himself, but an older David, well aware of the foibles and pretensions of his younger self. This allowed me as a dramatist, as well as the reader, to observe events from both perspectives at once: the callow youth and the older, wiser man. The novel is a tale of an unlikely but enduring friendship between two very different people, of the 'getting of wisdom' for the likeable, if occasionally pompous, youthful protagonist, of the differences between Highland and Lowland cultures, of the moral dilemmas induced by the politics of the time; but most of all, it is an engrossing adventure, a *tour de force* of the storyteller's art that represents my holy grail as a writer.

My appreciation of Stevenson certainly influenced my own original plays when I went on to write them. I learned so much from his finely drawn characters and vivid dramatisation of events. Now, when I find myself concentrating more on historical fiction than on drama, on novels and non-fiction rather than plays; I again find myself turning to Stevenson, remembering the qualities of his writing that have so engaged me over the years: enthralling stories, brilliantly told and real characters, vividly depicted.

The example that always comes to mind for me is the masterly portrayal of the friendship between respectable, conventional young lowlander, David Balfour, and the ferociously daring and dangerous Jacobite, Alan Breck. It is worth quoting David's, and therefore the reader's, first dazzling impression of him:

> He was smallish in stature, but well set and as nimble as a goat; his face was of a good open expression, but sunburnt very dark, and heavily freckled and pitted with the small-pox; his eyes were unusually light and had a kind of dancing madness in them, that was both engaging and alarming; and when he took off his great-coat, he laid a pair of fine silver-mounted pistols on the table, and I saw that he was belted with a great sword. His manners, besides, were

elegant, and he pledged the captain handsomely. Altogether I thought of him, at the first sight, that here was a man I would rather call my friend than my enemy.

We have all, occasionally, met those we would rather call friend than enemy. Like Tolkien's depiction of Aragorn, in *The Lord of the Rings*, Stevenson knew that a person does not have to be a villain to be dangerous, although Alan Breck has more genuine faults, more alarming failings than Tolkien's king-in-waiting. Later in *Kidnapped*, and after many hair-raising adventures, there is another key scene, where a feverish David has a serious quarrel with Alan, who has disastrously gambled away all their money. David challenges his friend to a sword fight, which Alan knows the younger man simply cannot win. Just in time, Alan realises how ill David really is:

'Can ye walk?' asked Alan.

'No,' said I, 'not without help. This last hour my legs have been fainting under me; I've a stitch in my side like a red-hot iron; I cannae breathe right. If I die, ye'll can forgive me, Alan? In my heart, I liked ye fine – even when I was the angriest.'

'Wheesht, wheesht!' cried Alan. 'Dinna say that! David man, ye ken...' He shut his mouth upon a sob. 'Let me get my arm about ye,' he continued; 'that's the way! Now lean upon me hard. Gude kens where there's a house! We're in Balwhidder, too; there should be no want of houses, no, nor friends' houses here. Do ye gang easier so, Davie?'

There is a heart-rending quality to this scene that almost moves me to tears every time I read it; a quality that makes me envy the achievement of it in the depiction of a profound tenderness without an ounce of sentimentality. I must confess that when I was writing my novel, *The Curiosity Cabinet* my islander protagonist,

Manus McNeill, owed a great deal to Alan Breck Stewart. I wanted Manus to be another unconventional hero, a flawed but honourable character whom one would rather call a friend than an enemy.

Moreover, because endings matter, because, as Stevenson well knew, novels should leave the reader giving a sigh of satisfaction, rather than a murmur of frustration, our last sight of Alan Breck in *Kidnapped*, before David enters the city of Edinburgh and a more or less secure future, is a small masterpiece of regret at a necessary parting that still gives me the same magical frisson, no matter how many times I read it.

> 'Well, good-bye,' said Alan, and held out his left hand.
> 'Good-bye,' said I, and gave the hand a little grasp, and went off down hill.
> Neither one of us looked the other in the face, nor so long as he was in my view did I take one back glance at the friend I was leaving. But as I went on my way to the city, I felt so lost and lonesome, that I could have found it in my heart to sit down by the dyke, and cry and weep like any baby.

Novelist and playwright Catherine Czerkawska's historical novels include *The Physic Garden*, *The Jewel* (about Robert Burns's wife, Jean Armour) and *The Posy Ring*. *A Proper Person to be Detained* (2019) takes the reader from Ireland to the industrial heartlands of England and Scotland, while other novels include *Bird of Passage* and *The Amber Heart*. Her novel *The Curiosity Cabinet* was shortlisted for the Dundee Book Prize.

The Hoose O'Shaws

ISOBEL REID

THE AMERICAN NOVELIST F. Scott Fitzgerald wrote: 'An author ought to write for the youth of his own generation, the critics of the next and the schoolmaster of the ever afterwards'. One of my Primary teachers followed this advice and introduced us to Stevenson and the delights of rote learning. As well as reciting poetry, we were asked to memorise some prose for homework: Chapter 6 of *Kidnapped*, 'What befell at the Queen's Ferry'.

I can still recall, with great clarity, the rhythm of the syntax and pace of language as I followed David Balfour into the Hawes Inn. Rote learning ensured I did not skim over the details and rush through the pacy narrative. Instead, I slowed down and focused on the details.

'As soon as we entered the inn, Ransome led me up the stairs to a small room with a bed in it and heated like an oven by a great fire of coal.' This was imprinted in my mind forever. The phrase 'fire of coal' rather than 'coal fire' with the reference later to the 'old coal-bucket burning on the Isle of May'. This sense of place was a revelation. Fiction, history, and geography fused together, and the landscape of Fife changed. This was not Queensferry but 'the Queen's Ferry'.

For me, this was an important threshold into the magic of Stevenson's prose. The inn existed. Where was the room? Was the fireplace still there? If the sense of place captured my imagination, the characters were also intriguing. Firstly, the unusual names – Ransome and Hoseason. Was the emphasis on the 'Ho' or the 'season'?

I dutifully recited the details of this 'tall, dark, sober-looking man' who sat writing… What? I could picture his 'thick sea jacket buttoned to the neck and the tall hairy cap drawn down over his ears'. He was all dressed up in front of the 'fire of coal'.

Rote learning is rarely used today in schools. Yet Stevenson's prose and poetry are still popular and part of the curriculum. I once rescued a set of abridged copies of *Kidnapped* from the recycling bin. They came in useful. One Thursday afternoon a challenging class of boys had completed the latest racy modern thrilling novel. Drugs, car theft and teenage pregnancy had caught their attention for a period, but it was time for the old master to placate them until 3.35pm.

Even in an abridged form, the magic returned. They settled to read and listen to David Balfour's adventures. Questions followed a period of concentration. 'Miss, can we draw the House of Shaws?' Although many lacked a love of reading, there were some talented artists in the class. 'Miss, you told us this house was near Edinburgh. Can we visit it? Can you arrange a trip!'

Alas, we have no Stevenson theme park or Potteresque merchandise to accompany Stevenson's prose. This group of pupils were intrigued by the sense of place and narrative. Stevenson captured the youth of his generation and continues to do so today. As critic Barry Menikoff commented: 'The books live, and they work their way into the lives of generations, long after the noise of writers' lives and critics' carpings have passed into oblivion.'

Isobel Reid was born in St Andrews and graduated from Dundee University in 1980 before teaching in West Lothian. As Principal Teacher of English at Bo'ness Academy she commuted each morning past David Balfour's route from Limekilns across the Forth. Now retired, she enjoys singing, reading, and walking in the countryside around Linlithgow.

Sing Me a Song of a Lad that is Gone

DAVID C. CLAPHAM SSC

'Sing me a song of a lad that is gone –
say could that lad be I?'
– Sing me a Song of a Lad that Is Gone, RLS –

I FIRST SAW the name Robert Louis Stevenson when I was given a copy of *Kidnapped* by a now very long-deceased aunt. I have that copy still. The date of reprinting is 1965, so I must have been around seven or eight years of age when I had the pleasure of reading *Kidnapped* for that first time. I have read much of RLS since – his novels, his poetry, his letters and his travel writing – but *Kidnapped* has a curious fascination for me, and I have reread it many times. My three children are all adults now, but each as a child was given a copy.

Boswell began his famous biography of Dr Johnson by saying that writing it was a 'presumptuous task' and Stevenson in his essay on Robert Burns commented that 'to write with authority about another man we must have fellow-feeling and some common ground of experience with our subject'. There I rest my case – I have no pretensions of Stevenson scholarship. I am just a plain man whose reading of Stevenson has enriched me and I have much fellow feeling. Even at a distance of more than half a century, I can still recall my childhood pleasure from the story of David Balfour and Alan Breck Stewart.

There is no denying Stevenson's gifts. He had a wonderful ability to weave plots from his imagination. He makes his characters real. Above all there is his gift for language:

> The sun began to shine upon the summit of the hills as I went down the road; and by the time I had come as far as the manse, the blackbirds were whistling in the garden lilacs, and the mist that hung around the valley in the time of the dawn was beginning to arise and die away.

The language which is priceless evokes time, place, atmosphere, smell, sound and surroundings. The debt of later Scottish novelists is considerable, and would it be disputed by Neil Munro, Neil Gunn, John Buchan or many others who came after?

I have come to appreciate that both David Balfour and Alan Breck were to some extent born of Stevenson's own personality. David Balfour is undoubtedly the sober, steady, reliable Presbyterian that no doubt Stevenson's lighthouse engineer father would have wished him to be; while Alan Breck Stewart is the brave, volatile, steadfastly loyal Jacobite of a sort that perhaps Stevenson would like to have been. Alan Breck was undoubtedly an adventurer – just as Stevenson himself, in his adult life, was in other ways an adventurer.

It was perhaps the character of Mr Rankeillor that made the biggest impression upon me. Even at an early age, I liked the idea of a lawyer as a man of business being buttonholed on many aspects of public and private affairs by those he met. If asked why I chose a career as a solicitor, I like to say – only half in jest – that it was because of Mr Rankeillor. Or maybe it was because, as a law student, I found a report of a case where the junior counsel was Mr R.L. Stevenson.

Alan, of course, would suffer no Gaelic to be spoken in David's presence and it was the references to it in *Kidnapped* that sparked in me a modest appetite for the language, satisfied only when I did a class on the subject in later life. All of the characters in *Kidnapped* are lifelike and carefully and realistically drawn – not just David and Alan, and Mr Rankeillor, but Captain Hoseason, Uncle Ebenezer, Mr Henderland, Neil Roy and all the others, including most poignantly poor James Stewart – James of the Glens, as he is referred to in the novel – whose memory is to this day perpetuated by the memorial at Ballachulish, where he was 'hanged on this spot for a crime of which he was not guilty'. He was, of course, all too real, but it was part of Stevenson's art that he was able to weave a novel out of a historical theme and to convey to the reader the flavour of divisions in eighteenth-century Scotland.

I wonder if all those who refer to a 'Jekyll and Hyde' character know they owe a debt to RLS. Surely Long John Silver has passed into legend?

If Stevenson is chiefly remembered for *Kidnapped* and *Treasure Island*, it is unfortunate that his poetry is not better known and more widely appreciated. I recently met a primary school teacher who was completely unaware of *A Child's Garden of Verses*. RLS's poem that resonates most with me is 'The Celestial Surgeon':

If I have faltered more or less
In my great task of happiness;
If I have moved among my race
And shown no glorious morning face;
If beams from happy human eyes
Have moved me not; if morning skies,
Books, and my food, and summer rain
Knocked on my sullen heart in vain:–
Lord, thy most pointed pleasure take
And stab my spirit broad awake.

The book of Genesis tells us that when Abraham died he was old and full of years, meaning he was old in a chronological sense, but also that he had used his time wisely. He had not wasted the time he was given. Stevenson died at the age of only 44. He cannot be said to have been old, but he was full of years. Despite the considerable challenges posed by prolonged ill health, he produced a remarkable canon of literature and poetry.

As these thoughts are expressed, the news is full of Brexit, which reminds me of David Balfour when he quarrelled with Alan on Rannoch Moor: 'Do you think it either very wise or very witty to cast my politics in my teeth? I thought, where folk differed, it was the part of gentlemen to differ civilly.'

I have often remarked that there is a book to be written about three fathers, Walter Scott Senior, William Burnes and Thomas Stevenson. RLS, writing on Burns, said that any view of Burns would be misleading which passed over in silence the influences of his home and his father (I doubt that I would be writing this without the influence of my own). Studying the life of RLS also requires an understanding of his distinguished lighthouse engineer forebears. Those who are interested in Burns, and his important place in Scottish literature, will benefit from reading Stevenson's views. No history of Scotland or of Edinburgh could be complete without reference to RLS, whose feelings for the sights and sounds of his country and his city were so intense.

RLS was also an important travel writer and his delightful book *Travels with a Donkey in the Cévennes* is a wonderful example of his ability to entertain with prose of the highest quality. Here he is on friendship: 'Of what shall a man be proud, if he is not proud of his friends?'

It was RLS who wrote that 'to travel hopefully is a better thing than to arrive', and 'I travel for travel's sake. The great affair is to move'. Move he certainly did, and I hope in his latter years he found some peace. His letters have an enduring quality of their own kind and are an indispensable source of light on his own life.

The prose simply walks off the page, as an enthusiast once told me. Stevenson's death meant that the sailor was home from sea and the hunter home from the hill, but let Neil Munro have the last word as he paid tribute to RLS following that fateful day in 1894:

O fine were these the tales that he narrated,
But there were others that he had in store;
Ours was the gain had he a little waited
But now our ears are vain for evermore!

David C. Clapham was educated at Hutchesons' Grammar School and the University of Strathclyde. As a solicitor, he is a consultant to Claphams, the law firm he founded in 1984, and he holds various part-time judicial appointments including part-time sheriff. He and his wife Debra have three grown-up children.

Stevenson and Weir

SARAH PURSER

IT WAS THANKS to an inspiring lecturer, the late Kenneth Simpson, that I first fell in love with the writing of Robert Louis Stevenson. Stevenson's works were not at that time, sad to say, on the syllabus in Scottish schools, and it was only because I chose a specific course on Scottish Literature at university that I became familiar with his writing.

Simpson introduced us to many extraordinary, often neglected, works of Scottish literature, but he had a particular passion for Stevenson, most especially for *Weir of Hermiston*. Simpson was not alone amongst academics to consider *Weir* Stevenson's finest piece of writing, and they are in good company: Louis thought *Weir* was the best he had ever written, so much so that the very quality of it frightened him... 'How shall I maintain the pitch?' he said.

Louis never did get to find out if he could maintain the pitch, as he died the very next day, at the tender age of 44. So, *Weir* stops mid-sentence. Unfinished. The thread left hanging. And it is this that first attracted me as a filmmaker. How great it would be to finish Louis's story for him and for us. To bring it to life again, and let it reach its happy, or unhappy, conclusion. To give Archie and Christina, the star-crossed lovers, at least a chance... The reader can imagine how the story might end, but wouldn't it be thrilling to see it actually play out?

Louis once wrote that 'Books are good enough in their own way, but they are a mighty bloodless substitute for life'. Cinema can breathe life into books and characters in a different way. The world one explores in a book, the visuals it conjures, is a private one, between the writer and the reader. With cinema, that world and those visuals can be universally shared and can give a story new life, often in quite unexpected ways. *Weir*, being an unfinished story, offers particular scope for that.

There have been countless film adaptations of Stevenson's work, over 100 versions of *Jekyll and Hyde* alone. But there has been very little of *Weir of Hermiston* on the big or small screen – and even less about the man himself – surprising, given the international regard in which he is held, and given the romantic, dramatic, and poignant life he led.

As I embarked on adapting *Weir* for the screen, I was increasingly drawn to Louis's Samoan life. That much of *Weir* is deeply autobiographical is broadly accepted – from Louis's own troubled relationship with his father, mirroring Archie's relationship with Lord Hermiston, to the need of both Louis and Archie to break away from the shackles of conformity that weigh heavy, along with the masterful depiction of the dark and brooding Edinburgh that both writer and creation inhabited.

It is beautiful, and moving, to picture Stevenson writing *Weir* from his home on the South Pacific island of Samoa, his very own treasure island, knowing he was never to return to Scotland. He describes in a letter in 1893 a 'wave of extraordinary and apparently baseless emotion' which made him literally stagger:

> And then the explanation came, and I knew I had found a frame of mind and body that belonged to Scotland... Highland huts, and peat smoke, and the brown swirling rivers, and wet clothes, and whiskey, and the romance of the past, and that indescribable bite of the whole thing at a man's heart, which is – or rather lies at the bottom of – a story.

The context in which Louis wrote *Weir of Hermiston* led me to think we should be doing more than a straightforward adaptation. What if we could not only bring *Weir* to life, but Louis as well – and allow him to finish his great masterpiece? We could intertwine both the story of the book, and that of Louis's life, allowing one to feed off and fuel the other, giving meaning and context to both. As Fanny wrote, 'Louis's work was always so mixed up with his home life', and testament to this is his beautiful dedication to her in *Weir of Hermiston*.

The cinematic opportunities in *Weir* are immense – the Four Black Brothers riding over the hill, the drama of the courtroom, the tragic beauty of the young lovers' romance. Also, the symmetry of the story, perfectly set up by Stevenson, that Archie – so judgmental of his father, and so opposed to the death penalty – could end up facing both the judgment of his own father and even the death penalty is ripe for the world of cinema.

When you add the Stevensons' life in Samoa to this rich palette – Mount Vaea towering above their home Vailima, Sosimo and the household staff (Louis's 'clan'), his extraordinary friendship with the Samoan chief Mata'afa, his battles in support of the Samoans against the rapacious empire building of the colonial powers – the possibilities are thrilling.

That Stevenson wrote cinematically is also a gift. Here he paints a picture of the very parallels we are drawing:

> Morning came, and showed mists on all the mountain-tops, a grey and yellow dawn, a fresh accumulation of rain imminent... and the whole harbour scene stripped of its tropic colouring and wearing the appearance of a Scottish loch.

It's described ready to be filmed, with emotional resonance for the actor in there, too.

Fanny said of Louis, 'His life had been one long romance, and he hoped to have a romantic end; the artist in him demanded that completeness... Could he have arranged his own life and death, how little things would have been changed.'

Louis's step-daughter Belle noticed at his funeral that from among the flowers, two Samoans 'had saved a little white tin cross trimmed with artificial flowers and fastened with cheap white ribbon... With what a tender smile would Louis regard this his monument'. Fanny also reflected: 'Nothing that money could buy would have pleased Louis more or more dearly touched his heart than this little tinsel cross.' Even in death, his life was cinematic.

When he wrote *Weir of Hermiston*, so very far away on the island of Samoa, Stevenson knew that he would never return to his homeland. Perhaps, though, with the magic of cinema, we can let him 'set his foot upon the heather' for one last time.

Sarah Purser formed Little White Rose Films with Tommy Gormley to bring the best of Scottish writing to the screen. As a producer and writer, Sarah has worked in theatre and film production as an assistant director prior to forming the company.

Writing RLS

JOHN PURSER

WE WERE STANDING in the hall at Vailima, my daughter and I, and the Samoan guide was concluding the tour before releasing us to explore as we wished. The guide was a young man who wanted to end with singing Stevenson's own epitaph. It was the young man's tune and his tribute. It was the simplest of things, sung without artifice but out of a genuine desire to express his own feelings – for us, yes, but for himself, too. We were both moved by his singing and he saw that and apologised after, as though he had perhaps touched on things that should not be touched. But, of course, he had touched on the things that absolutely should be touched. So there we were, on the far side of the world, a century and a quarter away from RLS himself, and there he was in spirit as alive as death can possibly allow.

The next day we climbed Mount Vaea to Stevenson's tomb. We were on a pilgrimage after all, though it was a struggle for me in the heat and humidity and in my old age, being overtaken by Samoans running up and down for their morning's exercise. But all were encouraging and finally, the sweat running off my brow and stinging my eyes, I made it. My daughter was there long since and there were two men mowing the plot, keeping the ever-greedy greenery from overwhelming everything. And out beyond, down the valley, beyond the pervasive greens, was the Pacific.

Why were we there? To any Stevenson fan that would be the silliest of questions, so perhaps I should explain *how* we were there. My daughter, Sarah, had asked me to join her in writing a film script combining Stevenson's last months in Samoa with the non-completion of *Weir of Hermiston*. I had been invited to New Zealand to give a series of talks at the New Zealand Gàidhealtachd in Whangārei Heads and this represented a last chance to get to Samoa. New Zealand is nearby, after all. Only it isn't. It's a four-hour flight from Auckland. That gives you some idea of the amount of time Stevenson must have spent at sea, and also the amount of distance he had put between himself and his past. To my delight, Sarah was able to join me. She has done all the research into Stevenson's family, but there were things even she discovered about them from the guide that are scarcely mentioned, if at all, in the extensive literature.

My own experience as a writer is that of a poet, music historian, and playwright. Three of my radio plays were Sunday plays for BBC Radio Scotland and Radio 3. All three were, for want of a better description, 'period dramas', one set in sixteenth-century Stirling, one in 1860s Oxford, and one in seventeenth-century Aberdeenshire. At least I was used to imagining and working with dialogue from different regions and different ages, so the late nineteenth century presented me with no terrors. Besides, my grandparents were born in the nineteenth century, so it was really no distance away at all.

Sarah had laid out the scenario for the film and chosen many quotations from RLS which gave life to the story of his last struggle with health and with the muse. She wanted to combine the two struggles and that meant imagining how Stevenson might have concluded *Weir of Hermiston*. I should say that right from the outset I realised that we had set ourselves a highly demanding task, blending all the storylines along with the complex realities of Stevenson's family life, the Samoan wars, and perhaps resolving the love story of Archie and Christina – or perhaps not. So we had to temper respect with our own need for narrative freedom – and this meant also a certain freedom from RLS's own narrative style. You cannot imitate Stevenson, and why even attempt it anyway? But you can take his work and his life as starting points. One thing we always wanted to retain was the power of imagination, the constant presence of fantasy. The sort of imaginative fun that can make stepping over a puddle a giant leap of faith. In other words, the world of childhood, but in a sometimes deeply alarming adult context.

Stylistically, RLS is of his time. Sentences are beautifully constructed. Dialogue is articulate and not frightened of including literary quality. Descriptions can be elaborate. Concision is not to the fore. In a play it should be; in a film script it has to be. So now and again quotations from RLS had to be doctored and descriptions re-written, never mind the editing of his narrative intentions. All this requires courage and a refusal to be intimidated by a great author. I am proud of the fact that rather than being intimidated, we have felt RLS as a constant source of inspiration without any fear of his ghostly retribution. When we have been stuck we have been able to go back to him again and again and there is always something, because the variety of his mind was rich and full of many environments.

In *Weir of Hermiston* Stevenson was ambitiously attempting to enter into a woman's mind more completely than ever before. Kirstie was the woman and she was central. But she was an early casualty in our script, appearing only as an independent-minded housekeeper, rather than a matriarchal force. We chose to give more attention to Frank as the source of Archie's weaknesses – and the ultimate provoker of his strengths. 'Enter Mephistopheles' – that's the title of the chapter which introduces one of the most vile and insidious characters in the history of literature. Iago is as close as any other author has got to such a hellish manipulator. But *Weir of Hermiston* was written by the author of *Dr Jekyll and Mr Hyde* and we were not going to be seduced by happy domesticity, abundant fruit, Pacific adventures and happy, gleaming Samoans. This film also has to confront the dark. *Et in Arcadia Ego.* It was not for nothing that Fanny wore a phial of cyanide around her neck, rather than be beheaded in some imagined Samoan misalliance.

But in the end, fear has to be conquered and trust has to be… well, trusted. That is the adventure. We have set ourselves out on an adventure and we shall see where it takes us. So far, the journey has indeed been demanding, but full of joys, and we hope our love of RLS will prove as worthy a homage as that of the young Samoan who sang to us in Vailima as though no time had elapsed, nor ever would.

John Purser is an award-winning writer, musicologist and composer. His published works include poetry; radio plays; *Scotland's Music* and, with Dr Meg Bateman, *Window to the West*. He is a researcher at Sabhal Mòr Ostaig, the Gaelic College on Skye, where he lives and crofts with his wife, Barbara.

An Unfinished Masterpiece
PAUL H. SCOTT

STEVENSON had no doubt that *Weir of Hermiston*, the novel on which he was working and left unfinished when he died in December 1894, would be his best. He told Belle Strong: 'I see it all so clearly! The story unfolds itself before me to the last detail there is nothing left in doubt. I never felt so before in anything I ever wrote. It will be my best work; I feel myself so sure in every word.' It was a book which reflected his strongest interests and feelings – first of all, about Scotland itself, to which his thoughts constantly turned, even – or perhaps particularly – in the very different atmosphere of Samoa.

You see this frequently in his letters. In November 1892, he wrote to J.M. Barrie: 'It is a singular thing that I should live here in the South Seas under conditions so new and so striking, and yet my imagination so continually inhabit that cold old huddle of grey hills from which we come.' Even more powerfully, in May 1893, he wrote to Sidney Colvin:

> I was standing out on the little veranda in front of my room this morning, and there went through me or over me a heave of extraordinary and apparently baseless emotion. I literally staggered. And then the explanation came, and I knew I had found a frame of mind and body that belonged to Scotland,

and particularly to the neighbourhood of Callendar. Very odd these identities of a sensation, and the world of connotations implied; Highland huts, and peat smoke, and the brown swirling rivers, and wet clothes and whisky, and the romance of the past, and the indescribable bite of the whole thing at a man's heart.

This passion for Scotland also includes Stevenson's love of the Scots language in which all the best dialogue of the novel is written. He spoke it constantly with Charles Baxter and other friends of his youth and, throughout his life, he often uses it in his letters to Baxter. When he wrote to him on 14 February 1886, to ask him to accept the dedication of *Kidnapped*, he said this: 'What's mair, Sir, it's Scotch: no strong, for the sake o' thae pock-puddens, but jist a kitchen o't, to leeven the wersh, sapless, fushionless, stotty, stytering South-Scotch thae think sae muckle o'.'

Book II of his collection of poems, *Underwoods*, is in Scots. He says of the language, in the first of these poems, the 'Maker to Posterity', that it is: *'Dear to my heart as the peat-reek/ Auld as Tantallon.'* And he says of it in a foreword to the book that it was the 'language spoken about my childhood', but he fears that 'the day draws near when this illustrious and malleable tongue shall be quite forgotten'. Unfortunately, it has certainly declined in use since Stevenson's time, but much fine poetry continues to be written in it and many people are devoted to its restoration.

You would not suspect from the novel, as it stands unfinished, that Stevenson in his youth also expressed a sympathetic response to the man on whom the character of Weir of Hermiston is based. The original was, of course, Robert McQueen, Lord Braxfield. One of Stevenson's early essays, published in *Virginibus Puerisque* in 1881, was 'Some Portraits by Raeburn', about an exhibition of Raeburn's in Edinburgh. His account of the Braxfield portrait (which you can see in the Scottish National Portrait Gallery) is almost affectionate. It begins:

If I know gusto in painting when I see it, this canvas was painted with rare enjoyment.

The tart, rosy, humorous look of the man, his nose like a cudgel, his face resting squarely on the jowl, has been caught and perpetuated with something which looks like brotherly love. A peculiarly subtle expression haunts the lower part, sensual and incredulous, like that of a man tasting good Bordeaux with half a fancy that it has been somewhat too long uncorked.

So, Stevenson continues in the same spirit, but later he tempers it with both admiration and an acknowledgement of Braxfield's brutality:

He was the last judge on the Scotch bench to employ the pure Scotch idiom. His opinions, thus given in the Doric, and conceived in a lively, rugged, conversational style, were full of point and authority. Out of the bar, or off the bench, he was a convivial man, a lover of wine and one who 'shone peculiarly' at tavern meetings. He has left behind him an unrivalled reputation for rough and cruel speech; to this day his name smacks of the gallows.

The novel, as it stands, displays only the aggressive and brutal side of the man. Perhaps his more sympathetic side might have appeared if Stevenson had been able to continue. He left a fairly clear idea of how the novel was to finish. Archie, following his conversation with the elder Kirstie about his association with the younger one, resolves to avoid conduct that might damage her reputation. Frank Innes takes advantage of this and seduces her. Archie has a meeting with Frank at the Weaver's Stone which ends with a duel in which Frank is killed.

Archie is brought to trial for murder before his father and is sentenced to death. Stevenson seems to have considered two different endings. In one the Elliot brothers, in good Borders tradition, invade the prison and rescue him. The other version ends with Kirstie visiting him in prison and reaching a final reconciliation with him.

David Daiches, in his book *RLS and his World*, said: 'On the last day of his life his imagination inhabited Scotland... Above all, his Calvinist ancestors, and his artistic bohemianism, working together in counterpoint, kept fertilising his imagination.' Curiously, Daiches puts so much emphasis on the Covenanters, on whom there is not much obvious emphasis in the novel. Certainly, it begins with a reference to the monument to the Praying Weaver of Balweary, shot by Claverhouse with his own hand, as an episode in his campaign against the Covenanters. In his childhood, Stevenson's imagination had been filled with tales of this kind by his nursemaid, Cummy. His first book, *The Pentland Rising*, was about the Covenanters. But it is more the atmosphere of the ballads and of the Border history of raids and forays which lies behind much of the novel with its four black brothers of the Cauldstaneslap.

Unfinished as it is, I have no doubt that *Weir of Hermiston* is a great novel and Stevenson's best work. It is a book which you can read many times and always with increased pleasure.

Edinburgh-born Paul Scott attended the Royal High School and Edinburgh University, served in the 52nd (Lowland) and 7th Armoured Divisions during the war, then joined the Diplomatic Service, in Berlin, Cuba and elsewhere. His books include *Walter Scott and Scotland*, *John Galt*, *Towards Independence*, and *Still in Bed with an Elephant*. Paul passed away, aged 98, in March 2019.

Stevenson:
the First Global Author

PROFESSOR PENNY FIELDING

STEVENSON has been absorbed into our cultural world in such a general way that it can be hard to imagine reading him for the first time. It's almost impossible now to think of the readers who started reading *Strange Case of Dr Jekyll and Mr Hyde* with no expectation of who 'Mr Hyde' would turn out to be. Neither can we project ourselves back to the readers of *Treasure Island* in the *Young Folks* newspaper who had no idea that the exciting treasure-hunting romance story, so familiar to them from Christian moralising novels such as R.M. Ballantyne's *The Coral Island*, would end with the nightmare memories of the young hero.

How, then, should we think about the radical innovations that Stevenson brought to literature? Even if we can't recreate the visceral moment of the first readers, we can still look back at the changes Stevenson brought about in the history of fiction. One way of doing this is to think of him as the first truly global writer – an author who exploited the expanding world of the nineteenth century both metaphorically and literally.

Stevenson burst onto the publishing scene at a time when the standard format of the bulky three-volume novel was falling in popularity. He flourished in a literary world that was becoming unbounded, both in its subject matter and in its readership. His works were rapidly sold to American publishers and very widely translated in Europe. After Stevenson had moved to Samoa, some first editions appeared in the United States – we can even think of a novel like *The Master of Ballantrae*, with its scenes in the North East wilderness, as an American novel as well as a Scottish one. In fact, Stevenson conceives of history itself as global and *The Master of Ballantrae* is set against a background of international warfare. At the start of the novel, the Jacobite Rising draws in forces from France and Ireland, and the travels of James Durie follow the centres of conflict during the Seven Years War – not only North America but also India, where Britain competed with France for trading positions.

This very wide global distribution in Stevenson's works comes at the same time as an information revolution. Stevenson's lifetime coincides with the opening-up of the globe to communications technology. 1866 saw the first successful transatlantic telegraph cable. In 1870, a cable was laid from London to Mumbai, and by 1872, India was linked to Australia. In the second half of the 1870s the telephone was being developed, just in time for Louis, in California with Fanny, to experiment with the new invention, as he tells us in *The Silverado Squatters* of 1883:

> But it was an odd thing that here, on what we are accustomed to consider the very skirts of civilization, I should have used the telephone for the first time in my civilized career. So it goes in these young countries; telephones, and telegraphs, and newspapers, and advertisements running far ahead among the Indians and the grizzly bears.

The technologically connected globe features in some expected places in Stevenson's work. The scientific explanation of telephonic communications is transmuted into the language of poetry and fiction. In one of his finest poems, written in the Gilbert Islands (now the nation of Kiribati), Stevenson thinks out the problem of global distance. He knows how telephones work and how the telegraph works, and he knows they are not the same technology. But the nature of poetry is that metaphor can supersede the logic of technological history. Stevenson knew how the telephone allowed you to hear a distant voice. And he knew that the transcontinental telegraph system could transcribe a voice in the sender's mind through a series of electronic signals to the eyes of a reader.

But as a poet he could transcend this scientific understanding to talk about the nature of friendship. 'To SC' is about the distance between where he is now in the Gilberts, and his memories of being in the London home of his friend and literary mentor, Sidney Colvin. As he walks on the beach, Stevenson remembers a time when he was in Colvin's house at night and 'heard far off / The unsleeping city murmur like a shell'. The metaphor of the seashell, in which one can hear the sound of the sea, acts as a kind of mnemonic telephone that connects the Pacific beach, where he is physically, with his memories of Colvin's house in London. Shells and telephones allow us to hear what is not physically present. Stevenson's telephonic imagination allows him to be in two places at the same time.

At the end of his writing career, living in Samoa, Stevenson was more aware than ever of a world where distances could be measured in miles or in seconds. *The Ebb-Tide*, one of Stevenson's late masterpieces, is a dark take on the treasure-hunting Romance story. In an ironic echo of imperial adventure novels such as *The Coral Island*, the three anti-heroes find themselves broke, sick and washed-up on a beach in Tahiti. Herrick, more educated than the other two, invents an elaborate story about meeting an old Arab seaman who owns a 'Travelling Carpet'. Herrick proposes that he use the carpet to return home to Britain:

> 'All right,' I said; 'and do you mean to tell me I can get on that carpet and go straight to London, England?' I said, 'London, England,' captain, because he seemed to have been so long

in your part of the world. 'In the crack of a whip,' said he. I figured up the time. What is the difference between Papeete and London, captain?

The American sea-captain, who is listening to this story, explains the 'difference' in terms of maritime technology: 'Taking Greenwich and Point Venus, nine hours, odd minutes and seconds.' Herrick asks about the time difference not to see how long it would take him to get there (the imaginary carpet ride is instantaneous) but to know what time it will be in London when he gets there. The experience of physical distance is abolished – temporal difference has become relative.

In this new magical world of instant communication, things that were previously far apart have come together. In another sense of the term, Herrick is asking how 'different' London, centre of the Empire, is from the Imperial outposts of the Pacific. As he goes on with his story of the magic carpet ride, London becomes a magical exotic place out of the *Arabian Nights*. Herrick's two companions chip in with suggestions of the cornucopia of food and wines they would tuck into in London. But, of course, this is a fantasy. As a rainstorm approaches them on the Tahiti beach they seek shelter in a disused prison – 'three sops of humanity on the cold coral floors'.

As in many of Stevenson's late Pacific works, the tables have been turned on imperial myth making. The oriental exoticism of the South Seas has been transferred back to the Imperial Centre, which now only exists for the three adventurers as a fragile fantasy. As the world was becoming more connected, Stevenson's writing was becoming more diverse and experimental. The technological advances of his lifetime freed his imagination to think about the relation of times and places in new ways.

Penny Fielding is Grierson Professor of English Literature at the University of Edinburgh. She is a General Editor of the Edinburgh Edition of the Works of Robert Louis Stevenson and editor of the *Edinburgh Companion to Stevenson*. She particularly enjoys teaching Stevenson's work to new generations of students.

Stevenson the Ubiquitous
IAN NIMMO

ALTHOUGH I HAVE NEVER seen it mentioned, or visible in any of the Robert Louis Stevenson photographs or portraits, Louis must have had a small bump on the middle finger of his right hand, left of first joint. I have one. So do all my old newspaper ex-hot-metal sub-editor friends from the old days before the introduction of computers to editorial departments. The lump is a badge of honour to that dwindling company, won by wielding a heavy editing pencil at speed, racing the clock over years and years. With Stevenson's daily writing output, scratching with his fast pen – essays, novels, poems, doodles, as well as being one of the great letter writers of his age – that tell-tale callus would have been unavoidable.

What a newspaper columnist or television pundit he would have made with his pungent views, independent mind, power of description and expression. Remember how his rhetoric enthralled members of London's Savile Club and in the artists' colony at Grèz-sur-Loing. His compassion for the underdog could have made him a great campaigning journalist. Remember his support for the heroic Father Damien de Veuster, Saint of Molokai, the leprosy island. Remember how *The Times* was so pleased to publish his comments and backing for the local islanders in the Samoan War. Remember how he was among the first of a new breed of insightful travel writers, breaking fresh ground, with his eye for detail and a vivid turn of phrase from outlandish locations.

Nearly 130 years after his death, Stevenson still surprises, and I keep bumping into him unexpectedly in the most unlikely places...

While working in West Africa – The Gambia, Nigeria, Ghana and down to Sierra Leone – I'm introduced to a man called Robert M'Fosa, who proudly tells me his full name is Robert Louis Stevenson M'Fosa. 'How did you come by that particular name?' I ask. He responds with a reprimand: 'I thought you would have known that. He was one of your country's greatest writers.' His father had studied at the University of Edinburgh where he fell under the Stevenson spell.

By chance I'm in New York, a few days after September Eleven, the city in shock. A sculptor friend takes me to lunch in the Century Club, one of the finest private clubs in the world, home of the American great and good. I chat with a Club executive and mention I'm following Robert Louis Stevenson's footsteps – next stops San Francisco, Los Angeles and onwards to Samoa. He gives me a strange look. 'Stay put, don't move,' he orders. A few minutes later he returns with a wooden box. Inside is an old flintlock revolver with the explanation that it once belonged to Robert Louis Stevenson. It was presented to the Century Club by the artist Joseph Strong, RLS's step-son-in-law, instrumental in taking the Stevensons to the South Seas. Highly collectable still in American art circles, Strong later became a prominent Century Club member.

I'm crossing Canada east to west, and stop for the night in the British Columbian town of Kamloops. It's late evening, there is only a bookshop open on what I take to be the main street. I stroll in, browse – and find a complete set of RLS's *Tusitala* edition in the tiny antique book section buried in the vastness of Canada.

I'm in Shanghai launching a new daily newspaper, casting an eye over the stories, and come upon a couple of paragraphs about a Chinese lady named Fang Guxiu who had translated *A Child's*

Garden of Verses into Chinese. It was incorporated in a book by her husband, Tu An, with other translations of British poets, and published by the Children's Book Publishing House of China. I resist the temptation to splash it.

I'm in Australia and visit Sydney's Union Club, where RLS was an honorary member in the early 1890s. The Club has changed premises since Louis's day, but is still an island of exclusiveness in the bustle of the city. I'm anticipating no sign of Stevenson. But, lo, his favoured leather armchair is a precious heirloom in the library, and a little known painting – more cartoon perhaps – of RLS striding the Club's old drawing room, arm raised in poetic exclamation or, it has been suggested, when composing his open letter of support for Father Damien. Startled faces of distinguished members gaze upon him in waking-up alarm. The exalted Union Club is unaccustomed to such agitated behaviour. The artist is George Molnar, the painting unlisted, and therefore exciting, and the Robert Louis Stevenson Club is permitted to publish it on the front page of its newsletter, once only, one edition, a world exclusive.

I'm driving north in coastal California. Someone tells me I should visit the Treasure Island golf course. I think my leg is being pulled. I swing down Stevenson Drive, Pebblebeach, and find the Spyglass Hill Golf Course. Magnificent. I make inquiries and find the first hole is named Treasure Island, and the second Billy Bones, the third The Black Spot, and so on to include Israel Hands, Captain Flint, Long John Silver, Black Dog, Jim Hawkins and Ben Gunn holes.

Years later I'm in California's Monterey, with the Robert Louis Stevenson Club, standing in what was the white-painted, verandahed French Hotel, Jules Simoneau's part-bar, part-barber's shop, part-restaurant below. Simoneau kept a watchful, fatherly eye on the strange, likeable, broke, young Scotsman under his roof. It's a museum now, holding some of the most cherished Stevenson artefacts in the world. One of his velvet jackets is on show, the narrowness of the shoulders a shock as it confirms what a bag of bones he was. Heriot Row furniture is on display, shipped to California via Vailima – RLS's travelling trunk, first editions of his works, photographs and paintings we do not recognise. Edinburgh is five thousand miles away, yet Stevenson feels close.

In the Santa Cruz wilderness, guarded by poisoned oak and giant redwoods, we track down the remaining boards and chimney of the old goat ranch. Here Stevenson was nursed after the ranch children found him unconscious, half-in, half-out of a nearby creek, his life almost at a dramatic end. We talk and think about him out there in the silence, and read some of his appropriate writings, and it is as if he is watching us.

We are heading for the Napa Valley, where RLS and Fanny spent their honeymoon in the Silverado bunkhouse, halfway up Mount Saint Helena in the Robert Louis Stevenson State Park. A large welcoming sign at the entrance to the Valley bears a quote from RLS. 'And the wine is bottled poetry,' it declares, taken from his essay on the Schramsberg Vineyards. On the flank of Mount Saint Helena is a little memorial topped by an open stone book in Stevenson's name. We again read from his work, near where the old bunkhouse stood, derelict even then, poisoned oak creeping through the floorboards, and we find the experience moving. Did the mountain wind rustling surrounding trees disguise past voices?

Stevenson's Heriot Row toy soldiers parade below, straight from the *Land of Counterpane*, now permanently barracked in the wonderful Stevenson Museum at St Helena, along with RLS's marriage certificate, his writing desk, a painting of the *Casco*, her original nameplate, Lloyd Osbourne's diary of their cruise, Fanny's and Joe Strong's paintings, photographs, childhood letters and some 11,000 other RLS artefacts. It is the largest RLS collection in the world. Frail old Ed Reynolds, a former curator and Hollywood scriptwriter, catches us off guard by reading his one-man play on Stevenson to us, and it is yet another unforgettable RLS happening.

The man is ubiquitous. If you seek him he will be found or turn up uninvited without prior notice. Travelling with the RLS Club, we found him at Yale University's Beinecke Library of rare books and manuscripts in New Haven, Connecticut; and on the train making for Saranac, along the Hudson, where actor John Shedden gave us an abiding Ticonderoga as the wheels turned, and we sensed Stevenson at the back of our carriage listening. At Saranac, the former sanatorium where he stayed in the dead of winter, temperatures plummeted to 30 below with RLS in a buffalo skin coat. Yet, it was there with a frozen blue nose he penned the first chapters of *The Master of Ballantrae*.

We felt sure he was smiling when we restaged that duel-by-bagpipe scene from *Kidnapped* between Alan Breck and Robin Oig MacGregor at Balquhidder, some of the finest pipers in the world giving us a blaw. In France we felt RLS's presence when we discovered the jail where he was interrogated after his arrest on suspicion of being a Prussian spy in the little French town of Chatillon-sur-Loire in the Central-Val de Loire region. When we joined the artists' colony at Grèz-sur-Loing and made merry as he did before us, we guessed he was in a corner, glass and cigarette in hand, enjoying it all over again.

For a moment we thought we saw his amused face on shore as we boarded the old sailing ship Tangaroa in Bristol, the Hispaniola's home port. The gentlemen among us daringly set sail in kilts – not too high up the rigging, chaps! – and headed for the sea as if we were setting sail for Treasure Island. The Mayor of Bristol came part of the voyage with us, and now The Long John Silver Trust has developed a Treasure Island trail around the historic harbour.

We found Stevenson when we plodded the 150 miles across the Cévennes, prodding that independent-minded animal Modestine along what has become the Donkey Trail after RLS pioneered the route with *Travels with a Donkey in the Cévennes*. As we descended from the high tops into the valleys at night he was at the heart of the festivities in his name, Robert Louis Stevenson banners and images slung high across village streets. More than 6,000 walkers now march the trail's magnificence every summer, and it has become an important element of the region's economy.

Both Stevenson and Sir Walter Simpson were just ahead of us all along our *An Inland Voyage* safari from Antwerp, in the wake of their canoes – the *Arethusa* and *Cigarette* – by canals and rivers all the way to Paris. Not so daft as to canoe ourselves, we walked and coached it, by the Scheld, past Boom, Willebroek, Maubeuge, through the forest of Mormal, and in the sunlight filtering through the trees did we glimpse two figures? Canoeists a-plenty these days all along those waterways.

On these excursions accents are always our giveaway and, like Stevenson, inevitably we carry our Scottishness with us. He did not wave a saltire or seek a soapbox to proclaim it, yet he was as Scots as 'Talisker, Isla or Glenlivet' or our Jekyll-and-Hyde weather. He was an international Scot, of course, with a wider view than from these shores alone, his accent forever Edinburgh, a Scot thirled to Scotland. And was there ever a writer with such an ear for Scots dialogue – the East Lothian of Tam Dale, the Capital's High Street of David Balfour's porter in *Catriona*, or the Highland of Alan Breck or Cluny Macpherson? The Scots tongue – the language of childhood and the heart – was as dear to him, he said, as peat-reek.

Remember that letter of reply to his fellow poet and Penicuik Free Kirk minister, Samuel Rutherford Crockett, written from the snows of Saranac in the Adirondacks. Stevenson signed off a very pleasant and amusing letter with a feigned rebuke because Crockett had used NB instead of Scotland in the address: 'Don't put NB on your paper: put Scotland, and be done with it,' he wrote. 'Alas, that I should be stabbed in the house of my friends! The name of my native land is not North Britain, whatever may be the name of yours.'

Remember, the year before he died, RLS's letter from Vailima to his friend Sidney Colvin:

> I was standing out on the little verandah, in front of my room this morning, and there went through me or over me a wave of extraordinary and apparently baseless emotion. I literally staggered. And then the explanation came, and I knew I had found a frame of mind and body that belonged to Scotland... Highland huts, and peat smoke, and the brown swirling rivers, and wet clothes, and whisky, and the romance of the past, and that indescribable bite of the whole thing at a man's heart.

That final year there was talk of him at last coming home. Those fond images of Scotland and his descriptions of them, often written long after the experience, would have been on his mind then...

> *I saw rain falling and the rainbow drawn*
> *On Lammermuir. Hearkening I heard again*
> *In my precipitous city beaten bells*
> *Winnow the keen sea wind...*

Such images came vividly to him when, half a world away in Samoa, he sat penning *Catriona*:

> There began to fall a greyness on the face of the sea; little dabs of pink and red, like coals of slow fire, came from the east; and at the same time the geese awakened, and began crying about the top of the Bass...

Likewise when he wrote *The Merry Men*:

> Over all the lowlands of the Ross, the wind must have blown as upon the open sea; and God only knows the uproar that

was raging round Ben Kyaw. Sheets of mingled spray and rain were driven in our faces. All round the isle of Aros the surf, with an incessant hammering thunder, beat upon the reef and beaches. Now louder in one place, now lower in another, like the combinations of orchestral music...

The tragedy is he never returned from Samoa. Never lived to confront the challenging new directions he had hoped to pursue as a writer. In that respect, Stevenson died unfulfilled and, as with so many other writers and poets who passed before their time, we are left to wonder at what might have been achieved.

Yet those in the Robert Louis Stevenson Club know almost 130 years after Stevenson's death he has never been out of print. Somewhere in the world, *Treasure Island*, *Kidnapped* or *Strange Case of Dr Jekyll and Mr Hyde* is being shown on screen or performed on stage. Discussion and debate at every level about Stevenson as a writer, and as a man, continue across the world. He is tangible to the pupils in the Robert Louis Stevenson School in Samoa, and at California's Pebble Beach, and up the Napa Valley. He is remembered at Sidney's Circular Quay; at Alaincourt on the Oise in the Hauts-de-France; on David Balfour's isle of Erraid off the Ross of Mull; at that sailing ship monument to him near Chinatown in San Francisco; in the Beinecke outside New York, at the Houghton collection at Harvard University, at Edinburgh Napier University and in Edinburgh's Writers' Museum, where a stream of visitors from across the globe enquire about him daily. The list goes on and on. And Stevenson remains, it seems, one of that small band of writers who, somehow, we feel is still around.

Ian Nimmo is a former long-serving newspaper editor and consultant at home and abroad, a lecturer, and a former chairman of the Robert Louis Stevenson Club. He is the author of ten books, including an investigation into the Appin Murder, the historical event around which Stevenson wove his fiction in *Kidnapped*.

The Resident Curator

NICHOLAS RANKIN

THE LETTER came from Hawai'i at the end of 2018. Rabbi Rita Leonard, the President of the not-for-profit Stevenson Society of America, needed new members and money for repairs to be sent to PO Box 607, Saranac Lake, New York 12983. Her letter began: 'Remember the lovely Stevenson museum in Saranac Lake you may have visited in earlier times?' Indeed, I did.

It was Saturday 11 August 1984 when I first walked along the green veranda and knocked on the door of what a tourist poster called 'the quaint old cottage', set behind a white picket fence on the eastern edge of the town in upstate New York. Beside the door, a 1915 bronze bas-relief by sculptor Gutzon Borglum depicted my quarry in trapper's furs: 'Here dwelt Robert Louis Stevenson during the winter 1887–1888.' Three days out of England, I was going around the world to write my first book, *Dead Man's Chest*, tracking the author of *Treasure Island* from Scotland to Samoa.

A young man my own age opened the door, a bluff-looking fellow with reddish hair. I introduced myself and my project and he stuck out a frank, friendly hand: 'Hi! I'm Mike Delahant.' I paid my dollar and he showed me around the few rooms of the house, 'Baker's', where the Stevenson family lived for six months in the 'stringent cold' of the Adirondack Mountains. They paid $50 a month plus $2 per cord of firewood while the consumptive but productive author, under the care of the physician Edward Livingston Trudeau (great-grandfather of the *Doonesbury* creator), put on weight and got his health back, walking in the snow in his buffalo robes and ice-skating on Moody Pond.

Turning 37, RLS was a success in the USA, 'really growing Bloated with Lucre', as he put it. *Scribner's Magazine* had offered $3,500 for a dozen essays and the dramatisation of *Dr Jekyll and Mr Hyde* had just opened at the Madison Square Theatre. I touched burn-marks on the mantelpiece from the roll-ups carelessly left by RLS himself, who favoured 'cigarettes without intermission, except when coughing or kissing'. Then I settled at a desk with some books. As Mike guided other visitors, I chipped in extra scraps of knowledge through the door. Afterwards he split the tips fifty-fifty; 'Fair's fair,' said Mike. We found we shared our birth-year too, exactly a century after Stevenson's.

At his invitation, I spent the rest of that weekend at the cottage, unrolling a sleeping-bag out back, exploring the museum's treasures, like RLS's narrow brown boots, stuffed with an 1897 Sydney newspaper; a velvet jacket with silk lapels; a handsome bronze head; some printing blocks carved by RLS himself for his stepson's tiny Davos Press; a few of his mother's scrapbooks. Endowed by the writer's friends in 1915 and incorporated as a not-for-profit educational entity in 1920, the Memorial Cottage and Museum was the world's first site dedicated to Robert Louis Stevenson. Mike was the third generation of Delahants keeping an eye on it. His dad Jack first suggested he sleep there as a kind of security guard, in September 1980; it was essentially a 'crashpad' for the young man.

I next saw Mike Delahant 10 years later. With the publication of *Dead Man's Chest* forthcoming, I had got a job as a BBC talks scriptwriter, and by autumn 1994 I was a staff producer at the World Service, making a three-part radio version of the book for the centenary of Stevenson's death falling that December. Arriving in New York City on the way back from Polynesia, I stretched my BBC budget to make a flying day trip 300 miles north to Saranac Lake in its fall colours. Mike picked me up at the tiny airstrip, we bought burgers at a drive-thru and I interviewed him on my (pre-digital) Sony Professional cassette-recorder. We chewed over the quid of our lives: marriage, children, the death of parents. Karla LaDue had moved in with Mike, galvanising him to action. Her brother Brian helped Mike fix the house – insulating, re-wiring, plumbing, etc. – and she made a home, with flowers.

The radio programme was able to use pre-publication excerpts from the Yale University Press *Letters of Robert Louis Stevenson* because I was reading the proofs for its editor, the remarkable retired civil servant Ernest J. Mehew. He had got into Huntingdon Grammar School with an essay on what Jim Hawkins overheard in the apple barrel, and he never stopped reading RLS thereafter.

Mehew never went to university or owned a computer. Having worked for Rupert Hart-Davis on the Oscar Wilde letters, he took on Stevenson's correspondence in 1968. Assisted only by his wife Joyce Wilson, he meticulously edited 2,800 letters in eight volumes, with concise links and footnotes.

Volume Six has over 130 pages written from Saranac Lake in 1887–88. Baker's, the hunter's home where fur-clad Stevenson could play 'a rank Saranacker and wild man of the woods', was freezing, but ink flowed freely. *The Master of Ballantrae* was conceived one frosty night on the veranda, 'the air extraordinary clear and cold, and sweet with the purity of forests'. Stevenson also completed the dozen essays for *Scribner's*, remembering dreams, childhood reading, boyhood games, descending in a diving suit in Wick harbour, thinking about beggars and gentlemen, art and morality. His stepson Lloyd Osbourne drafted *The Wrong Box* at Saranac Lake, and the quarrel between Stevenson and the poet W.E. Henley (the crutch-wielding original of Long John Silver) erupted here after Henley suggested that Stevenson's wife Fanny was a plagiarist.

A dozen years passed before I saw Mike Delahant again. Twenty-first-century academia had struck gold in the Stevenson seam; exegetical strip-mining was under way. Biennial international Stevenson conferences started in 2000; *The Journal of Stevenson Studies* in 2004. When Saranac Lake hosted the 2006 Transatlantic Stevenson conference, I attended, staying with Mike and Karla and the dogs at the repainted, repaired, centrally-heated Memorial Cottage, where I saddle-soaped and polished Stevenson's high-laced Australian boots and slept among the museum treasures that now included the pinkish pebble Jorge Luis Borges gave me after I read aloud to him Stevenson's fable *The Touchstone*, an event I described in the prologue to *Dead Man's Chest*. Borges enjoyed RLS's prose as he did the taste of coffee, and he thought him 'not only a great writer, but a great man' and a personal friend. 'If you don't like Stevenson,' Borges once remarked, 'there must be something wrong with you.' On the last night, Mike and I got trumpeting drunk on my duty-free Scotch. 'I like water (fresh water I mean),' Stevenson had written to Henry James from Saranac Lake in early October 1887, 'largely qualified with whisky.'

When Mike and I first met, we were light-hearted youths; Philip Mason called *Dead Man's Chest* 'essentially a young man's book'. Age, with its stealing steps, has changed that. Now grumpy and grey-haired, Mike and I are both a quarter of a century older than RLS was when the stroke felled him at Vailima. We are not kin, but we are kith, forever bound together in the clan who attend the same chief, 'the lean man' as he called himself in Samoa.

What inspires loyalty? At the October 1915 unveiling of the Borglum bas-relief, Lloyd Osbourne pointed out that Stevenson had read *Don Quijote* at Saranac, even stumbling through it in Spanish, and said that RLS identified completely with the deluded Don Quixote, who, as Cervantes says, 'was not only well loved by those of his household – *bien querido de los de su casa, sino de todos cuantos le conocían* – but by all who knew him'. The

Irish American publisher Sam McClure, who came up to Saranac Lake in November 1887 to offer the author $8,000 for a sequel to *Kidnapped*, said Stevenson had qualities which 'made one eager to serve him in every possible way'.

Stevensonian duty unexpectedly knocked at my door. When E.J. Mehew, editor of the Stevenson letters, died in 2011, he was lodged in a bleak care-home with Joyce, who by then had dementia. They had no children or family who understood their scholarship. Ernest's disciple of more than 40 years, Dr Roger G. Swearingen, lived 6,000 miles away in California. Time for a clansman to step up. So, I registered Ernest's death, found his will, conducted his cremation, and became his executor. This involved selling their little house in Stanmore to guarantee better care for Joyce. Roger and I ensured that their papers went to the National Library of Scotland and their books reached Edinburgh Napier University, with a dedicated room for the Ernest & Joyce Mehew Collection. I posted a full set of the Yale *Letters* to Saranac Lake, where my own Stevenson books will go one day.

Mike Delahant had no idea how much service would follow his first agreement to bunk at the house. What RLS called 'the romance of destiny' has become his lifetime's work, staunchly maintaining the Memorial Cottage, explaining it in the pages of the *Adirondack Daily Enterprise* and enduring all the boredoms and satisfactions of meeting pilgrims. Mike has poured thousands of his own dollars into the place. He has defended it from the brutalities of time and climate (RLS experienced 40°C below), and even against a cabal on a previous board of the Stevenson Society of America who tried to evict him. One damning accusation was 'permitting the unauthorised handling of collection materials' by Nicholas Rankin. (Yes, I polished Robert Louis Stevenson's boots.) My friend the Resident Curator has weathered all storms.

[This article first appeared in the *Times Literary Supplement* on 12 April 2019.]

The Resident Curator

Nicholas Rankin grew up in Kenya and spent his twenties in South America and Spain. An encounter with Jorge Luis Borges led to his writing *Dead Man's Chest: Travels after Robert Louis Stevenson* and joining the BBC World Service, where he worked for twenty years, winning two UN awards. His other books for Faber include *Telegram from Guernica*, *Churchill's Wizards*, *Ian Fleming's Commandos* and *Defending the Rock*.

Re-reading Robert Louis Stevenson's South Sea Tales

JANE ROGERS

I FIRST READ Robert Louis Stevenson's *South Sea Tales* 17 years ago. They are wonderful but seem strangely little-known. So I pitched to adapt them for radio. At long last, thanks to the magical addition of David Tennant to the cast, the project got a green light. Two of the best of these tales, 'The Beach of Falesá' and *The Ebb Tide* became radio dramas in 2016.

Adapting a book is a sure-fire way of discovering its strengths and weaknesses; its plot must prove truly dramatic; dialogue must not only ring true, but simultaneously reveal character and advance the action. Stevenson's *South Sea Tales* were my tenth foray into adapting for Radio 4's *Classic Serial* slot and, from Edith Wharton to Dodie Smith by way of John Wyndham, I have never felt more privileged to be let loose on another writer's work than this.

Both tales (novellas, in fact, at 70 and 131 pages respectively) were written while Stevenson lived in Samoa, 1890–4, in the final years of his tragically short life. He brought to them all the literary skills he had developed over his career as a best-selling writer, but beyond skill and confidence, these tales have a savage political and moral engagement, a real-world vision, and a bleak black humour, which is more distilled here than in anything else he wrote.

Stevenson and his wife Fanny set off for the South Seas in 1888 when he knew he was under sentence of death. He'd been suffering lung haemorrhages for years and doctors advised a warmer climate. Exploring the islands gave him a new energy and engaged his passionate curiosity about the islanders, both colonisers and colonised. From the start his attitude to the indigenous people, who included cannibals, differed widely from that of most other Europeans. In the second chapter of *In the South Seas* (his journalism about his travels), he reveals that he found many resemblances between them and Scottish Highlanders and Islanders of the eighteenth century:

> In both cases an alien authority enforced, the clans disarmed, the chiefs deposed, new customs introduced, and chiefly that of regarding money as the means and object of existence... Hospitality, tact, natural fine manners, and a touchy punctilio, are common to both races: common to both tongues the trick of dropping medial consonants... These points of similarity between a South Seas people and some of my own folk at home ran much in my head in the islands; and not only inclined me to view my fresh acquaintances with favour, but continually modified my judgment.

He cheerfully recommends this method to other travellers: 'When I desired any detail of savage custom, or of superstitious belief, I cast back in the story of my fathers, and fished for what I wanted with some trait of equal barbarism.'

Stevenson, Fanny, and numerous relatives, visitors and Polynesians settled in an estate he named Vailima, in Samoa, in 1890. He learned to read and speak the language. His increasing knowledge of, and involvement in, island politics, and his back-breaking work clearing paths through the jungle on the estate, all fed into the fiction he wrote there. It was fiction so different from *Kidnapped* or *Dr Jekyll and Mr Hyde* that his fans were dismayed, and Oscar Wilde wrote, 'I see that romantic surroundings are the worst surroundings possible for a romantic writer.'

'The Beach of Falesá' tells the story of trader Wiltshire who is welcomed by another white trader on the island, Case, and offered a native wife. Case organises a grotesque parody of a wedding between Wiltshire and Uma, and feigns ignorance when Wiltshire finds himself instantly tabooed. No one on the island will trade with him. Gradually the truth emerges. Case has driven other traders from the island and indeed helped to kill a couple of them; the natives are in thrall to him, convinced he has devilish powers, thanks to his fake church of devil-worship in the bush. Blunt, racist, atheist Wiltshire is an unlikely hero, but he is revealed to be thoroughly decent and courageous, and he falls in love with Uma who is herself quite extraordinarily brave. Stevenson's depiction of a strong, intelligent native woman is based on observation. In his journalism he reports that among the islanders, power resides in rank not gender. For example, Nei Takauti was older, wiser and higher ranking than her husband, and he was obliged to wait on her.

It is Wiltshire himself who relates his story, opening with:

> I saw that island first when it was neither night nor morning. The moon was to the west, setting, but still broad and bright. To the east, and right amidships of the dawn, which was all pink, the daystar sparkled like a diamond…

This beautifully sets up the conflicts to come, night and day, dark and light, death and love. Sentiment is anathema to him, and romantics must be satisfied with this assessment of his 20 year marriage to beautiful Uma: 'She could throw a London bobby over her shoulder… there's no manner of doubt that she's an A1 wife.' In a letter to his close friend Colvin, Stevenson called it 'the first realistic South Seas story; I mean with real South Sea character and details of life'.

It is fascinating to trace that realism back to actual events described in his and Fanny's journals. In the Gilbert Islands a native woman proudly displayed her marriage certificate to them. It stated that she was 'married for one night' and that her white 'husband was at liberty to send her to hell when he pleases'. Stevenson notes that she was 'none the wiser for the dastardly trick'. Uma's marriage certificate, which she guards jealously, contains the same wording, and as Wiltshire falls in love with her it gnaws at his conscience sufficiently for him to eventually request a proper marriage by a missionary.

Details of daily life at Vailima creep into moments of high drama. Fanny hit on the following method of scaring thieves away from their piglets and chickens:

> I took the round top of a small meat cask and painted on it a hideous head... Instead of hair, flames radiate from the head. These flames, the iris of the eyes, and the pointed teeth I have painted in luminous paint. It almost frightens me.

When Wiltshire finally uncovers Case's devil-church:

> I saw a shining face. It was big and ugly, like a pantomime mask, and the brightness of it waxed and dwindled, and at times it smoked. 'Oho!' says I, 'Luminous paint!'... Any poor Kanaka brought up here in the dark, with the harps whining all around him, and shown that smoking face in the bottom of a hole, would make no doubt but he had seen enough devils for a lifetime.

Stevenson wrote to Colvin that Wiltshire's story 'shot through me like a bullet' as he laboured alone trying to clear a path in the jungle at Vailima. He recreates that moment in the fiction, when our hero heads into the jungle to find Case's church:

> The brightest kind of day is always dim down there. A man can see to the end of nothing; whichever way he looks the wood shuts up, one bough folding with another like the fingers of your hand; and whenever he listens he hears always something new – men talking, children laughing, the strokes of an axe a far way ahead of him, and sometimes a quick stealthy scurry near at hand that makes him jump and look to his weapons… the whole place seems to be alive and looking on.

Stevenson's letters record that *The Ebb Tide*, two years later, was painfully difficult to write, and although it still contains glints of comedy, the story is dark indeed. The tone is set in the first sentence: 'Throughout the island world of the Pacific, scattered men of many European races and from almost every grade of society carry activity and disseminate disease.' Three down-and-outs are malingering on the beach at Papeete, scrounging food from Polynesian sailors. Davis is a disgraced American sea-captain, Huish a thieving Cockney, Herrick an Oxford-educated failure. Their fortunes are reversed when Davis is given captaincy of a schooner which no one else will touch, because the captain and mate have died of smallpox.

Our three desperadoes set sail with a Polynesian crew, and are soon tucking into the cargo of champagne and squabbling horribly. Their plans to steal the ship are thwarted by a shortage of stores, and they put in at a private island. There they find a 'huge dangerous looking fellow. His manners and movements, like fire in flint, betrayed his European ancestry'. He is Attwater, the most villainous villain you are likely to meet this side of Kurtz (and I am not alone in thinking Conrad may owe the older and, at that time, more successful Stevenson, something of a debt for *Heart of Darkness*). Attwater has combined missionary zeal with ruthless efficiency in running a pearl fishery, and 29 of his 32 slaves have recently died of smallpox. The dinner to which he invites his three guests is a masterpiece of suspense, over which he presides with veiled menace: 'A cat of huge growth sat on his shoulder purring, and occasionally, with a deft paw, capturing a morsel in the air.' (A prototype for Blofeld's cat in the James Bond movies?)

Here's a morsel of dialogue from that dinner. The conversation has turned to Attwater's method of slave-driving:

> 'Wait a bit,' said Davis. 'I'm out of my depth. How was this? Do you mean to say you did it single-handed?'
> 'One did it single handed,' said Attwater, 'because there was nobody to help one.'
> 'Ope you made 'em jump,' said Huish.
> 'When it was necessary, Mr Whish, I made them jump.'

Herrick, the Hamlet of the piece, crippled by indecision, listens in silence. Note the Captain's drowning figure of speech, apt both intellectually and by way of reference to his career. Note Attwater's upper-crust 'one', and his insulting mispronunciation of Huish's name. As for Huish, his accent is written in.

Snobbery, the greed and cruelty of whites, religious hypocrisy and the casual destruction of native cultures and lives are all grist to Stevenson's mill. Yet he succeeds in exploring these dark themes in tales of high drama and suspense, with wicked humour and an infectious open-heartedness towards all his characters. They are exposed, but rarely judged.

[This article first appeared in *The Guardian* in December 2016.]

Jane Rogers, FRSL, writes novels, radio drama, and short stories. Historical novels include *Mr Wroe's Virgins*, which Jane adapted as an award winning TV drama. Her contemporary and future fiction includes the ManBooker longlisted *The Testament of Jessie Lamb*, winner of the Arthur C Clarke Award 2011. Her latest novel, *Body Tourists*, is set in 2045.

Literature, Travels, Friends, and Life
KUMIKO KOIWA

I WAS A CHILD who loved stories. I enjoyed books and comics, and watched TV animation. Any story was fine – I didn't distinguish literature from ordinary writing.

Until I read one book.

When I was a junior high school student, I liked the animated version of *Treasure Island* on TV and read the original. I was fond of this famous novel, and attracted to the character and the dramatic life of the author introduced in the afterword. It also taught me that the author was famous for his style, so I reread the novel several times carefully, trying to enjoy the writing itself. It's fortunate that I had a very good translation – I found I liked this author's style very much. This was the first time the idea of the art of writing touched me, the importance of how to write, not only what to write. Literature. Without this encounter with Robert Louis Stevenson, I would not have read books more seriously than before, and might not have graduated from the Faculty of Letters in later years.

Anyway, when I was 15 years old and got a rough but vivid image of this Scottish writer, I was totally hooked. I said to myself that I would visit his grave in Samoa within ten years. During my years at university, I read all the major Japanese translations of his works. Most of them were old publications; in my country

Stevenson was less popular than before the last war and I needed to search for them in second-hand bookshops or in big libraries. This search was not easy, though it gave me great pleasure for many years each time I found a book.

Just before graduation, I visited Edinburgh. Unfortunately, the Writers' Museum – the only one of the countless places in Stevenson's hometown about which I could find information before leaving Japan – had closed the Stevenson room in the basement because of staff shortages. I peered into the dim room beyond the iron gate for a while, but had no chance of entering. The museum staff suggested visiting the houses Stevenson had lived in instead, and drew a simple map in my notebook. Following it, I walked to 17 Heriot Row and 8 Howard Place. This was my first, humble RLS pilgrimage – later I became more knowledgeable.

I had been an office worker for three years when I found that ten years had passed since I promised myself I would visit Stevenson's grave. In the early 1990s there were just some hundreds of Japanese who visited Samoa each year, most of them international volunteers or businessmen. But somehow I went to Western Samoa in my 25th summer for the first time; it was also my first trip abroad by myself. In that small South Pacific island country, I strolled in the shade of trees on the waterfront, went to the unbelievably beautiful beaches, and was deeply impressed by the strong sunshine, vivid colours of greenery, flowers, and the ocean, and the friendly smiles of the local people. Those were surely the things which impressed Stevenson about 100 years ago on the same island.

I visited Vailima, Stevenson's former home, then the official residence of the prime minister of Western Samoa. I walked through the gates and the 'Road of the Loving Heart' into the big front garden and saw the building; it did not look much changed from the original one I'd seen in photos many times. And I walked by the house to the trail climbing up Mount Vaea to visit the author's grave.

Thus my pilgrimages have gone on to Scotland, England, the United States, Europe, and the South Pacific. It's always a pleasure to follow in the footsteps of Stevenson, to see the same scenery he must have seen a long time ago. The places he was sent when health deserted him were singularly beautiful. On these travels abroad I have often brought two books of Stevenson's – in English and the Japanese translation – and enjoyed comparing the descriptions to the real scenery.

In earlier years, I had only a few acquaintances I could talk with about Stevenson, but on my travels I have naturally met many people who have knowledge of and interest in him. When I visited the Stevenson House in Monterey, the museum guide was very kind and said I could stay in her house on my next visit (and I've stayed with her several times since then). When I was queuing for a small concert focussed on Stevenson in the Fringe Festival in Edinburgh, I happened to get talking with a lady in the same queue, and on the following day she took me to Swanston Cottage (she was one of the members of the RLS Club). On a chilly rainy day, the living curator of Stevenson Cottage in Saranac Lake let me stay in their living room and lit a fire in the wood stove; there I spent the whole afternoon with Maggie Stevenson's diary in my hands and the curator's kitten Maggie on my lap. Soon I came to call these Stevensonians my friends. They have taught me a lot about the author and his works, and their Western lifestyle and ways of thinking have helped me to understand the cultural background of Stevenson.

Travelling abroad and seeing foreign scenery and customs inevitably influences our philosophy. Through my travels I've learned that although people and cultures are different from each other, our natures are not so very different and we can find kindred minds anywhere, that we can make our wishes come true if we know what we want and have some courage.

Now, as I look back and look around, I find many old and new books on my bookshelves, over a hundred photo albums from my travels, and a pile of greeting cards that come from various countries every December. And many quotes – words written by the long-gone Scottish author – which pop into my mind in so many situations in my daily life and are intertwined with my own thoughts inseparably. I owe them all to Robert Louis Stevenson, and I cannot picture my life at all without having read *Treasure Island* as a schoolgirl.

Kumiko Koiwa is a Japanese office worker who was born, grew up and lives in Yokohama. Never a scholar, she has been an enthusiastic reader and fan of RLS for about 40 years.

— STEVENSON —
THE TRAVELLER

A Stevenson Haiku

NIGEL PLANER

ALL HIS LIFE, 'Chaudhuri strove both to express his Bengaliness and to escape it', wrote the novelist Amit Chaudhuri of his namesake Nirad C. Chaudhuri, the famous writer on English traditions and culture. And I feel the same could be said of Stevenson and his relationship to Scotland. Although a great part of his life was spent escaping from his birthplace, it is nevertheless still present in all his work, not just the 'Scottish' novels, but in his travel writing – from France and America to the South Seas.

Also, like Nirad C. Chaudhuri, Stevenson could be a little verbose at times. So, I have tried to be brief and decided to summarise my thoughts in a seventeen-syllable haiku:

Edinburgh's so cold
RLS was ordered south
Glad to get away.

Nigel Planer was an original member of *Comedy Store* and *Comic Strip*, which were at the centre of the 'alternative comedy' movement in the 1980s. He is now a successful actor in TV, theatre and radio, and author of novels, articles, and radio and stage plays. His poetry is published in anthologies and a collection.

Walking with RLS
GAIL SIMMONS

I FIRST met Robert Louis Stevenson one grey autumn morning on the platform of High Wycombe railway station. It was 1874. The fledgling author was 24, and in the throes of an ill-fated love affair with an older, married woman when he alighted at this flint and brick station, built just 20 years previously. His aim was to walk across the Chiltern Hills to Tring, a three-day journey he describes in his essay, 'An Autumn Effect', as a 'little pilgrimage'. He was sporting a black velvet jacket, a moustache and a knapsack – his fashionably Bohemian appearance a little out of place in this workaday Buckinghamshire town.

At least, that's how I like to picture the slender young Scotsman as he set out on his Chiltern journey. The truth is, I can't know for certain what he was wearing, although photographs of him around that period show him in his favourite velvet jacket, and with that trademark wispy facial hair. We do know he was carrying a knapsack, as he mentions this in his essay, along with a 'sufficiency of money' he had with him for the trip.

Now, almost 150 years later, I too left the train at High Wycombe station to begin my own 'little pilgrimage' in RLS's footsteps. I wanted to chronicle the changes in the countryside since he walked here, and at the same time reprise my youth in a nearby commuter village. I also wished to record for posterity a landscape that will be altered irrevocably by the HS2 railway which, if all goes to plan, will tear through these modest chalk hills from 2026.

For three days, RLS and I travelled side-by-side, now under 'a pall of grey cloud', now in 'thin golden sunshine'. Typical autumn weather, in fact. Together, we strolled across the hills, over 'brown ploughlands', passing hedgerows 'shot through with bright autumnal yellows' and through 'russet woods'. We stood and looked over valleys, largely unchanged in the century and a half since RLS was here, when the fields were exposed before him 'like a map'. One such view – over the Misbourne Valley whose ancient field systems and sunken lanes have remained little altered for 400 years – will be soon bisected by HS2.

There were times on our walk that RLS and I lost sight of one another, he faded like a ghost as our experiences diverged. 'An Autumn Effect' is full of references to the birds he saw and heard throughout his journey. He mentions yellowhammers and blackbirds, but above all, it was the song of the skylark he noted. He writes of the 'wonderful carolling of larks', of the air being 'alive with them from High Wycombe to Tring', concluding that they formed 'so integral a part of my conception of the country, that I could have baptised it "The Country of Larks"'.

I, too, listened out for skylarks. But where RLS heard the 'uninterrupted carol of larks innumerable overhead', for most of my journey I strained to hear even one. Since I grew up here in the 1970s, we've lost some 60 percent of our wildlife, with the skylark suffering a serious decline in recent decades. It is now listed by the RSPB as an endangered species, mostly due to the intensive agriculture that was unknown to our peripatetic author.

There were other sounds that RLS heard, and that eluded me. I didn't catch the 'sweet tumultuous tinkle of sheep-bells', as arable farming has mostly replaced pastoral in the Chilterns. And while he heard 'the ploughmen shouting to their horses', the fields I passed through were mostly silent, but for the occasional clattering of farm machinery – now doing the job of a whole village a century ago. Instead, there were sounds RLS could never have imagined: the growl of traffic from distant roads, the whine of aircraft overhead, the incessant whirr of strimmers, leaf blowers and lawnmowers.

But perhaps most noticeable was the absence of people working in the countryside. RLS noted the fields 'busy with people ploughing and sowing', the hedgerows hiding jugs of ale from which the plough-teams would drink, in 'as it were, a spirit of picnic'. Always interested in people, always pausing for a chat, RLS was also a social chronicler. His walk coincided with the tail-end of British agriculture's golden age, just before the great depression in agriculture kicked in. He even describes how the driver of the dog-cart which took him from Wendover to Tring was 'all in praise' of the agricultural labourer's way of life, singing *O fortunatos agricolas!* 'in every possible key'.

I met no crooning labourers on my walk in RLS's footsteps. The closest I came was a tenant farmer who emerged from one of the few traditional Chiltern farmhouses not yet converted into swish executive homes, furnished with electronically operated gates. It was he who showed me the tract of Iron Age Grim's Ditch lying on his land – along with a hay meadow rich with wildflowers and fertilised only with sheep droppings, soon to become a spoil heap for HS2's tunnelling works. My only other living companions were the occasional dog walker or horse rider, plus squawking rooks and red kites squealing in the thermals above.

Although the lovesick RLS began his walk in good spirits – 'in the most enviable of all humours', as he himself put it – his mood did occasionally dip as he walked alone through the Chiltern Hills. He describes the lanes as 'profoundly still', adding that 'they would have been sad but for the sunshine and the singing of the larks'. Instead there came over him at times 'a feeling of isolation that was not disagreeable', and yet was enough to 'make me quicken my steps eagerly' when he saw someone before him on the road.

I, too, felt an exquisite melancholy as I walked the same deep twisting lanes, tree roots like arthritic fingers emerging from earth banks. Over the same chalky hills, my boots scrunching on flinty soil, and through the same beechwoods – so characteristic of the Chiltern landscape – described by RLS as having 'a dim green forest atmosphere'. It was easy to envisage him here, deep in the countryside where much of the old England still remains, despite the busier roads, housing estates and the looming menace of HS2.

RLS, perhaps ailing from the illness that killed him aged just 44, or maybe suffering the pangs of unrequited love, opted to take a 'dog-cart' on the final leg of his journey to Tring. I decided to walk on, alone now. We reunited once again in Tring – not in the old market town itself, but at Tring station set a mile and a half outside the centre. As RLS noted, the 'good people of Tring' held the new-fangled Victorian railway 'in extreme apprehension'. I couldn't help reflecting on how much more apprehensive they must now be as a massive new rail project endangers their – and my – cherished Chiltern landscape.

It was here, then, that Robert Louis Stevenson and I parted ways. He went back to London and on to greater things, penning such classics as *Treasure Island*, *Strange Case of Dr Jekyll and Mr Hyde* and *Kidnapped*. But before reaching worldwide fame as a novelist, it was another journey he took which most captivates the travel writer in me. Hailed as a 'pioneering work of outdoor literature', *Travels with a Donkey in the Cévennes* has motivated many hikers to retrace his steps along what is now the long-distance path, GR 70 – also known as *Chemin de Stevenson*. Just as RLS's Chiltern journey inspired me to take a short walk across the gentle hills of my childhood home.

Walking with RLS

Gail Simmons and RLS crossed paths when, after a lifetime of journeying that took her far from her Chilterns homeland, she returned to write about the impact of the HS2 rail ink on her beloved childhood landscape – RLS's description of which inspired the title of her book, *The Country of Larks*.

Visiting the World in Stevenson's Way
CHRISTIAN BROCHIER

WALKING IS A SLOW ITINERANCY, a human-scale approach at low speed. Exploring an area on foot with its villages, its heritage, its inhabitants, respecting the human body pace, the rhythm of one's own breathing, here is a genuine way of looking at the world, here is a radically different way of apprehending a territory.

'One ought to have meditated long on a landscape before beginning to enjoy it to the full,' wrote Robert Louis Stevenson. The beauty of the landscapes crossed by the Cévennes trail which bears the writer's name – and more generally the beauty of any nature trail – can only be enjoyed to the full at the slow pace walking implies, this meditative, swinging movement which puts one in harmony with the world.

Pausing in front of a chapel, a patchwork of lava-coloured stone ranging from *terra di Sienna* to black with a steeple in the shape of a comb; or a thatched house with granite walls, or a moor covered in broom, scattered with granite rocks; or a centuries-old oak. Slowing the pace, then starting again, listening to the whisper of mature barley in the wind, or to the gentle noise of a mountain burn running on schist rock – all these are little pleasures that only a walker can enjoy, just around the nearest corner of the path.

Landscape can only be enjoyed at a contemplative pace, by completely immersing oneself in it. The age of motorcars and commercial estates has taken life away from the heart of small towns, from villages even. True enough, there are still quiet roads, but it is not easy to park, one is bothered by metal, noise and fumes, none of these making it easy to encounter people – and drivers are totally taken up by the machines which prevent them from seeing and approaching people and landscapes.

People have to be met face-to-face, at ground level, in their usual environment. The farmer in his field, the gardener in his garden, the pedestrian as he is! Meeting other people is part of the beauty of walking tours – meeting walkers from all over France, Europe and elsewhere.

But first and foremost it's about meeting the local people: shopkeepers, tourist professionals or cultural service providers, and in particular hosts, with whom the relationship will be closer as they welcome and cater for the walkers, and are delighted to tell them about their little corner of land.

A donkey is an ambassador for nature. Walking in the company of a donkey, as our friend Robert Louis did, is another way to travel in which the natural environment appears quite differently. Seen through the donkey's eyes, nature looks like a huge food store! To understand it from a human point of view, you have to imagine being in Hansel and Gretel's gingerbread house, where all the environment is edible! Values are completely reversed. Grass often appears as an enemy to city dwellers, who are constantly trying to prevent it from invading their flower beds and lawns by weeding and cutting – but for the walker travelling with a donkey, grass represents a vital source of strength, a reward for one's companion who will feast on it at each pause. Nature which appeared hostile is then perceived as good and bountiful.

The donkey's presence is also comforting for beginners who may sometimes be frightened by creatures such as spiders, snakes or wild boars which can be found in the Cévennes and elsewhere.

Donkeys are at home in this environment which sometimes seems hostile to humans. The sounds of their hooves frighten reptiles away, while aggressive dogs must beware of being kicked. In the company of a donkey – a docile mammal with an average weight of 200 kilos – walkers feel safe. The paths are familiar to the donkeys, who tread them regularly, and the walkers more or less expect the animal to lead the way!

A donkey is also a priceless ambassador in making contact with people you come across on the way: elderly people who remember the time when each farm kept donkeys, children walking with their parents, animal lovers of all ages, and virtually anybody else. Who can remain indifferent to a donkey? I remember a walker who had crossed Le Pont-de-Montvert to take his donkey to the communal green on the other side of the village, and who had been greeted by most people he had met on his way. Walking back to the hostel, he felt rather vexed when nobody looked at him – earlier on, it was in fact the donkey that had been greeted!

Walking a historical trail changes the walker's outlook when it is seen through a writer's eyes. This trail through the Cévennes has a story, and one can sometimes realise that the landscape that Stevenson crossed and described 140 years ago has not changed much, as can be seen from the following anecdote. In September 2008, on the occasion of the 130th Anniversary walk as the party of about 60 walkers and a dozen donkeys were passing through the hamlet of Fouzillac, a rather unfriendly-looking old lady poked her head out the window to see what was going on. Just to see what would happen, I asked her the way to Fouzillic (another hamlet situated about half-a-mile away along the same road). She eventually replied very reluctantly, yelping at me that she did not have the slightest clue. She looked really hostile and, immediately after she banged her shutter closed. I felt speechless at such unexplainable behaviour – an exact replica of what Stevenson himself had experienced when he arrived in Fouzillac and was sent on the wrong path when he asked the way. Was this down to everlasting animosity between the two hamlets? Defiance of travellers and strangers? Whatever, I felt suddenly sent back in time 130 years, and quite pleased after all to find intact the memory of the places visited and described by the travel writer.

Indeed, travelling across a territory like Stevenson did, on foot and accompanied by a donkey, does affect one's outlook – and the way of discovering and appreciating a place and its human dimension.

[Translated from the original French by Odile Guigon.]

Christian Brochier used to hire out donkeys in the Cévennes. For 12 years he chaired the Association *Sur le Chemin de Robert Louis Stevenson* (On the Robert Louis Stevenson Trail) and now chairs the Council of Europe's European Cultural Route *In the Footsteps of Robert Louis Stevenson*.

Stevenson and James Watt in France
HERVÉ GOURNAY

SCOTLAND AND FRANCE have many bonds over and above their long-standing friendship: a sovereign, Mary Stuart, wife of François II, and Queen of France in the years 1559 and 1560 ('Farewell to this agreeable and pleasant country of France, my dearest homeland'); the works of Robert Louis Stevenson, an author who is both Francophile and Francophone; and James Watt, a universal benefactor and inventor of the steam engine. Stevenson and Watt merit special recognition in a project started by the Community of Maroilles in the district of Northern France and due to be completed in 2021.

Just outside the town of Maroilles – famous for its cheese – stands the Hachette lock house, opposite lock No 2 on the river Sambre which was canalised in 1834. The Sambre and the lock house form an important part of Maroilles's modern industrial heritage. Once this river was rendered navigable, it linked several Belgian canals directly with Paris. The railway line which passes by Hachette was built in 1855 and has conveyed many famous people travelling from Liège and Brussels to the French capital.

On the 1 September 1876, Robert Louis Stevenson and his good friend Walter Simpson were canoeing on the river Sambre as tourists and passed by the Hachette lock. At this time RLS had yet to publish his first book. Written in 1877, his tale of the journey through Belgium and France, from Antwerp to Pontoise, was published the following year. *An Inland Voyage* was not translated into French until 1900 under the title of *À la Pagaie* (To the Paddle). In it, RLS describes in detail the countryside and the people he encountered. After the two canoeists left 'Pont-sur-Sambre' under lashing rain, RLS noted that only Simpson had a raincoat. They eventually reached the edge of the Mormal forest after some two or three hours on the water – 'a sinister name to the ear but a place most gratifying to sight and smell', says Stevenson. He perhaps had doubts about the true origin of the name 'Mormal', likening it to a 'violent death' (*mort violente* or *mal-mort*). 'Mormal' in fact means a raised plateau. He did, nonetheless, show great appreciation for the countryside and the forest smells;, 'and the breath of the forest of Mormal, as it came aboard upon us that showery afternoon, was perfumed with nothing less delicate than sweetbriar: I wish our way had always lain among woods'. In a century and a half nothing has changed. The Mormal forest still offers its wooded pleasures to visitors. It has been preserved by nature and one can still admire the same bucolic scene that so seduced RLS.

One can safely surmise that 'Stevenson the author' was born in 1876 on the banks of the river Sambre, thanks to his authorship of his 'water' voyage, which was initially planned to be an observation of the ethnography and geography of the area. His decision to write *An Inland Voyage* must surely have been inspired, in part at least, by his previous experience and knowledge of the rivers and seas of his native Scotland.

His first published work, however, remained largely unknown in Belgium and France until recent times. For a long time in France, Robert Louis Stevenson was known for his adventure novels and fantastical accounts destined to be read by adolescents. Do we not still reckon this period in the life of young people, their *Treasure Island* age, as being synonymous with light-heartedness and awakening dreams?

It turned out that 1876 was an all-important year for RLS in another way. As he passed through the Hachette lock, he did not know that a few days later at the end of this continental journey in the forest of Fontainebleau, he would meet the beautiful American lady Fanny Van de Grift – at that time the wife of Samuel Osbourne. Some four years later, on 19 May 1880, he would marry Fanny in San Francisco.

James Watt, surveyor of Scotland's Forth and Clyde canal in 1767, is best remembered as the designer of the steam engine named after him. Alongside the Sambre canal one of his engines can still be viewed at the Hachette lock No 2, along with a steam-driven lifting machine known as *'à Robert'*. The building that houses it consists of three rooms and boasts a boiler, a steam engine and an Archimedes screw. They came into service in 1859, so they would have been seen by RLS as he and Walter Simpson canoed down the river in 1876. This machinery was used to compensate for the loss of water caused by each opening and closing of the lock, as well as water loss due to normal leakage and evaporation. It has not been in active service since 1974 and it is believed to be the last remaining model on the continent of Europe.

As coincidence would have it, the busts of these two great characters, Stevenson and Watt, are to be found in close proximity in Edinburgh's Scottish National Portrait Gallery. At Hachette, the lock house and the building that houses the steam engine are merely ten metres apart and will soon be open to visitors. In this way the talented man of letters and the brilliant inventor, both Scots, will remain united in this Maroilles Community project.

[Translated from the original French by Andrew Brown.]

Hervé Gournay was born in the north of France and now lives in Maroilles, on the banks of the Sambre., He rediscovered Stevenson's books thanks to *An Inland Voyage*. He is President of the Maroilles History Society which plans a permanent exhibition about Stevenson's canoe voyage in the old lock house at Hachette, near Maroilles.

From the Cévennes Diary and Poems, 2008

JIM BERTRAM

FRIDAY 23 MAY – Le Puy-en-Velay: Hotel Bristol, room with a view! But what is behind these prison-like shutters? Why drab neutral colours for all? Is there only conformance with predictability? And does predictability hold hands with conformance? Paint your shutters vibrant colours of Charlestown yellow, or New Orleans green – new world colours, spirit-lifting colours, nature's brightest colours. An ethereal whisper says: 'I am the Cévennes, and I am very old. You are not here to change, but to be changed.'

The view from the Christ statue on the hill is roofs. The monument presides over the town and was made from melted down World War I guns, and perhaps a few girders. Tiled roofs, bright yellow tiled roofs and brown tiled roofs; rows of geometrically pitched tiled roofs. All is roofs. They look ploughed between the roads, which predate city planning, and the river which uses the valley to escape to other places. Geography once ruled the ways of man. Yet, religion is another thing, and seeks the higher ground.

Bought some Le Puy lace for Emily. Could we but buy life's best, wrap it in red tissue paper, and give it to our grandchildren? Alas no, but I will tell them of a goodly heritage. Yes, but will they listen?

The Cévennes are:

FROM THE CÉVENNES DIARY AND POEMS, 2008

A garden of verse for the poet
A garden of produce for the gourmet
A garden of light for the artist
A garden of delight for all others.

SATURDAY 24 MAY – Le Puy to Monastier, where 130 years previously Stevenson's chosen mode of four-legged transport was met with incredulity: '*Et vous marchez comme ça?*'

Fanny, the woman he loved, had said no, and returned to America. Perhaps her memory lived on in the naming of the donkey Modestine.

'Modestine'

Sweet Modestine to thee is owed
My obligation in an ode.
For your own, and gentle way,
And for the starring role to play.
Fame's candle burned for but a day,
And you carried the master's story.

What fortune brought for us, to please
Sweet lassie of the Cévennes?
The foil of innocence imbued
On such as you, his burden moved
Yet meekly through the pages trod,
And you carried the master's story.

Oh! man in love is sic an ass.
He has no thought but o' one lass,
And so to kind of muddle through
He placed his troubled soul on you.
His blistered hopes, his tattered trews,
And you carried the master's story.

Now divvy praise as praise you dare,
Vie lass and ass for glory.
The one a ghost of 'might have beens',
But loyalty 'marche' the whole way.
To Modestine the author's Queen,
You, you carried the master's story.

WEDNESDAY 28 MAY – Pradelles to Cheylard-l'Évêque, along a route reputedly haunted by a giant wolf, the 'Beast of Gévaudan'. The fear of which a French peasant refused to leave the safety of his cottage to show Stevenson the way: '*Mais je ne sortirai pas de la porte.*'

'Fear' (Lupus canis)

Behind those yellow tunnels of light,
The gray wolf lopes through the mind of your night.
Close your eyes tightly, but it doesn't undo
You seeing him, seeing him, watching you!

An afforested pavement of no one you knew,
The way opens up for you to pass through.
In a flash, there's those eyes in fateful review,
He's there watching you, seeing him, watching you!

You encamp at day's end for sake of repose,
But just at that time, quite naked of clothes.
These eyes of you fear continually pursue,
With back to the fire, you watch him, watching you!

THURSDAY 29 MAY – Notre-Dame-des-Neiges to La Bastide, the monastery of Our Lady of the Snows where Stevenson 'blessed God that 'I was free to wander, free to hope, free to love'. Morning walk down the hill from the monastery, Jim and Ruth and solitude. That is not quietness, for there are sounds to be heard, but they are in concert, and I must speak softly to sing my part. Order, order, all is in harmony and there is no one to hear but Jim and Ruth. Hail solitude, give me your hand.

'Free to Love'

The place where nettles bloom,
Where cuckoos call in three.
Wild pansies smile beside the road
And history bends her knee.

The way to La Bastide
Is for the pilgrim poor,
Where nothing is too heavy
Avec l'amour dans le Coeur.

The radio in the café in La Bastide is playing 'The Theme from the Titanic' as we enter, and Ruth begins to sing. What is it about that song? It lodges by the heart and speaks of love. '*Deux cafés s'il vous plaît.*'

Next song is 'I Believe I Can Fly' and Ruth sings on. This another song of aspirations, and the lady who just came in now joins us and we sing along. She has her hopes buried in this song and soars on wings of aspiration. She is happy, perhaps even in love.

At the monastery where we had spent last night, the monk who had unloaded all our luggage unassisted, said: 'With love in your heart nothing is too heavy.' Such is freedom, such is love.

'Aspiration's Song'

As sparks that doth by nature upward fly
In cold black night as if to try

For heaven's crown and join the sky
Of starry aspirations.

Or butterfly on cobweb wings
Lift to the sun of hoped for things
And lofts the garden wall to cry,
Of soaring aspirations.

So let this token love has brought
Be to you when troubled thought
Does shutter expectation's port,
A trove of aspirations.

WEDNESDAY 4 & THURSDAY 5 JUNE – Florac: 'On a branch of the Tarn stands Florac with an old castle, an alley of planes, many quaint street-corners, and a live fountain welling from the hill.' Two roads diverged in a yellow wood, and I followed Ian across the stile, and that made all the difference. This hillside path was bedecked with orchids, and he knew them all. My favourite was the Bee Orchid, but all were splendid. Robert Frost's poem 'Two Roads' would be read this evening. I'm sorry for those who took the other path.

'The Stile'
To Ian G, with thanks for showing us the orchids

To what does this stile portend
That lifts my spirits so?
The journey is but at its end,
On downward path laid long ago.

No, not a gate for walking through
Nor fencing wire to bend and pierce.
A lovely wooden stepping stile
Exhorts its magic through release.

From the Cévennes Diary and Poems, 2008

Leaving behind the man made woods,
Dead to themselves in twilight gloom.
A shameful shameless stockade stood
Save where the roadside flowers bloom.

Here now a wall to bind day's thoughts
Unto themselves as so they should.
And file in libraries of time
A floral famine to conclude.

But now escape! A vaulting stile
Lifts up and over this redoubt
And sets us down in wonderland
What's this, that's scattered all about?

Here did the orchid fairy come
From runrig plantings on the moor.
But she had mused away the day
As many a mortal's known to still.

Thus with her basket yet half full
She could not gain the master's smile,
And so she tipped the lot upon,
The place, beyond the stile

'Festina Lente' the Gardener said, *(make haste slowly)*
And hurt there not a one.
They are the children of this world,
And we must softly come.

So hike we all the ways of life
As hike the hike we can,
To mount the stile on Florac's hill,
And come down the better man.

Hear the song of Florac, for she is singing her song. Sung in a Celtic tongue, sung in a lilting voice, sung by Eyna, dark and broody across the town square. I am the call from long ago, the echo of times long past. The one who long remembers.

'Florac'

I am the bell, hear me ring,
I speak to you of the ancient thing.
This place, once fort to Rome,
Is now the lammergeyer's home.

I am the river, watch me flow,
I'll tell you things from long ago.
Of peasant poor, but honest toil,
Raised a family from this soil.

I am the rampart's frowning brow,
Looking down both then and now.
I saw oppression, poured upon,
As the Stone Age spear of religion.

I am the graveyard, fertile loam
Worthless and worthy now call home.
And shout, into the black hole of time,
'I have lived and doth now repine!'

Sing on, sing on, from the twin Bose speakers in the craft shop, on the square. Let its stone artwork speak of Florac, for it is hard, and it is polished, and it is very old.

From the Cévennes Diary and Poems, 2008

Jim Bertram was born in Glasgow during World War II, and trained as an engineer in the family tradition – encouraged by his English Teacher! He left Rolls-Royce and Scotland for the United States, and now lives in South Carolina. He is thankful poets don't make good lighthouse engineers, and engineers don't live off their poetry.

Brief Encounter

DAVID REID

LE PUY-EN-VELAY is the starting point for two pilgrimages of contrasting character. On the road more travelled, the faithful labour towards distant Santiago de Compostela; the one we took was the Grande Route Pedestre 70, the 'Chemin de Stevenson'. It was the very September week of Stevenson's own trek through the Cévennes, and we were using it to walk more extended stretches than we had done before. Our base for the central and southern reaches was a *gîte* in a village hacked from the Mont Lozère granite, where, from blue-shuttered windows, we could look across the valley to the trail itself.

On the Grande Route there are still tracts which RLS would immediately recognise, when he could afford to lift his eyes from his recalcitrant donkey's rear. The track down the green slope from Monastier to the ford across the Gazeille is still as he trod it. On the path approaching the white outlines of the monastery of Our Lady of the Snows, on the 125th anniversary of Stevenson's arrival, we saw a monk with a spade on his shoulder, recreating a scene from 'any time these thousand years', just as RLS had found. The corkscrew path dropping down towards the Tarn still displays 'the stony skeleton of the world' on the high ground, before it picks up the pools and rapids of the stream which follows the wooded valley down to Le Pont-de-Montvert. In the valley of the Mimente there is still the old castle above the trail – though the Grande Route now follows the line of the disused railway. And you can still hike the route with a donkey – though without having to fight it tooth and nail every inch of the way.

But at Our Lady of the Snows, the welcome is no longer muted: the busy coach park is the first indication of an open-door policy and the monks run a souvenir shop doing a brisk trade in produce labelled *methode artisanale*, with the monastery logo. There is just one old doorway surviving from the building Stevenson knew. The route from Cocurès to Florac is now a throbbing highway and the Grande Route takes to the hills to escape it. Of course, RLS couldn't celebrate the end of the trail with a restorative glass in the Bar Stevenson in Saint-Jean-du-Gard.

As we follow the winding trail we weave in and out of Stevenson's world. However, we cannot, at every step, experience the route as he saw it, and far less as he lived it, even with his own account for a handbook; but we can at certain points feel an affinity. Some have even sensed that he was their companion on the road. I can't claim that much for the brief encounter we had on the highest point of the Grande Route, but it had a resonance.

We had turned our backs on the Chalet de L'Usclade, as untidy and featureless a cluster of buildings as ski centres out of season tend to be. The green path climbs alongside the fence lines which clutter the slope to mark out the *pistes*. As we rose above them, there was no temptation to look back; we were leaving the twenty-first century behind. The medieval stone pillars which marked Stevenson's way still mount the hill, some bearing the faintly carved outline of a Maltese cross. They led us to the col, and onto a terrain Stevenson himself knew. From the summit itself – the very highest point of his journey – we could see ahead and around, the view he had described 125 years before, unchanged and through his eyes.

And as we looked back towards the col, just for a moment it seemed that he had reappeared as a figure in his own landscape, stepping up the slope towards us. I remember him as if it were yesterday: a lean, rangy figure, suntanned, with tousled dark hair, a moustache and small beard, in a loose shirt and breeches, with a knapsack – but without a reluctant donkey and clearly not a ghost.

As we passed the time of day he told us he was not on a Stevenson pilgrimage; he was a *randonneur*, ticking off the Grandes Routes as we collect Munros, so we had an instinct in common. He gave us to understand that he preferred to walk on his own and form his own impressions of scenes and encounters along the way, without distraction. But 'like all the world' he knew Stevenson from childhood and our pursuit made as much sense to him as did his own. We had brought out the little hip flask which we carry to every mountain top; at 1,699 metres the Sommet de Finiels outranks Ben Nevis, though you don't have to climb it from sea level. We invited our fellow traveller to join us in a dram from Braemar to celebrate achieving the summit and to honour the memory of Stevenson. He courteously explained that he did not, as a rule touch alcohol, but on this occasion he would be pleased to take a measure – to salute, as he said, the man who wrote *L'Île au Trésor*.

We parted – for him to continue south on the waymarked trail, following in Stevenson's footsteps, while we took another route off the hill. In my fanciful mind's eye, as I watch him dropping down the slopes still 'stubbly with rocks', I sometimes see a donkey trotting alongside him.

It was an encounter in which the world Stevenson knew merged momentarily with our own, and a shared sense of him enlivened three minds brought together by chance. Stevenson should have been there to recount it, with so much more grace, humour and humanity. But in a happenstance, quirky way, maybe he was.

David Reid was Chairman of the Robert Louis Stevenson Club from 2015 to 2019. Around the age of seven he was captured by the alliance of RLS and Dudley D. Watkins in the graphic version of *Kidnapped* published by D.C. Thomson in the 1950s. In many re-readings since, Watkins's figures still linger in his mind's eye.

Following Stevenson
LORD STEWART

IN ITSELF LE MONASTIER-SUR-GAZEILLE is no more remarkable than dozens of other little towns in the French provinces. It stands high on the west-facing slope of its river valley, at an altitude of 2,000 feet, 15 miles from Le Puy in the department of Haute-Loire. It has a mayor. It has an ugly cemetery which dominates the approach from the north. It has a tax-gatherer, a small sausage factory, a slightly bigger twisting mill partly powered by the stream of the Gazeille, a feudal castle, an abbatial church, 2,500 inhabitants and enough drinking shops to accommodate them all comfortably at the same time. But for children – children of all ages – who dream of the Great Adventure without Danger, this little town holds a special place in the imagination. It was from here in the autumn of almost 100 years ago that Robert Louis Stevenson and his four-legged companion, Modestine, set out on the journey recorded in *Travels with a Donkey*.

It was something of this dream, I suppose, that brought us to Le Monastier, to hire our own donkey and follow their path through the pasture lands of the Velay, across the moors of the Gévaudan, over the peaks of the Cévennes and down into the Midi at Saint-Jean-du-Gard. I hope Monastriens can forgive us for imagining from a distance that they might be unconscious of their place in literature. Stevenson and Modestine are local celebrities commemorated by a plaque in the Place de la Poste, expounded upon to the curious visitor – and gossiped about as if they left only yesterday: 'He took a mistress you know. But of course.' Passages from the book are cited to put the matter beyond doubt; and her name is breathed in the hushed tones of a current scandal.

In many ways, it is still the same town where 'Monsieur Steems' spent 'a month of fine days'. The citizens retain a lively interest in hard drinking, colourful language and political dissension. If you are lucky, you will find a lacemaker, sitting out of doors with her cushion on her knee. The fountain is still there, the old houses with their ornamental ironwork, and the miraculous little Virgin of L'Anglade who drove away the English free-booters.

It was at L'Anglade, the northern quarter of the town, that we found a donkey or, should I say, *the* donkey – for it turned out in the age of the motorcar to be the only one within 40 miles. The owner was M. Marcel Bonnefoy, a cattle merchant. Some whim had prompted him to buy the beast from a peasant the year before, with a little cart and harness thrown in. But, in essence, M. Bonnefoy is not a sentimentalist. Once he got his price, or thereabouts, and the deal was settled over a glass of pastis, the donkey was ours to do with what we wanted.

But what exactly *do* you do with a donkey? The cattle merchant had been short on advice: 'He only drinks when he's thirsty.' Not very helpful – but on reflection I guessed that M. Bonnefoy wished to make the distinction between donkeys and other mortals, such as cattle-merchants, for whom imbibing is a gratuitous activity.

The first thing, by local consensus, was to get her shoed. (Yes 'he' was a 'she' – funnily enough, the French are not so punctilious when it comes to the gender of animals.) We found a smith ten miles away in the village of Fay-le-Froid, now called Fay-sur-Lignon so as not to suggest a chilly welcome for tourists. He did the job – new shoes specially forged, fitted and prettied up with a coat of black grease – for the charitable price of 40 francs.

The next thing was a pack – for the purpose of the donkey was to carry the baggage. Something was cobbled together in a very provisional way really, but with an air of assurance and expertise to forestall an invasion by the regiment of would-be pack-makers gathering in the wings. Any sign of weakness might have meant days of delay as these theoreticians competed for the honour of equipping us with their own particular system of knots.

We left the town on a beautiful morning, hurrying down the track that led to the banks of the Gazeille. Across the river and under the beech trees, hidden from the threat of a public calamity with beast or burden, we climbed at a leisurely pace on a sun-dappled path towards the village of Saint-Martin-de-Fugères. Our first camp was in the pine woods above Goudet. Below us Château Beaufort stood sentinel over the old pilgrimage road where it crosses the infant Loire. The donkey slept standing up – her own choice – tethered to a tree beside the tent.

Except where it is unexpectedly riven by the steep valley of the Loire, richly wooded, the country to the west of Le Monastier is a wide, undulating grassland. All the farms are clustered together in the villages, jumbled up with the houses. The fields are divided off by low stone dykes, ineffective as a means of enclosure. It is a land of cowbells and cowherds, where the gathering in and sending out of the cattle marks the peaceful rhythm of the day. It is a pretty country to walk through, following paths that wind between brilliant hedgerows full of prickly things for a donkey to eat, across meadows, through copses of beech and pine, and coming every two or three miles to a red-tiled, stone-built hamlet.

The country people here are frank and friendly; and their advice on the road to follow can be trusted. With the help of local knowledge, it is easy enough to follow Stevenson's route on paths, tracks and unsurfaced roads. But, I must confess, we elected not to recreate every detail – such as the frustrated wanderings in the dark when he lost the way to Cheylard between Fouzilhic and Fouzilhac in the marches of the Upper Gévaudan.

In one thing we had no choice – the weather, which determined to be authentic. It hailed at Cheylard. It thundered at Luc. It rained at the Monastery of Notre-Dame-des-Neiges where, thankfully, the Trappist rule enjoins hospitality for all comers. It rained from there to Chassarèdes, and again from there over the Goulet to Le Bleymard. It was still raining as we climbed above the pine woods and on to the ski slopes of Mont-Lozère. The only comfort for the traveller, in this land of rainswept moors and forests, is the smell of wood-smoke rising through the mist from isolated farms. But it is not worth imagining what might be cooking on those unseen wood fires: from a gastronomic point of view, the Gévaudan is a bleak no-man's land of lard between 'la cuisine au beurre' of the north and 'la cuisine à l'huile' of the Midi. Stevenson's judgment must stand: it is a dull country.

From Notre-Dame-des-Neiges to Alès, his proposed destination, Stevenson's chosen route seems at first sight absurd. He made a long detour to the south-west, where the road took him over one mountain after another rising in places to well over 4,000 feet. The purpose was literary. With the idea of a historical romance in mind, he determined to enter the High Cévennes and visit the ancient strongholds of the Camisards – Protestant insurrectionists against Louis XIV, whose peasant generals held at bay three Marshals of France in a war of heroic ferocity.

To this day, the religious frontier is strictly drawn on the summit of Mont-Lozère, the highest peak. Here and there, in the fields and thickets on the southern slopes, you can see the little cemeteries where Protestant families still bury their dead. The High Cévennes is a Scottish style of country with a Scottish style of history. There were conventicles and dragoons, there was psalm-singing and butchery. The revolt flared into open war in July 1702 when the Abbé du Chayla was hacked to death in his prison-house at Le Pont-de-Montvert. This southern

Archbishop Sharpe had favoured the 'Squeezers' a close cousin of the 'Boot' used to test Covenanting principles in the basement of Edinburgh's old Parliament House. What with these instruments of mutilation, and the Maiden and the Guillotine, the Scots and French have a grim affinity.

Du Chayla's house still stands – restored by Catholic piety – beside the hump-back bridge that joins the two halves of Le Pont-de-Montvert across the river Tarn. It is a quaint little town of narrow alleys and steps, hugged in on all sides by the hills. It is the sort of place where you might have difficulty changing travellers' cheques – unless you enlist the help of the mayor and the tax-gatherer. But in the Hôtel des Cévennes where Stevenson dined it has what must be, with its homely atmosphere, superb cuisine and encouraging prices, the best small inn of the region.

The Lozère is a watershed in many ways. This is where we found the sun again. This is where a Mediterranean influence starts. Coming down to Le Pont-de-Montvert, pine woods give way to oak, which in turn give way to chestnut groves on the banks of the Tarn. Towards Florac – a pretty name for a pretty town – you find the first vineyards where they grow the succulent Muscat grapes. The warm air of the valleys is rich with the scent of mint and thyme, and of honey from the hives stacked by the peasants on terraces beside the road.

Between Cassagnes, in the valley of the Mimente, and Saint-Germain-de-Calberte, in the valley of the Le Gardon de Mialet, there is another watershed – Le Plan de Fontmort – which divides the waters of the Garonne from the Basin of the Rhône. Looking south from this pass you can see the land falling away through a hazy tumble of foot-hills to the Mediterranean plain and the sea. An obelisk beside the road, erected in 1887 by the descendants of the Camisards, commemorates the centenary of the Edict of Toleration. It is hard now to imagine the time when Cassagnas 'made a figure in the history of France'. It has retired into its sleepy fold in the hills. Its railway has been axed.

It has no shops and depends for provisions on the twice-weekly grocer's van from Florac.

And Saint-Germain-de-Calberte no longer boasts an inn. We got directions to a place for camping which, wrongly understood, led us into the orchard of a Protestant minister. When he saw the donkey, Pasteur Charpiot took the intrusion in good heart. At dinner, he produced champagne and, afterwards, fetched down his copy of *Voyage avec un Âne dans les Cévennes* to refresh his memory of the route.

It is extraordinary how well known Stevenson is throughout the land where he travelled, and particularly in the Cévennes. He was the first outsider to project the Cévenols' image of themselves – something they could believe in and be proud of. Everyone has something to say about Stevenson and the commonest greeting on the road is no longer 'Où est-ce que vous allez comme ça?' but 'Alors, vous faites le voyage de Stevenson'. Here and there his passage survives in oral tradition – like at La Vernède, where they still talk about 'the Englishman's tree' – an oak where he camped near the road. It is charming to think that the story must have started with the father and son who surprised him over breakfast on their way to work in the woods.

Our last day was the first Sunday of September, a date of double significance in the region. It marks the great Protestant fête when thousands gather at the Musée du Désert near Alès to fortify their faith among the relics of the persecutions. And it marks the opening of the hunting season. On this sacred morning, long before we took the road from Saint-Germain-de-Calberte, the countryside was full of sound of slaughter. There were reputedly 100,000 enthusiasts at work in ours and the four neighbouring departments blasting everything from turtledoves to wild boars with their shotguns.

In the late afternoon, we left the banks of the Gardon de Mialet and took the old road which leads from Saint-Étienne-Vallée-Française to the Col de Saint-Pierre. The sun was setting as we reached the summit. It was night before we came down into Saint-Jean-du-Gard. In the main street we passed the hitching ring where Modestine was tied for the last time. It added up to 140 miles in 12 days – the Stevensonian schedule.

The journey back to Le Monastier in a van took four hours. It was with a touch of sadness that we returned our donkey to her barn in L'Anglade. M. Bonnefoy had been worrying about lawsuits. We set his mind at rest. She hadn't bitten any children. In fact she had been perfect – pretty, gentle, uncomplaining and affectionate. And it is true, she hardly drinks at all: and when she does, it is in the dainty, sipping sort of way which is lovely to watch.

Lord Stewart is a retired Scottish judge who first donned his advocate's wig and gown in 1975, exactly a century after RLS. He received *Travels with a Donkey* on winning the RLS Club Prize at Edinburgh Academy, Stevenson's old school, and in 1976 he and his wife, Jenny, hired a donkey and followed Stevenson's trail.

Living with Louis

CHRISTOPHER RUSH

I HAVE ALWAYS FELT a great affinity with Robert Louis Stevenson, even a close link. Not that I was aware of it as a child, but we were both brought up on the same stories, particularly those from the Old Testament and other religious 'horror' stories involving massacres and hangings and witches and ghosts and the like. Thomas Hardy, born only ten years before Stevenson, had exactly the same childhood experience at the hands of his grandmother, and it spills over darkly into his work. Louis died in 1894, still recalling his nurse Cummy's renderings of these stories with something of a glad shudder. I was born 50 years later, in 1944, and am glad to say – without a shudder – that the language in which those stories were clothed was still that of the King James Bible (KJB) and not the colourless lingo tricked out in most churches today from the New Revised Bible or other even more accessible translations, 'accessible' meaning with all the thrills and theatre and poetry washed and ironed out of it, so that instead of the little frisson of *And after the Fire, a Still, Small Voice*, you get something like 'there was a faint murmuring sound'. As if Jehovah couldn't do better as a public speaker. A faint murmuring sound. What dull dog dished that up, I wonder?

Like Louis, fortunately, I didn't have to wonder at the time. Old Epp, my great-great aunt, gave it to me as hot and strong as

Cummy and in the same good old Jacobean prose: 'For dust thou art, and unto dust shalt thou return.' I was three years old, and that was me told, and in no uncertain terms: 'Ye shall surely die.' As for what followed, after death, that was no less certain: it was 'the burning fire', as Epp called it, the place of eternal torment. 'And not one drop of water will you get, to cool your parched and blistered tongue!' Thank you, Cummy; thank you Epp. You kept us trembling in the dark and cowering under the covers, struggling to shut out images of death and damnation, torture, and bloody deeds. But the point is that the world I entered in 1944 was as close in some ways to 1894 as 1894 was to, say, 1611, the year of the KJB. Even after the revolutions of industry and medicine and science and two world wars, some things had not changed all that much, unlike now, only a single lifetime later, when the world that Louis and I shared has disappeared practically without a trace.

And not before time, some would say – adding no doubt that if they'd been our mentors today, both Epp and Cummy would most probably be up on child abuse charges, ignoring the fact that the terror was in one sense positive, or at least productive; it was the penalty paid at the time for the creativity that was to come. And it was not all fear and trembling. Years later, in one of his *Songs of Travel*, Louis recalled his childhood: 'Dear days of old with faces in the firelight, / Kind folks of old, you come again no more.'

Nostalgia colours memory all too falsely, as I know all too well. Nonetheless these lines whisk me back to the time of the old oral tradition (television did not enter our village until 1954, when I was ten), a time of stories round the fire and the faces that told them, the old remembering mouths. My mother's folk were fishermen, my great-uncle was a sailmaker, and the stories they told were about shipwrecks and sharks and castaways and exhumations, and the crabs that dined sweetly on drowned sailors. Ugh! I have never been able to eat crab in my life, the result perhaps of this early introduction to literature – of the folk variety, not unlike the old ballads in atmosphere, presentation and effect.

Reading actual books – that was something that came later. And the first book I read was *Treasure Island*. I was still unaware, when I read it, of the affinities between its famous author and my obscure self: Calvinism, a hellfire-breathing old female, a father problem (which was to loom large in both our lives), a terrorised mind and fevered imagination. Or that I would one day become an Edinburgher, inhabit what Stevenson calls his 'precipitous city', and light out from it, too, following his troubled footsteps across the Cévennes, with a four-footed companion, having also lost a woman – not as he did, to another man, but to that grim seducer, cancer. And indeed, one of the wonderful things about *Treasure Island* is that there is nothing in it that could have told me at the time anything at all about its author. Re-reading it now, more than six decades later, I can of course see scores of clues. The book is a treasure trove in more ways than one; it is eloquent of its creator's personality, apart from being a thoroughly ripping yarn.

One thing did strike me with peculiar force at the time of that first reading; the characters of the book, exotic and flamboyant as some of them were, seemed to me not at all that far removed from everyday life. Our village of a thousand souls was almost an island: swept by the stormy North Sea on one side and by fields on the other, all the way to the beckoning skylines, but shut in like Robinson Crusoe by the bolts and shackles of land and sea. For my first 12 years I never left that island, nor wanted to, nor even thought about it, or that there was anywhere else to go. There was no Forth Road Bridge, we had no car, no telephone, and even the local railways were soon to fall under Dr Beeching's axe. There was little social mobility; the radius of my travels rarely exceeded one mile in any direction and marriages were mainly between couples from the same or neighbouring villages, most of whom were vaguely related to one another in a sort of unconscious tribal incest. We did not suffer from grinding poverty, but we had no spare cash and often not enough.

It all opened up in the sixties, but I had read Stevenson in the early 1950s, when the place was still fossilised geographically, historically, socially, theologically. Before television arrived and ended the era of the faces in the firelight (they were caught now in the cold blue flashes from the box in the corner) our entertainment lay out in the streets and on the beaches. There was a one-legged man who used to haunt the harbour with a spyglass. He was the local barber, and when trade was slack he'd hobble out of his shop looking for ships on the skyline and tell me sea stories. He kept a half-bottle of rum in the side pocket of his jacket. It was called Black Heart. Does he sound familiar? Another eccentric, an ancient sailor with a gold earring and a white beard jutting over his sea-waistcoat, once grabbed me and hissed into my ear: 'I've seen monsoons and typhoons and baboons – and teaspoons!' I never forgot the line. Out in the firth lay the mysterious May Island, where I'd never been. And there was the Bass Rock, where the hero of *Kidnapped* and *Catriona* was incarcerated, and where old Epp told me I'd come from, and not, apparently, out of my mother's womb – the Book of Job had got it wrong. And if I was bad I'd be taken back to it to join the Covenanters who'd been marooned out there, and whose long-powdered bones whitened its cliffs – they weren't seagull droppings after all.

The Bass crouched like a blue bear waiting for me, and Berwick Law stood like a pyramid on the other side of the water. These were the faraway places, glimpsed only by my grandfather and my uncles, who took sea-chests with them when they went out on long hauls. They also took charts and came back laden with half-crowns that tumbled out of their blue- spotted neckerchiefs and clattered on the table like Spanish doubloons and pieces of eight among the marmalade and crumbs. Stevenson's world not only fitted exactly into mine, I grew out of it. I lived and breathed on *Treasure Island*.

All the more astonishing that by the time I did come to Stevenson, familiarity had bred not a particle of contempt, and the figures of the book sprang from it fresh-minted in my imagination. When I went to the pier-head, lay flat on my belly, looked into the water and saw the flounders lazing on the clear green sunbed of the bottom, there he lay – Israel Hands – all hunched up, two bullet-holes in his head, his brains oozing out, staining the sea, and the quick glinting fishes nibbling him down to the bone.

When I took stores down into the belly of my sea-cook uncle's boat, Long John sat waiting for me in the galley, to fry me up an egg. Being the youngest member of the crew Uncle Billy started off on board as cook. All he lacked was the one leg and the crutch. And he was not Billy Scott – he was Billy Bones. Up above the cries of seagulls converted easily into those of Captain Flint, perched on Silver's shoulder, just like the seagull my grandfather had tamed with scraps of fish to swoop down and land on his, and to sit there to be fed. Pieces of fish, pieces of eight. There was even a blind man, the village's very own blind Pew, swinging his stick wide at our legs as he paced the pier, counting the steps to the edge. He was out to get me – because of course we boys tormented him, as little boys do in their cruelty. And the booming of the Caribbean surf about the Fife coasts, I heard it day-long, night-long, and all through my dreams. Just like Jim Hawkins.

That was *Treasure Island* for me in 1954 – an open book; just as its author was a completely closed book. In spite of the clues, I neither knew or suspected anything of Louis the great traveller, although the story surely throws a window wide open on the personality and future life-style of the man who felt a constant need to:

Rise and go
Where the golden apples grow,
Where below another sky
Parrot islands anchored lie'

Free in other words, from the repressive moralities of Eden (Epp and Cummy-style), or Edinburgh, and the grand inquisitors who had ordained that apples were strictly off the menu. So a sick boy, the author in embryo, lies in bed dreaming about islands; later the writer takes his little hero, his young self, off to one of these islands, and in the end takes his older self off to Samoa, where he becomes his own tribal chief, and even his own god.

All this I came to understand much later. But along the way there was a stepping- stone. I began my secondary schooling in 1956 and for the first few years it was a grimly demoralising time (the father problem had much to do with it) in which I felt an inadequate and miserable failure. One afternoon, sitting in the dingy school library I picked up at random a *Reader*, a book of verse and prose for boys and girls, presented in all the dullness of the day, and which I had taken only because we were not allowed to sit down before we had chosen a book. The librarian loomed and hovered and I opened it obediently and acted the part of the bookworm. A moment later I was no longer acting – I was entranced, transfixed. The extract in front of me was *Travels With A Donkey*. and was Stevenson's account of his night among the pines on Mont Lozère, sleeping *à la belle étoile* while Modestine munched her black bread and he drank ice-cold water, smoked a rolled cigarette and thought of the woman he loved. Beyond the pine-tops the Milky Way was a faint silvery vapour above his head and the only sound was the quiet conversation of the stream over the stones. I thought at the time what an incredibly liberating and exhilarating experience it must have been, and it freed me from bondage to that miserable moment and sowed a seed for the future. Louis's description had fired my imagination.

Years later, a happily married man, I read the whole of the *Travels* along with *An Inland Voyage*, and my wife and I talked of how lovely it would be if we could go down the Loire, like Louis follow the Oise, or cross the Cévennes, or take a barge. We never did. One summer my wife fell seriously ill with breast cancer and died early that autumn. It was a swift and aggressive attack which left me and my young children devastated. Wandering the streets of the capital in the dim dawns, unable to sleep, I found myself one early morning outside 17 Heriot Row. It was no accident. My unconscious feet had drawn me naturally, and as I stood there looking at Louis's old house, I remembered how he'd felt when Fanny Osbourne left him to return to her husband 3,000 miles away across the Atlantic. 'A miserable widower' was how he described himself; she was dead to him now, or as good as. And I remembered also how he had reacted: by going to France and buying a donkey and setting out across the mountains.

Of course. After all it's the obvious thing to do when you lose your partner, your life's companion. Why doesn't everybody think about it? Thinking about it was no longer enough. That summer, I was in France making inquiries and arranging to hire a donkey. And on 22 September, just before nine o'clock in the morning, I was standing in the Place de la Poste of Le Monastier in the pouring rain, watching it pelting down an inscribed plinth which told me that Monsieur Robert Louis Stevenson had set off from this exact spot on the same day over a century ago: *D'ici partit le 22 septembre 1878 Robert Louis Stevenson pour son voyage à travers les Cévennes avec un âne.*

He came back from his travels and wrote a book about it which is now famous. I came back from my travels in his footsteps and wrote a book about it which is now out of print. Louis also went to America, brought back the woman he loved, and made her his wife. That was a journey I could not make. Even Orpheus failed in the attempt. I knew that it was not the book that mattered. Or matters. It's the journey. And I knew that the first childhood link with Louis had only been the beginning, the start of a lifetime's journey which, if you travel in the same spirit, is one that never ends. Nobody has put it better than Louis himself: 'to travel hopefully is a better thing than to arrive, and the true success is to labour'.

Christopher Rush

Christopher Rush was born in St Monans, Fife, in 1944. Graduating from Aberdeen University as the English Medallist, he taught for 30 years at George Watson's College in Edinburgh. For memoirs such as *Hellfire and Herring'* and *To Travel Hopefully,* and his novels *Last Lesson of The Afternoon* and *Will*, his alma mater made him a Doctor of Letters.

From An Inland Voyage Diary and Poems, 2011

JIM BERTRAM

> Landrecies: It is not the place one would have chosen for a day's rest; for it consists almost entirely of fortifications. We visited the church. Here lies Marshal Clarke. But as neither of us had ever heard of that military hero, we bore the associations of the spot with fortitude (…) It reminded you that even this place was a point in the great warfaring system of Europe, and might on some future day be ringed about with cannon smoke and thunder, and make itself a name among strong towns.
> - *An Inland Voyage*, RLS (1876) -

WEDNESDAY 19 AUGUST – We must not miss the prophetic poignancy of these remarks by RLS as Verdun is off to the left and the Somme to the right. We had visited the railway carriage where the ending of all wars had been signed. It would take only a generation! The poem by Wilfred Owen with the line: 'Gas! GAS! Quick, boys!' had been recited two nights previous.

Lochnagar Mine Crater Memorial, La Boisselle, Somme: A stop at what was once a great battlefield of World War I. You can't tell, but then there is no woodland, and again you may get to seven when counting cemeteries that are in plain sight. Each with its white picket fence, and a well-kept paddock of white wooden crosses, some with names, some without. Yes, this must have been a hell of a place. 'Look! There by the roadside a posy of wild poppies.'

Jim Bertram

'Names'

Names are sacred things
That tie men to their times.
Where death, as spring forget-me-nots
Breaks through in crosses bearing names.

War's black horse rode out
A quota needing yet for claims.
To scythe, to reap, to plant,
A crop that harvests only names.

That soldier was a man
Who passioned in his day.
T'o'rd love of life; alas,
His glories but a name.

In some far distant time
A finger traces the riven line,
In wee, wet, words to ask again,
'Is that all; just a name?'

Embodied in this poem are the conflicting questions posed by an engineering mind, and a Christian faith. I visited Arlington Cemetery USA, the Vietnam War Memorial USA, and these battlefields of France, in a short period of time.

Each generation must count its crosses on the hill.

From An Inland Voyage Diary and Poems, 2011

'Once upon a Question'

If a man die shall he live again?
If a widow cry shall she sing again?
If a son sigh shall he rise again?

Is Time the enemy of living things
Or just an agent of life and death?
Is she sweet kindness to the young
And tortured cruelty to an aged breast?

By what command does she constant fly
To measure all since time began
Who knows her look, her want, her way?
Will Time yet die for 'eternal' man?

Jim Bertram was born in Glasgow during World War II, and trained as an engineer in the family tradition – encouraged by his English Teacher! He left Rolls-Royce and Scotland for the United States, and now lives in South Carolina. He is thankful poets don't make good lighthouse engineers, and engineers don't live off their poetry.

Stevenson has a Home in Monterey
MONICA HUDSON, LINDY PEREZ
& ELIZABETH ANDERSON

'The Pacific licks all other oceans out of hand; there is no place but the
Pacific Coast to hear eternal roaring surf. When I get to the top of
the woods behind Monterey, I can hear the seas breaking all round
over ten or twelve miles of coast from near Carmel on my left,
out to Point Pinos in front and away to the right along the sands
of Monterey to Castroville and the mouth of the Salinas'
- *RLS Letter to W.E. Henley, 1879* -

THE MIGHTY PACIFIC OCEAN, dramatic scenery, fascinating cultures, and supportive friendships that Robert Louis Stevenson found in Monterey influenced his future travels and writings. He turned his keen observation to the local landscapes, history, and peoples to capture a vision still seen today. We, who know and love this place, think: 'He understood us. Monterey looks and feels so much like his descriptions.'

Stevenson's brief stay in Monterey during the fall of 1879 was a gift to our small coastal community. Many visitors include Monterey on their itinerary to see the dunes and craggy coastlines, which resemble settings described in *Treasure Island*. And, just as his first book lives on in popular culture, so do beliefs about Monterey as a place of mystery, drama, and buried treasure.

For decades, pilgrims have walked in the footsteps of RLS:

from the adobes in historic Monterey to the goat ranch in Carmel Valley, from the church retreat in Pacific Grove to the old mission of Carmel, from the lighthouse at Point Pinos to the windswept beaches curving around the bay. We appreciate his skill in recording these memorable places; he understood the importance of our history and cared about our future. The Monterey Peninsula's historic sites are now some of the most celebrated and best-preserved in the American West.

But Stevenson's time in Monterey was not easy. Soon after his arrival, he was confronted with Fanny's ambivalence about divorce, which caused him an agonising wait before their marriage. Fortunately, while Fanny made up her mind, Montereyans befriended and supported the affable visitor from Scotland who told stories so well. As a traveller in a weakened state of health who had risked his family's support, Stevenson had to rely on strangers. Venturing out to camp in the Carmel Valley, he fell severely ill, and a couple of goat ranchers found and took care of him until he was fit to travel again. Back in Monterey, acquaintances became close friends.

'A place does not clearly exist for the imagination, till we have moved elsewhere… Hence it is that a place grows upon our fancy after we have left it.' So writes Stevenson in his essay on Simoneau's at Monterey. He goes on to describe the warmth and company Jules Simoneau offered at his small restaurant near the French Hotel. At his table sat a French baker, an Italian fisherman, a Portuguese whaler, and a 'polysyllabic' newspaper editor. Along with shared meals, these friends supplied lively conversation and – unbeknownst to Stevenson – a little money to support his writing. Among his friends in Monterey, character was more important than money, occupation, formal education, or family background; kindness, congeniality, and honesty mattered. His intimate correspondence with Jules Simoneau is a lasting testament to the bonds he made with those who shared his optimism.

His future stepson, Lloyd Osbourne, noticed Stevenson's talk was all about the people he was meeting in Monterey. It was in Stevenson's nature to look past class and race and perceive the inherent value in people he met. He saw and admired Indians singing Gregorian music in the ruined Carmel Mission, Chinese practising ancient customs in a segregated village, and Mexicans living with grace and decorum despite their declining status in the land that once was their own. The diverse population of Monterey today recognises Stevenson as a man ahead of his time, believing in the unique contributions of every culture.

Despite physical and financial hardships during his stay, RLS gained insight into his own strengths and vulnerabilities. He came to feel he had done the right thing striking out on his own. He found the ability to persevere. We still admire his acceptance of poor health and suffering and his will to survive. In a letter to his friend Edmund Gosse, back in England, he wrote:

> I don't know if I am the same man I was in Europe… my head went round and looks another way now; for when I found myself over here in a new land, and all the past uprooted in the one tug, and I neither feeling glad nor sorry, I got my last lesson about mankind… that I could have so felt astonished me beyond description. There is a wonderful callousness in human nature which enables us to live.

The rambling old adobe where Stevenson lodged was then called the French Hotel. Fortunately, the building was spared demolition, the fate of many neglected historic adobes. In 1949, the Stevenson House was opened under California State Park ownership as a museum dedicated to the memory of Robert Louis Stevenson. It is home to the largest collection of RLS's personal possessions found anywhere.

Monterey RLS Club members and other volunteer docents greet visitors seven months of the year and share our affection for RLS – for the man and his writing. As ambassadors for his legacy, we find ourselves welcoming people from all walks of life and from countries all over the world. We love to share the many reasons why he continues to be an inspiration today, and visitors teach us what he means to them. Today, as well as during his lifetime, his vulnerable and rebellious nature appeals to those who see something of themselves in his struggles and aspirations. His kindness, gentle humour, modesty, moral integrity, advocacy for the underdog, and courage are evident both in his stories and in the accounts of those who knew him.

Spreading the word about Stevenson naturally generates positive connections and lasting friendships here and abroad. An experienced docent explains it this way:

> What drew me in is his life story. He could have been a snob because of his family background; he could have been consumed with self-pity because of his poor health; but instead, he dealt with his setbacks and pursued his dream of living an adventurous and creative life. Once we start talking about him, people want to know more and more. We encourage them to rediscover Stevenson and his writing; he lives on here.

His best story, of course, is his own life, and the most fascinating and enduring character is Robert Louis Stevenson himself. He has made storytellers of us all.

As members of the RLS Club of Monterey, Monica Hudson, Elizabeth Anderson and Lindy Perez have all served as volunteer guides at the Stevenson House in Monterey, California. Monica is an author, researcher and a fellow traveller in Stevenson's footsteps around the world. Elizabeth is a cultural resources planner and writer who rediscovered her admiration for RLS in a museum archive on Maui. Lindy Perez is a retired social worker, drawn to extraordinary people, travel, history and literature, which led to her researching Stevenson's Monterey period.

Two Poems

ELAINE PARKS

AFTER DISCOVERING *Travels with a Donkey*, I delved deeply into the world of RLS, searching out all of his travel works, completing my collection of the novels, and reading old and new biographies. I composed a set of poems which were inspired by Stevenson's life and some of the people he encountered. I reflect on Louis in Edinburgh as a young man, his time in France at the artists' colony, his decision to leave for America, living in Monterey and San Francisco, his winter in the Adirondacks, on the sea, in Hawai'i, and finally his life in Samoa.

These two are from Louis and Fanny's honeymoon at the Silverado mining camp.

'Silverado'

A three-room cabin high on a mountain side
Sun brilliant in morning, sky bluer than in dreams
The new husband watches his wife pour water
Its drops flash silver in the clear light
He cannot believe this California day is his
And this bronzed woman his, too

So far away are the Scottish glens
Heathered hills and sad winds blowing
Rain in sheets needling grey pavements
Breath like smoke, and blanketed knees
Heavy cities with castle towers

Now this woman in a blue dress
Makes coffee over a wood fire
The husband ceases his morning writing
To watch and remember this scene
The past is already many pages behind

This new wife has gold-brown eyes that see clear
Love burns his heart

'The Kingdom By Night'

Among sweet bay trees
The King and Queen of Silverado
Survey their honeymoon encampment:
Platform built into rockface,
A huge theatre stage their home,
Their unseeing audience the tops of trees
Rooted in the deep canyon below.
Nutmeg scent and cedar
Invade the night air in gusts,
Framing the edges of all thought.
Valley winds spring up, then die;
Far away boughs shake with gales
Then sleep silent once more.
Red rock overhanging the old bunkhouse
Looms bold in outdoor candlelight;
The night sky unfurls a thousand diamonds.

The tallest pine tree cradles a silver moon
Until she swims out of reach;
Twisted roots of madrona trees
Snake grey coils underfoot in the moonlight.
Perfumes of tree resin spice the cool air,
Brush and chaparral clamber
Over rock stained with cinnabar and iron;
White azalea bushes
Glow palely and ghostlike,
Welcoming the royal guests.

Elaine Parks has worked in print and film archives, television news, and education. She is particularly interested in the art, literature and social movements of the 19th century. Besides writing poetry, she contributes travel and event reviews to *The William Morris Society of Canada Newsletter*. She lives in Toronto, Canada.

RLS: Writer in Eternal Residence
PROFESSOR ALAN RIACH

I VISITED SAMOA for three days in 2000, arriving on the evening of 17 October. I had my return ticket but when Stevenson arrived, he didn't know he'd be staying. There had been some talk in the press at the time about returning his bones to Scotland. My friend Sina Va'oi, then Professor of English at the University of Western Samoa, shook her head: 'No,' she said. 'He is our writer now, our writer in eternal residence.'

So many years before, for me, a wee boy in Lanarkshire, it was *Kidnapped* and *Treasure Island* in the Dudley D. Watkins illustrated books, two pictures per page, a short paragraph underneath each: not Stevenson's words, but based upon them, so that when I came to read the works themselves, the images and language, the style, speed and insight, were so much greater and went in so deep. And the legacy was multiple: the adventure, the quest, the map (or maps), the treasure, whatever it might be, and Scotland – its geography encompassed and traversed, its meaning through history and language and politics, and its purpose as modernity approached.

It was my grandfather's legacy first – five or six copies of the Tusitala Edition with which I set out to complete the set. And one day in Voltaire & Rousseau, Glasgow's labyrinthine second-hand bookshop – full of lights and shadows, catacombs of books, piles and shelves and pyramids, marvellously fragrant, entered through a close-mouth like a cave in the tenements around it, then revealing its treasures within, and the treasures in each book awaiting – I found, tucked in unobtrusively between much larger, heavy tomes, a slim blue spine with a palm tree: the last of my collection!

Later came films, at my Uncle Glen's home – out for a beer in the local pub, then back to turn on the TV just before 9 pm, and Spencer Tracy in *Jekyll and Hyde* began. Two hours passed in unbroken attention. Each horrible turn of the story, each bagatelle from victim to villain, each unravelling of possible hope, each revelation of sympathy as the depths of what humanity might turn to, was followed to its saddening end, that optimistic curiosity turned to understanding and failure, human potential at its worst. Wisdom and adulthood, childhood's dreams, all turned dark and poisonous. And in the cinema in Airdrie, the beginning of the all-colour *Kidnapped* of 1971, a bright green field all covered in bloody corpses: Culloden's awful aftermath.

I went to New Zealand in 1986. In 2000, I knew that I was coming back to Scotland in January 2001. The chance at last had to be taken: get to Samoa, visit him there. I booked a ticket, got a flight, went.

That first night, the small coach from the airport is taking me past billboards: 'Vailima – Samoa's own beer – welcomes you.' It is a rough road, the houses set back from it on stilts, and young people, single or in small groups, are walking. It's after midnight now and the ocean is shining in the moonlight. Dogs, at least a dozen loping around, are sitting by the roadside, watching us drive by, likewise, cats.

To the Hotel Insel Fehmarn. The bus conductress asks me why I'm here. 'It's a pilgrimage,' I tell her. 'Do you read Stevenson?'

'Oh yes,' she says, 'we read his history a lot. He was here, you know – only a few blocks from the hotel – for, three, four, five years, till 1894. They were happy years for him. Happy years. You are Scottish?'

'Yes.'

'Ah!' She beams and nods. 'I understand why you come here now.'

The next morning, breakfast is Samoan banana porridge, coffee, papaya fruit and Samoan pancakes.

'What makes them "Samoan"?' I ask the waiter.

He smiles and tells me: 'They are very good. They are made with fruit in the mix.'

Simon Va'oi is waiting for me, takes me up the hill to Vailima. The road in is beautiful, spacious, surrounded by trees and flowers, all eloquently curved and cared for. The residence is grand and gracious, broad, a wide-angle lens building, especially since the later wing was added. It's 9.15am. A guide will take us around; we're the first of the day. The day is all high blue, white clouds over Mount Vaea, a shoulder rising, a lookout; the eye goes up to its summit easily from the grounds as you approach, from the windows once inside. Stevenson's view of the place of his own grave is not possible since the later wing was added. The guide is careful, generous and slow, reverential, but immediately open to our questions and humour. RLS's mother's room has a big portrait of Christopher Columbus. I make some remark about her formidable look; he laughs, speculates she may have bought it for the pioneering spirit she discerned in her son also.

A photograph on the wall in RLS's study catches my eye: a native 'helper' dressed in tartan (RLS gave them all Royal Stewart cloth to wear) with a native-patterned cloth behind him. But no one can tell me who the man was, or his name. Then, the famous 'group' photograph – of the 15 people, eight are named (Joe Strong, Mary the maid, Margaret the mother, Lloyd the stepson, RLS, Fanny, Belle the stepdaughter, her son Austin). The other seven 'servants' or 'helpers' are unnamed, native Samoan people. The man on the right, leaning on the post, is looking at Lloyd as if he suspected bad things of him; the man on the far right is holding a big wood-axe, eyeing the edge of it.

Three moments I remember most intensely. Coming into RLS's library and study, where he wrote, dictated to Belle, lay on the little single bed (a photograph shows him playing the flageolet, knees up under the counterpane). You come in the door and look around the big broad room, its spaciousness, the bookshelves; then your gaze turns right to the corner where the small bed is. Suddenly, I want to cry. There is a catch in my throat, and I turn away again quite quickly. From the front windows, you can see the blue Pacific, a mile or two away, the white waves; certainly you feel the ocean breeze.

Then, coming down the broad staircase into the great hall and dining room. Solid Californian wood, no give or creak, another wide-angle view.

And then, of course, the small veranda at the back of the dining room, facing the outhouse where the cooking was done, where, standing making mayonnaise, the final stroke came down. 'They carried him in here and this is where he died,' says the guide. Well, whatever it is, it is for a moment, invisible, the fingertips, anonymous, drumming a quiet roll upon my spine. He was 44. I am 43.

It's 6.30, twilight almost, and Sina and her husband, Sale, pick me up and we drive back up the hill to Vailima. As we reach the entrance, Sale pulls over: the gates are closed, the side- road has a chain across it.

'Curfew,' he says. The local villagers have closed everything for 20 minutes while they say prayers. Within a few minutes, there are half a dozen taxis on either side of the gates, some having dropped delegates off, trying to get out, some trying to take delegates in. There are two coachloads of delegates stuck behind us, and two other cars parked beside us, waiting. A host of other colorfully-clothed nationals are all in their vehicles, puzzled and inconvenienced. Sina laughs delightedly.

Someone opens the gates; the cavalcade drives through. We follow up the Robert Louis Stevenson Avenue to Vailima in late twilight, all lit up, the greensward in front of it, marquees, people going up the steps. We are greeted by the Prime Minister and his wife, who is also Head of Sociology at the National University of Samoa, and find ourselves in the middle of the happy crowd of delegates and officials and their parties, drinking iced wine and chilled Vailima lager.

Waiters and waitresses circulate with trays of raw tuna and soya sauce, small savoury parcels, fish or curried morsels, fatty roast pork and crackling with bright green seaweed-like tentacles, more beer, juices and wine. Everyone seems jolly and untroubled; it's strange. There will be neither speeches nor demonstrators of any active kind. There is a sequence of performances, dances by a national group who are about to take part in a traditional dance competition in Noumea. There are fire-eaters and firestick jugglers. The floodlights are on the performers in the open sward; we watch them, all the bright colours and costumes, and Vaea, looming.

I'm introduced to the British Honorary Consul. 'You're British?' he asks. 'Well, keep your passport about you and stay out of jail.' I tell him I will, and hope not to see him again.

The lights are going out. We are among the last to leave. Then, the dark – and up there the stars, and out there, almost palpable, the phosphor of the sea.

The next day, I get a taxi to the offices of the *Samoa Observer* to meet Sano Molifa, the paper's editor and publisher. He's also a poet and a novelist. I had met him five years earlier at a conference I helped organise at the University of Waikato in New Zealand. He's one of those people you can recognise as genuine immediately, a big man with a shy smile, a warm look, a cautious but firm and decisive voice, welcoming, yet also shy. 'Stevenson's story we know,' he says. 'Tell me your story, now.'

On the last day, Sina's friend, Chantal, picks me up and drives us to the car park at Vailima and we set off.

'Which way,' she asks, 'the easy route or the hard one, straight up?' We go straight up. It's not too bad, no scrambling, all walking. And after many pauses, drenched in sweat, we get to the summit and look back down. We meet an Australian honeymooning couple, we talk about RLS. We go back down the easy, roundabout way.

I ask about the name 'Vailima'.

'It means five rivers,' Chantal tells me.

'Where are they? Are they named?'

'Sure,' she says. 'River number one, river number two, river number three . . .'

Halfway down, I say I can hear a river, the sound of running water.

She pauses. 'No,' she says. 'That is the rain – it will be here soon.' And in two minutes it arrives. It's a warm, refreshing shower, drenching us both like a last benediction, in the last half hour's walk back to the car park.

It's one in the morning. The stars are everywhere. The coach arrives to take me to the airport, through the dark, starlit night. All of this is navigation, coordinate points. Something now summed up, something to recall. The scars of Billy Bones, the loneliness of old Ben Gunn.

I'm thinking of Stevenson's hands, his fingers on the flageolet, his gentle pressure on the paper and the holding of the writing instruments, and of how the words themselves remain, so deep, like stars in the darkness.

Airdrie-born Alan Riach is a poet and Professor of Scottish Literature at Glasgow University. Recent books include *The Winter Book* (2017), *Homecoming* (2009), *Arts of Resistance: Poets, Portraits and Landscapes of Modern Scotland* (2008) and *Arts of Independence: The Cultural Argument and Why It Matters Most* (2014). He visited Samoa in October 2000.

From the North American Diary and Poems, 2013

JIM BERTRAM

FRIDAY 13 SEPTEMBER – Manhattan to Saranac. The best way to get from Manhattan to Saranac is to take a group of RLS friends, as we did, and a train up the Hudson River Gorge. It put me in mind of doing a similar journey on a previous occasion, out of Lyons and going to Le-Puy-en-Velay. The Hudson is found at the bottom of a steep-sided valley, which it probably authored, and runs north out of the city to 'Upstate New York'. Along the way the scene dramatically changes from a metropolis whose skyline consists of tall buildings and polluted atmosphere, to a wilderness of tree and lake surrounding crystal clear air and stream. I like Saranac.

'Saranac'
To Mike and Friends at Baker Cottage

I have been to Saranac
A place of lake and hill.
Wrapped in forest wilderness
Where thoughts do linger still.

Adirondack is a singing word
The tongue delights to frame.
And senses anticipate the best
With the saying of the name.

The people bear the pith o' man
And know the honest face.
Where handshake is a sacred pledge,
And kindness commonplace.

Came we to this lovely town
Following a less trod way.
To meet their Stevensonians,
On a crisp September day.

We sang the song of friendship,
We danced beneath the pine,
And sealed it up with friendship's cup,
For Auld Lang Syne.

And should I meet the stranger,
Who's sad for New York home.
I'll ask him 'Is't Saranac?
Or just some other town.'

I stood at the main intersection in Saranac to ask myself the poet's question, 'what do you see, what do you hear, what do you feel?' but was asked in short order by one motorist, and two pedestrians, 'Can I help you?'

MONDAY 15 SEPTEMBER – Saranac to Boston. The following lines were written in the middle of the night in Boston against a challenge set by a RLS Club member on the second last day of the trip. The poem was read at dinner on the last evening. Tusitala was the Samoan name given to Stevenson and means storyteller. The island of Samoa was where he died. The poem mimics the epic poem by RLS which is his *Requiem*, which closes with these lines: 'Home is the sailor, home from the sea, and the hunter home from the hill.' This is my small tribute to genius.

It is a sadness that so many Scots stravaig, but...

'Tusitala'

Why go ye from Scotia's land
To scribble o'er the main?
The soul of 'Storyteller' says,
Tusitala, is my name!

Oh sailor, hunter, won't you come,
Why lie ye not at hame?
The soul of Louis Stevenson says,
'Tusitala, is my name!'

Jim Bertram was born in Glasgow during World War II, and trained as an engineer in the family tradition - encouraged by his English Teacher! He left Rolls-Royce and Scotland for the United States, and now lives in South Carolina. He is thankful poets don't make good lighthouse engineers, and engineers don't live off their poetry.

Tusitala Still Matters to Samoans, after 130 Years

JAMES WINEGAR

IN THE STYLE OF TUSITALA, this story is full of chance meetings, new relationships, and exotic destinations, with multiple side 'happenings' along the way.

On 7 December 1889, the Reverend W.E. Clark, Headmaster at Malua Theological College, looking seaward spotted a small schooner underway with full sails and the wind pushing it toward Apia. He decided to go to town and see who might be on board the sleek, fast, little vessel, the Equator. And there they were – Robert Louis Stevenson in his sailing togs, Fanny in a loose-fitting holoku and a broad-brimmed hat carrying a guitar, and Lloyd wearing a striped pyjama-like garb with a banjo over his shoulders. They looked every bit like a small band of gypsies roaming the world with no apparent objective other than going from place to place. In our time, they would have been dismissed as a group of common hippies stopping to make some extra money to resupply their stash of mind-expanding substances.

Interestingly, the good Reverend made friends almost immediately with this eclectic group. He saw in RLS a light of genius burning brightly and, over a very short period, the two bonded. American-born Harry J. Moors also witnessed the precarious disembarking of the eccentric travellers. He recognised immediately something different about this little group and in the usual and expected fa'a Samoa, or Samoan way, Harry offered the unusual visitors accommodation at his Tivoli Hotel on the waterfront.

Harry and Louis got further acquainted and their lives became intertwined. Louis felt invigorated in the wonderful tropical climate; the natives were accepting, the culture seemed friendly and the mail service, on which Louis was so dependent, operated on a scheduled basis with a stop each fortnight. But important in his decision to stay was that he had found in Harry a like-minded friend. After the passing of Louis, Harry's own affectionate book *With Stevenson in Samoa* attests to this.

The subsequent five years were filled with fantastic growth, satisfactions, drama and a change of pace for each member of the family. Fanny's pioneering skills and general toughness were a key to their success as they homesteaded and developed Villa Vailima, but then, as still today, the house is a reflection of how RLS saw himself.

His love for everything Samoan prompted him to declare that Polynesians were one of 'God's sweetest creations'. Despite periods of sickness, his Samoan years gave him some of the best years of his life. He and Fanny developed and built Villa Vailima into a respectable island plantation – a labour of love and determination to make Samoa their permanent home. And, why not? The circumstances were ideal.

Then suddenly, near the end of 1894, Tusitala was gone. The shock and disruption to the household was absolutely devastating.

After a short period, following his mother's return to Scotland, the rest of the family decided to return to California. Life without Louis in Samoa was too unbearable. After a time away, they decided to return to see if they could revive their idyllic life, but after months of valiant efforts, they realised that the plantation could not survive without its heart, Tusitala. A wealthy Russian-German merchant, Gustav Kuntz, purchased the property, and the original cast of characters embarked on their separate journeys. Interestingly, each was different but there was a common thread that ran through all their lives: their relationship with Tusitala defined who they became.

Kuntz's ownership didn't last long and the property eventually became government-owned, the home of whomever the governing official happened to be. And, why not? It was the most beautiful plantation home in all of Oceania and it was located conveniently near the seat of government in Apia. And so it stood for all those years of protectorate rule and through the painful process of Samoan Independence – a symbol of honour and prestige. Malietoa Tanumafili II declared it the official residence of the Head of State and took occupancy, but eventually found that his own plantation best suited his lifestyle. Villa Vailima still stood as a symbol and icon of government, but it never lost its identity as the home of Robert Louis Stevenson.

Fast forward to the 1980s. Three ambitious and energetic former missionaries to Samoa realised the value of Villa Vailima to the islands' history. The building itself, though cosmetically retaining its outward architectural elegance, was showing and feeling inwardly the ravages of old age. The building was literally a pile of dust held together by multiple coats of paint, and badly in need of rehabilitation.

Each of the three missionaries had their own relationship with Samoa, returning often and for various reasons. In 1989, they joined with a world-class ethnobotanist, Dr Paul Cox, a former missionary like them, to save 30,000 acres of prime, low-lying rainforest land at Falealupo, Savaii. In celebration of this achievement, cultural Samoan matai titles were bestowed. Nafanua, Tilafaiga and Taima – honoured names from Samoan mythology – were given new life and meaning in our real world.

The environmental preservation of the rainforest profoundly influenced the historic preservation of Villa Vailima, igniting a desire to carry out a project that would benefit all of Samoa, just as the rainforest had benefitted the Falealupo area. The wish of the chief players to 'give back' to Samoa was evident in their lasting commitment to the preservation of Villa Vailima.

Rex Maughan was bestowed the Tilafaiga title. At the beginning of the 1990s, and with the encouragement of his former faife'au Mamona associates, an ambitious restoration plan for Vailima took shape which was presented to the sympathetic Prime Minister Tofilau Eti Alesana. The busy year that followed saw the development of written submissions to the government. Then in 1990, Cyclone Ofa hit Samoa with the force of an angry Mother Nature. One year later, as the proposals were discussed and debated, Cyclone Val struck Samoa again, this time inflicting severe damage to Villa Vailima. The twin cyclones sealed its fate and a decision had to be made: either finish the demolition or take advantage of the offer to restore and preserve it, as the newly created Robert Louis Stevenson Museum Preservation Foundation, Inc. had proposed. Prime Minister Tofilau led the development and passage of the RLS Parliamentary Act, and the restoration plan began almost immediately. Through ensuing months of intense construction activities, Tilafaiga made certain that the home of RLS was preserved for ages to come. Visitors now come to Samoa because of RLS and discover why he loved Samoa with all his heart, or for its beauty and culture and discover RLS and his family at the museum.

During the time of consideration and acceptance of the proposal, the restoration team was very busy carrying out intense research on the building of Villa Vailima, poring over volumes of materials that Louis and Fanny had left in various forms. Because of the many international visitors to Samoa, there were also references to the home, the ambiance, and the occupants. Major decisions were made weekly to keep the work going.

During the process, several writers and biographers stopped by to see for themselves what all the fuss was about. The team was delighted to welcome one of Tusitala's distant cousins, Mrs

Jean Leslie from Edinburgh. She came with the notion that if the Scots were not happy with the restoration results, they might take his bones back to his homeland. It was made clear to her that any attempt to implement such a strategy would be unthinkable in Samoa and it would be met with resistance stern enough to ensure that Tusitala's bones and Fanny's ashes would never be disturbed from their final resting place atop Mt Vaea.

We forgave her, and she did see for herself the beauty and appropriate place Samoa had provided for the fulfilment of Stevenson's wish to be buried 'under the wide and starry sky'.

Meanwhile, another prestigious visitor was Hunter Davies, in the process of writing a book tracing the multiple stops Louis made on his way to his discovery of Samoa. He was on the last leg of that memorable journey and was well received. His reflections were eventually published in his widely read work *The Teller of Tales*.

With months of preparation, research and the usual problems arising when working with skilled craftsmen, carpenters, landscapers, contractors and so on, the place was a beehive of activity. The typical 'coconut wireless' rumour mill was very much in evidence with stories such as 'Malietoa has been kicked out of his assigned residence' and other such preposterous suggestions as only the undercurrent in Samoa can conjure.

As work toward the dedication day proceeded with the usual bumps and unexpected problems, the team was invited to Scotland for the christening of the locomotive to be named The Robert Louis Stevenson, for the daily high-speed service between Edinburgh and London. It took some quick planning and logistical manoeuvring, but we managed to take the reigning Miss Samoa to Scotland to break the magnum of champagne over the nose of the powerful engine. We were treated royally by the Scots and were given a first-hand look at the multiple places in and around Edinburgh that still have Stevenson's fingerprints all over them. We also had the opportunity to kiss and make-up with RLS's cousin Jean Leslie. Eventually, she was very comfortable with the way Villa Vailima was being treated and conceded that Samoa was the only place that should ever house his bones. How could we not agree?

The work was nearing completion and it was decided to present the completely restored and beautifully landscaped Villa Vailima to the public on the Centenary of Stevenson's death. The show went on with local celebrities, food and a historic group trek to the gravesite assisted by students from our neighbouring Avele College. It was a day not to be forgotten in Samoa.

Now, after 25 years of operation, we, the Board and Directors and Staff of the RLS Museum Foundation Inc., are pleased to do what we can to raise the awareness of the importance of the history, the environment and the love that has been expressed by former missionaries. Their respect and *alofa* could have been made manifest in other ways, but God blessed them to be able to show it in a unique and lasting manner.

The Foundation's own Jubilee celebration, in August 2019, brought together kindred spirits from far-flung corners of the earth, with Professor Joseph Farrell of Glasgow University as the guest speaker at our Memorial Garden Party. The Scottish Government has promised its support for cultural links and the Jubilee, with its rich variety of other events and activities, was reported in the *Samoa Observer* – as well as featured in *The Scotsman*.

Long after all of us and our readers will have passed on, the memory of Tusitala will still burn brightly in very meaningful ways in Samoa. Thank you, Tilafaiga.

And thank God for Tusitala.

In the late 1950s, James Winegar and his friend, Tilafaiga Rex Maughan, served in Samoa as young missionaries for the Church of Jesus Christ of Latter Day Saints. Returning to the USA, they pursued projects to repay their love for Samoa, culminating in the restoration of Villa Vailima. Jim died in October 2020, while this book was in preparation.

Lord, Teach Us the Lessons:
Revisiting the Vailima Prayers

NEIL ADAM

AFTER TWO WEEKS of touring our Stevenson Show in New Zealand, we flew into the Apia airport and were met in the arrival hall by local musicians playing ukuleles and guitars and singing Pacific songs in four-part harmony. A tired-looking immigration official asked: 'Why are you coming to Samoa?' We said we had a concert at Vailima. There was no response as he continued to examine our passports. 'Stevenson's house,' I added. He smiled, saying: 'You don't have to tell Samoans about Stevenson and Vailima.' *Lesson Number One*.

Two minutes later, my wife asked the car hire man about the speed limit on the island. He asked: 'Why would you need one?' Soon, we learned why you don't: dogs, pedestrians, cyclists and brightly coloured buses carrying religious messages all took equal rights on the roads. Cars drove at a speed dictated by the surface, and those who shared the road. *Lesson Number Two*.

We were the only people staying in the small, family-run 1930s' hotel, and the staff were tremendously helpful. The next morning, with our Scottish friends Mitchell and Rex, we found our way out of town, up the hill to the RLS Museum. We climbed Mount Vaea in great heat and were overtaken in the process by small children, pregnant women, and people running up and down as part of their fitness regime. A runner of about my age slowed down long enough to tell me about his farm in the valley and to enquire whether his son would be safe moving to Melbourne. The view out over the ocean from Stevenson's grave was unforgettable.

The four of us, in varying states of disrepair, arrived at the museum, to prepare for our Stevenson show the next day. The show consists of Stevenson's life story, and much of it is told through the autobiographical content of his poems, which we have set to music and turned into songs. To walk around in Vailima with my guitar over my shoulder, and to sing his songs in the rooms where he wrote them, was just an extraordinary experience. We began to wonder whether the emotional lumps in our throats were going to interrupt the flow of the show the next day. We were right to wonder, because they did.

A few months earlier, I had picked up a copy of Stevenson's *Prayers Written at Vailima* (Zodiac Books, 1939) in the Oxfam bookshop on Morningside Road in Edinburgh, and I had the book, with its lovely hand-cut paper pages and linocut dustjacket, with me. A second walk around the house and garden, with the Zodiac book in my hand, was another emotional event. Soon a plan was hatched to see whether, when we got home, I could turn some of these prayers into songs.

Like Stevenson, I had at least one intensely religious Edinburgh parent and, like Stevenson, I also caused some rumpus when I announced that I would no longer attend church with my family. Like his, my religious upbringing left me with a well-defined sense of right and wrong, and an understanding in later life of the value of its learnings. Much has been written about Stevenson's Christianity and its 'rebirth' in his final years. Yet the feeling I get from the prayers is of a profound humanism. They read less like the sometimes-tedious homilies of my churchgoing days, and more like lessons drawn from events at Vailima during that particular working day. As daily life continues, in a very different social, environmental, and political milieu, so Stevenson's prayers continue to have a message for us all in how to manage daily struggles.

Taking up the writing task has been a great pleasure in the time since our trip to Samoa.

Below is one of the Vailima prayers – first the original, then my song version below it. Anyone who has stood on the upstairs veranda at Vailima and looked through the forest to the summit of Mount Vaea will remember 'the uncounted millions of the forest'. The social and environmental messages of this prayer ring as loudly now as they did when first read to the evening prayer meeting of the Vailima community in the early 1890s.

> Stevenson's Prayer: Another in Time of Rain
> Lord, Thou sendest down rain upon the uncounted millions of the forest, and givest the trees to drink exceedingly. We are here upon this isle a few handfuls of men, and how many myriads upon myriads of stalwart trees! Teach us the lessons of the trees. The sea around us, which this rain recruits, teems with the race of fish; teach us, Lord, the meaning of the fishes. Let us see ourselves for what we are, one out of the countless numbers of the clans of Thy handiwork. When we would despair, let us remember that these also please and serve Thee.

The Song: Teach Us

Rain falls on the many miles of forest
The trees drink at their ease
So few handfuls of people
Yet so many myriad races of trees
Lord, Teach us the lesson of the trees

The ocean falls and rises all around us
And Teems with more than we could wish
On the coast handfuls of people
Yet in the sea so many races of fish
Lord teach us the lesson of the fish

As last night we watched one star shooting
In the firmament of many million stars
So We are just one clan amongst many
Let us see ourselves for what we are
Lord teach us the lesson of the stars

When we would despair, let us remember
That others serve and live both near and far
We are just one clan here amongst many
Let us see ourselves for what we are
Lord teach us, Lord teach us.

Postscript:

When we returned to the airport prior to leaving, the hire company office was closed. I rang the number on the door and asked where we should leave the key. After silence at the other end, a voice asked what I meant. It quickly became clear that the key was the means of starting the car, not a security device at all. 'Just leave it in the car park where I can see it,' he said. 'With the key in it, of course.' *Lesson Number Three*, from our first Samoan trip.

Neil Adam comes from an Edinburgh family with a generations-long interest in Stevenson. He and his wife, Judy Turner, have toured their show 'Sing Me A Song' in Australia, New Zealand, Scotland and England. Their latest recording is of songs based on Stevenson's 'Vailima Prayers'. More details at neiladamandjudyturner.com.

A Beautiful Adventure

JOHN SHEDDEN

'The most beautiful adventures are not those we go to seek'
- An Inland Voyage, RLS -

THE LIST OF FICTIONAL CHARACTERS an actor portrays in his career is long and varied. I've played clowns, tramps, adventurers, professors, politicians and kings. I've even climbed into Sherlock Holmes's housekeeper Mrs Hudson's corsets and peered imperiously through Lady Bracknell's pince-nez! If I consider the historical characters, then the list is eye-watering: John Knox, David Livingstone, Joseph Lister, David Garrick, John Buchan, Eric Liddell, Robert the Bruce, William McGonagall and Stan Laurel! One man, however, stands out, whose character I have inhabited over many years in different guises: the incomparable Robert Louis Stevenson.

Like most boys, I avidly read the adventure stories, the exciting challenges faced by Jim Hawkins and David Balfour. Growing up in Shetland, I knew the appeal of islands on the imagination. Having trained as an actor at the Royal Scottish Academy of Music and Drama in Glasgow, my burgeoning career in radio gave me countless opportunities to broadcast Stevenson's essays, short stories and poetry. I read *Travels with a Donkey in the Cévennes* for the popular *Book at Bedtime*. There followed readings of 'Thrawn

Janet', 'The Body Snatcher' and a dramatised version of *Dr Jekyll and Mr Hyde*. Then a memorable adaptation of *Kidnapped* for the Royal Lyceum theatre where the back wall of the theatre was opened to reveal the majestic Edinburgh Castle!

In 1994, I effectively 'lived' Stevenson for 12 months. To honour the centenary of his death, various plans were arranged, and I was fully involved. In 1992, I'd had a couple of award-winning solo plays written for me by John Cargill Thompson – *Every Inch a King* and *Port and Lemon*. Now John would write a third, *The Laird of Samoa*, to be premiered at the Café Royal for the Edinburgh Festival Fringe. The scene 'Vailima', with RLS alone on stage, would take us back with him in time to relive his life. The convention would mean imagined conversations with unseen family and friends. His father, mother, cousin Bob, his wife Fanny, and his friends Henley and Colvin all appear and disappear on this pilgrimage. In little over an hour, we follow Stevenson from childhood to maturity, Edinburgh to France, America and finally to Samoa. It would be by turns witty, pensive, evocative, irreverent, moving and, most important, unmistakably Scottish. The critics were gratifyingly unanimous in their praise of *The Laird of Samoa*:

'Performed by John Shedden with depth and finesse; he is alive to every nuance of the text, with a remarkable ability to switch from character to character.'

'It is written and delivered with charm, nonchalance and authenticity. Cargill Thompson's script evokes so convincingly the voice of the writer that it is sometimes impossible to tell if the words are Stevenson's or his own.'

That autumn, I was asked to portray Stevenson in two major exhibitions: *Jekyll or Hyde* at the City Arts Centre and *Treasure Island* at the Royal Museum of Scotland. Jenni Calder was responsible for my contributions to the latter. The exhibition was a Samoan setting with appearances by myself as Tusitala, under the palms presenting favourite passages from poems and stories to children and adults alike. The universal appeal of *A Child's Garden of Verses* seems never to diminish; but there were so many other pleasures, including descriptions of Stevenson's first landfall in the Pacific:

> Few men who come to the islands leave them; they grow grey where they alighted; the palm shades and the tradewind fans them till they die... No part of the world exerts the same attractive power on the visitor... The first experience can never be repeated. The first love, the first sunrise, the first South Sea island are memories apart and touched a virginity of sense.

Stevenson's words express exactly the emotions that I, and all our Edinburgh party, felt as we arrived in Apia, Western Samoa, to take part in the official Centenary Celebrations. On 3 December, the Grand Parade through Apia was led by Samoan bands and bagpipes as our float, suitably bedecked, had the 'Stevenson family' aboard. Actually, it was our Edinburgh RLS Club group, around ten of us.

The pre-dawn service on Sunday 4 December at the entrance of the Road of the Loving Heart heralded a quite unforgettable experience. After a Samoan priest said some appropriate words, the combined College choirs sang the 'Requiem' sublimely. Then holding candles in the rainy, misty atmosphere to light the trail, everyone began the ascent of Mount Vaea and the quest for Stevenson's tomb. The steep track was tricky and slippery underfoot; it was Indian file most of the way. The young, uniformed students from Avele College, sprightly in bare feet, their clothes unmarked, helped those who were labouring upwards. At last, the summit. Day was breaking. Our candles were extinguished.

Flowers and other small tokens, some brought specially from Edinburgh, were laid beside the tomb, Stevenson's chosen resting place. Festoons of yellow and white hibiscus flowers, and candles decorated the plinth. Then, exactly 100 years after Stevenson's death, John Cairney and I shared the spoken tribute in RLS's own words:

> You who pass this grave put aside hatred; love kindness, be all services remembered in your heart and all offences pardoned; and as you go down again among the living, let this be your question. Can I make someone happier this day before I lie down to sleep? Thus the dead man speaks to you from the dust. You will hear no more from him.

The famous 'Requiem' followed, which graces one of the two bronze plaques which flank the plinth. As it was being recited, some of the College choir started to hum the setting they had sung earlier that morning as crowds gathered beside the gates of Vailima. People joined in with the closing lines: *'Home is the sailor, home from sea /And the hunter home from the hill.'*

A hushed, poignant silence fell, broken only by the clicking of cameras capturing those treasured moments. Then a piper began to play 'The Flowers o' the Forest', that most moving, beautiful Scottish lament, to honour perhaps the greatest of Scottish writers.

It was indeed an honour and a privilege to have played my part in these memorable Centenary celebrations. Since then, I have been regularly involved in Stevenson events and travels with fellow enthusiasts: to Fontainebleau, the Cévennes, Paris, Antwerp, London, San Francisco, Saranac and Boston; and of course, a the airts of his beloved Scotland. In recent years as a Club Committee member, I have formed lasting friendships with ardent Stevenson devotees whose aim is to keep alive an interest in the man and his work. How fitting now to celebrate the Club's centenary with this unique book and to join others who have been similarly inspired by the vision and humanity of RLS.

His friend and great admirer Henry James said: 'He lighted up one whole side of the globe, and was in himself a whole province of one's imagination'.

In John Shedden's career as an actor, he has found it a rare privilege to perform many Stevenson classics and portray the man himself on stage. Stevenson's compassion, courage, versatility and charm are shining qualities, John says, adding: 'Why is there no Cairn in his native Edinburgh to honour this citizen of the world?'

Robert Louis Stevenson is Still with Us
CHRISTIAN BROCHIER

TODAY, ROBERT LOUIS STEVENSON is more and more present in the imagination and language of Europeans. His two most famous novels *Dr Jekyll and Mr Hyde* and *Treasure Island* are often quoted, as well as his essays on travel and on walking. A commercial for the latest Audi S7 shows a black car emerging from a fog to the sound of Dr Jekyll's voice changing into Hyde, evoking the pleasure and feeling of freedom this transgression gives him! One may regret such a commercial use of the text of our favoured author, but it is also a measure of how his talent should be recognized in describing the complexity of the human mind.

Fortunately, Robert Louis Stevenson is also a source of inspiration, thanks to the values he advocated all his life and which can be found in his writings. Freedom of thought and of leading one's life, open-mindedness, tolerance, rejection of injustice, anticolonialism, celebration of nature, respect of minorities... all values that can be considered the basis for today's citizenship but were then ahead of his time and values still to be fought for.

The several groups of Stevenson enthusiasts in France, Belgium, and more recently in Germany and Spain, who joined with the Robert Louis Stevenson Club in Great Britain to help create the European network 'In the Footsteps of Robert Louis Stevenson', were not wrong. It is indeed as a 'European Cultural Network' that they now proceed together. And when one looks closer at the Council of Europe's criteria for renewing certification one realises the values are exactly the same as Stevenson himself advocated. Respect of human rights, freedom of speech and association, rule of law, democracy, equality and protection of minorities, equal rights for men and women, child protection – all these themes are fundamental.

The actions of the network include exchanges between the different regions, in particular among young people with school exchanges. These celebrate the culture which is common to Europeans with the aim of revitalising economically and socially deprived territories through sustainable tourism, respectful of nature. The Stevenson European network also works at making walking paths and heritage accessible to the visually impaired and to people with other physical disabilities. They also take part in actions denouncing modern slavery and organise events in favour of mutual understanding and peace.

The strength of this network is particularly obvious in the way member groups cooperate in a friendly way always trying to get to know 'others' and their territories better. It can thus be observed that, 125 years after his death, Robert Louis Stevenson is still alive and continues to travel, gathering around him humans and their territories.

[Translated from the original French by Odile Guigon.]

Christian Brochier used to hire out donkeys in the Cévennes. For 12 years he chaired the Association *Sur le Chemin de Robert Louis Stevenson* (On the Robert Louis Stevenson Trail) and now chairs the Council of Europe's European Cultural Route *In the Footsteps of Robert Louis Stevenson*.

— STEVENSON —
THE SCOT

A Far Cry from Edinburgh
EILEEN DUNLOP

IN AN ESSAY presented at the British Library as winner of the 2018 PEN Pinter Prize, and printed in *The New Statesman* in January 2019, the Nigerian novelist Chimamanda Ngozi Adichie took as her starting point a question she had been asked at a book event in Lagos some years before: 'Are you an African writer?'

Initially, Ngozi Adichie thought the answer obvious; she was born and raised in Nigeria, is an Igbo speaker, loves Nigerian story-telling and writes vividly and with passion about her home country. Although she is now based in New York and regards America as a second home, she visits Nigeria regularly and holds only a Nigerian passport. Of course she is an African writer.

Yet the question, she quickly realised, was intended as a challenge; it was not, as she put it, about geography, but about loyalty. Her willingness to tackle thorny questions about Nigerian society, notably on women's and LGBT rights, has raised hackles among her more conservative critics. What the questioner hoped for was a statement of the sort of patriotic identification – 'my country, right or wrong' – that condones easy lies about abuses and stifles debate in a nation. Therefore, believing that freedom of expression is a writer's most precious possession, she answered, 'No'. Ngozi Adichie is proud to be African but, as a privileged voice, will not give up the right to criticise, through her fiction, what she sees as flaws in the patriarchal society of her homeland. To some of her compatriots, intent on presenting the best possible face of their nation, this candour has given offence.

Although Ngozi Adichie was born more than 80 years after his death, there is much in her awareness of the tension between national identity and desire to escape what she has perceived as a narrow-minded and defensive society that calls to mind the career of Robert Louis Stevenson. Stevenson never pretended to be other than he was, since, like most Scots, he regarded his nationality as a mark of distinction. His broad Lowland accent, much remarked upon by his London friends, was unmodified by the many years he spent roaming the world. His relationship with cold, windy Edinburgh and the house in Heriot Row where, as a child, he had been deeply loved, but was also fed the terrifying Calvinist doctrine of salvation and damnation which he later violently rejected, is a recurring motif in his work.

The critical note in Stevenson's writing was struck early. *Edinburgh: Picturesque Notes*, published in 1878, combines fine descriptive writing with frankness about the city's weather, 'raw and boisterous in winter, shifty and ungenial in summer and a downright meteorological purgatory in spring'. The gross social inequality in a city where 'from their smoky beehives ten stories [*sic*] high, the unwashed look down upon the open squares and gardens of the wealthy' is castigated, its poorer inhabitants described as 'skulking jailbirds, unkempt, barefoot children, big mouthed robust women... and a dismal sprinkling of mutineers and broken men of the higher ranks of society, with some mark of better days upon them'. The proud parade of the Heralds and Pursuivants of Scotland is mocked as 'a tawdry masquerade' and, most humiliatingly of all, the capital of Scotland is dismissed as 'not so much a small city as the largest of small towns'.

Unsurprisingly, such descriptions drew indignant protest, as did the remorseless dragging-up of Edinburgh's unsavoury and not-so-distant past, when witches were burned, graves desecrated and plague victims hanged at their own doors. This was not the image of Scotland's capital that proud and upright citizens cared to project and, in exposing its uglier face, Stevenson was regarded as letting the side down. But he, like Ngozi Adichie in our own day, claimed the right to speak the truth as he saw it, merely noting 'with pain and merriment' the offence he had caused; though we suspect with more merriment than pain, since a chief complaint was that the book had given 'proportionable pleasure to our rivals in Glasgow'. Nor did he confine his candour to his native city. Writing elsewhere of a summer placement in Caithness as his father's unwilling apprentice, he sourly described Wick as 'one of the meanest of man's towns, and situate certainly on the baldest of God's bays'. Not words easily forgiven.

There were several reasons why Stevenson could not settle down, either as a lighthouse engineer or – his father's second choice – as an Edinburgh advocate. The risk to his health in a city where, he said, 'the delicate die early' was one he quickly recognised, but there was also the realisation that by refusing to enter the family business he had deeply disappointed his father. There had been violent rows and hard words spoken. He knew, too, that both his parents were hurt by his rejection of their religious practices and embarrassed by small-city gossip about his bohemian appearance, disruptive behaviour at university and rumoured sexual laxity.

The old harmony at 17 Heriot Row had been shattered since the innocent days so poignantly recalled, 20 years later, in *A Child's Garden of Verses*. The air was thick with huff and disapproval, and the suffocating atmosphere of church going, judgmental, 'unco guid', Victorian Edinburgh middle-class society became too much to bear. Young Stevenson knew that if he was to salvage his relationship with his parents, and claim a writer's freedom of expression, he had to escape the city of his birth. And he did, physically at least – to London, to France, to the United States (where he married a divorced Californian ten years his senior) and finally to Samoa, as far a cry from Victorian Edinburgh as it is possible to imagine.

And through all his brief years he wrote, essays, short stories, novels, travelogues and polemics, many with no connection to Scotland – *The Ebb-Tide*, *The Black Arrow*, *The Silverado Squatters*, 'The Treasure of Franchard', 'The Isle of Voices', 'The Bottle Imp', 'Olalla' – drawing on his experience of different peoples, cultures and lands. He commented fearlessly on Samoan politics, writing long letters to *The Times* and embarrassing the British government. In 1889, he came furiously to the defence of Father Joseph Damien, a Roman Catholic priest and missionary to the leper colony of Molokai, whose memory had been traduced in the correspondence columns of the *Australian Star* by a Presbyterian nonentity, the Rev Dr C.M. Hyde. The force of Stevenson's diatribe was electrifying, and the only thing to be said in Dr Hyde's favour is that – contrary to Stevenson's expectation – he did not sue for libel.

Stevenson went to the ends of the earth to break free from the constraints of Scotland and its small-town capital, and to claim his right to freedom of action and speech. Yet in an emotional and imaginative sense, he never broke free at all. Through all the long years of his self-imposed exile, the places of his boyhood haunted him, and he kept returning to them in what is now regarded as his finest work. Apart from *Treasure Island*, set on the south-west coast of England and an imaginary island in the Caribbean, all of Stevenson's greatest novels, and much of his poetry, are inspired by an intense recall of the land he fled. *Kidnapped*, *Catriona*, *The Master of Ballantrae*, the unfinished *St Ives*, these all take the grey towns, heather hills, liquid skies and rockbound, restive seas of Scotland for inspiration. Although his chilling masterpiece of the Calvinist 'divided mind', *Strange Case of Dr Jekyll and Mr Hyde*, is supposedly set in London, it is a tale of Edinburgh through and through. Then there are the poems, with their famous first lines – 'In the Highlands and the country places', 'Blows the wind today, and the sun and the rain are flying' – and the heartbreakingly beautiful verses found tucked into the manuscript of his uncompleted but potentially greatest novel, *Weir of Hermiston*.

I saw rain falling and the rainbow drawn
On Lammermuir. Hearkening I heard again
In my precipitous city beaten bells
Winnow the keen sea wind. And here afar,
Intent on my own race and place, I wrote;

So, we return to the question. Is Stevenson, who tried to embrace a world so much larger than his native land, a Scottish writer? In one way, it seems obvious but, faced with the kind of loaded question put to Chimamanda Ngozi Adichie in Lagos, when terrible words like 'post-truth' and 'fake news' are in danger of losing their power to shock, and writers worldwide are threatened and imprisoned for challenging governments and exposing lies, is it not probable that he too would have answered, 'No'?

And yet, Ngozi Adichie tells a story of how, when her first novel was shortlisted for but failed to win the Orange Prize, she was approached by a Nigerian woman who assured her: 'We will win next time.' When, some years later, she did win, she recalls being hugged and congratulated by strangers, and was touched by the realisation that many of her compatriots saw her success as a prize for Nigeria. And is not that how we Scots feel about Robert Louis Stevenson? He may have offended our ancestors, but now we are proud of his reputation as a great writer of the world, of his moral courage, humanity and the fearless defences of the causes that moved him. We salute his free spirit, and are glad that he is one of our own.

Eileen Dunlop published 21 novels for young adults between 1975 and 2003. She has since pursued her interest in Scottish biography, and is the author of *Queen Margaret of Scotland* (2005), *Robert Louis Stevenson: The Travelling Mind* (2008) and *Sir Walter Scott: A Life in Story* (2016), all published by NMS Enterprises.

My Father and RLS: a Life in Parallel

MAGNUS LINKLATER

ROBERT LOUIS STEVENSON presided over our dinner table. Not just because his books lined the dining-room shelf (the Tusitala Edition, I think); nor because we were encouraged to read and learn *A Child's Garden of Verses* by Miss Pirie at the Nigg School, then tested on it at meal-times; nor even because we were enthralled by *Kidnapped*. It was more that *Weir of Hermiston* used to sit at one end of the table – in the person of my father, the poet and author Eric Linklater.

Here is how RLS describes the fearsome judge, Lord Hermiston, in the novel that bears his name:

> When things went wrong at dinner, as they continually did, my lord would look up the table at his wife: 'I think these broth would be better to sweem in than to sup.' Or else, to the butler: 'Here, M'Killop, awa' w' this Raadical gigot – tak' it to the French, man, and bring me some puddocks!'
>
> Then, as his distraught wife held out a sopping pocket-handkerchief to seek his forgiveness: 'You and your nonsense! What do I want with a Christian faim'ly? I want Christian broth! Get me a lass that can plain-boil a potato, if she was a whüre off the streets.'

It was a line my father relished. Here is how my brother, Andro, described the scene at meal-times at our home in Easter Ross:

> Meals took place in an atmosphere which I recall as being so charged, the squeal of a knife on china or the slurrup of soup on lip could trigger an explosion. 'If you can't eat like a civilised human being,' he bellowed, 'you can finish your meal at the bottom of the garden.'
>
> At his most irritable, he had a habit of addressing us through my mother as though she were the NCO of a slovenly platoon he had to inspect. 'Marjorie! Have you seen this boy's tie? Does he have to come to table looking like a slum child?' or, on the occasion I first tried to carve a chicken, 'Marjorie! What's that bloody boy been doing? The bird looks as though it's been attacked with a Mills grenade.'

Just as, in the household of Lord Hermiston, nothing seemed to measure up to expectations, so life at Pitcalzean, the house we were brought up in, often teetered on the edge of disaster: 'For all his shouting, deficiencies continued to appear on every side,' wrote Andro:

> Plates were served cool when they should have been hot, drinking water was tepid instead of cold, and spoons were dull instead of sparkling. There was, in consequence, no mistaking who was at the centre of the conspiracy – the woman responsible for plates, spoons, children and, most infuriatingly of all, for boiled potatoes which either dissolved to flour or split as crisply as apples.
>
> 'Good God, woman, look at this!' he bawled in disbelief. 'After 23 years of married life you still haven't learned to boil a potato.'

And then, Hermiston and Linklater dissolved into one: 'Get me a lass that can plain-boil a potato,' he would roar, 'if she was a whüre off the streets.'

There was a lighter streak to the wrath. Hermiston disappeared into his study with 'a twinkle of humour'. My father would lob a potato down the table towards my mother, 'though either because she was only a silhouette against the light, or out of good manners, he usually missed'.

My father loved Stevenson because he saw himself moulded in that tradition – the Scottish writer who travels widely, taking Scotland with him as he went, but not weighed down by it. He set his novels in America and China, in Italy or the Faeroes, as often as he did in Scotland – just as Stevenson chose France or the South Seas. Like Stevenson, he rarely wrote in the Scots dialect, though when he did, it was pitch-perfect. In the great dispute that divided literary Scotland during the 'Scottish Renaissance Movement' of the Thirties, he was pitted against Hugh MacDiarmid and Lewis Grassic Gibbon, preferring to champion the richness of the English language rather than accepting that a writer could not consider himself properly Scottish unless he wrote in the demotic. On this, Stevenson and he would have agreed.

Stevenson shared, with my father, an admiration for the old Scots of Dunbar, Henryson and Drummond of Hawthornden. But he thought that it had declined into a dialect that was celebrated for the wrong reasons. Here is Stevenson on Scottish poetry:

> It is somewhat too much the fashion to pat Scotch literature on the back. Inhabitants of South Britain are pleased to commend verses which, short of a miraculous gift of tongues, it is morally impossible they should comprehend. It may interest these persons to learn that Burns writes a most difficult and crude patois… that there are not so many people alive in Scotland who could read his works without

a furtive reference to the margin… any Englishman need not be ashamed to confess he can make nothing out of the vernacular poems except a raucous gibberish – which, it is the honest belief of the present reviewer, is about the measure of his achievement.

Eric Linklater echoed the feeling:

> The Scottish tongue no longer spoke a national language. It spoke a dialect, and that which had been its proper pronunciation of Scots became in English merely a Scottish accent. It is true that the remnant dialect, with a stiffening of archaic forms, was later to be fashioned into the most popular of all contributions to literature: but the language of Burns was an artefact, a literary convention. I am not decrying his genius – it would not matter if I did – but his language, in comparison to Dunbar's, is patently a slight and precarious thing.

Both loved words – one critic called Stevenson 'essentially an artist in words', coupled with 'an extreme appreciation of style'. He wrote a long essay on the techniques of writing – the rhythm, cadence and 'melody' of a well-balanced phrase. My father said he owed his love of good prose writing to the experience of learning the classics at Aberdeen Grammar School, where English was taught in much the same way as Latin, with the accent on grammar.

Above all, both were story-tellers with a keen ear for narrative – and place. Read *Kidnapped* and you are in the grip of a story that takes you headlong through the Highlands, leaving you not much space to catch your breath, but with a clear picture of the landscape in which it is set:

> The mist rose and died away, and showed us that country lying as waste as the sea; only the moorfowl and the peewees crying upon it, and far over to the east, a herd of deer,

moving like dots. Much of it was red with heather; much of the rest broken up with bogs and hags and peaty pools; some had been burnt black in a heath fire; and in another place there was quite a forest of dead firs, standing like skeletons.

My father's best novel, *The Dark of Summer*, opens in Shetland:

> (...) there is, at the top of summer, no darkness at midnight. The day puts on a veil, the light is screened, and the landscape that, in fine weather appears at noon to be almost infinite – in which long roads and little houses are luminously drawn – becomes small and circumscribed, and the hills and the shore, the sheep in the fields and the glinting sea, are visible, as it were, through a pane of slightly obscuring glass.

Both were wedded to literature and to their Scottish roots. Both ranged far and wide to find their inspiration. My father's most successful novel, *Juan in America*, was set in the United States of prohibition and the flapper era. Stevenson set the *Silverado Squatters* in the Napa Valley of California.

But I caught up with Stevenson in France, walking through the Cévennes, as he had done with Modestine, his donkey. We were heading south-west for the Pyrenees, and wherever we went there was a Rue Stevenson, or a Route de Modestine. They offer donkey trips through the hills, and his books are on sale in every auberge and hotel. We followed his trail across the Goulet, through the country of the Camisards, the Lozère and the valley of the Tarn. I kept a diary most of the way, but could not match Stevenson's powers of description. As we passed the village of Pradelles, I turned to his account:

> Pradelles stands on a hillside, high above the Allier, surrounded by rich meadows. They were cutting aftermath [the late grass] on all sides, which gave the neighbourhood, this

gusty autumn morning, an untimely smell of hay. On the opposite bank of the Allier the land kept mounting for miles to the horizon, a tanned and sallow autumn landscape, with black blots of fir-wood and white roads wandering through the hills. Over all this, the clouds shed a uniform and purplish shadow, sad and somewhat menacing, exaggerating height and distance, and throwing into still higher relief the twisted ribbons of the highway. It was a cheerless prospect, but one stimulating to a traveller. For I was now on the limit of Velay, and all that I beheld lay in another county – wild Gévaudan, mountainous, uncultivated, and but recently deforested from terror of the wolves.

Ah, the words. I could never have dreamed up the 'tanned and sallow landscape', or the 'twisted ribbons of the highway'. I think my father could. But then he and Stevenson had the ear for it.

Magnus Linklater has been Editor of *The Scotsman*, and columnist and Scotland Editor of *The Times*. A former President of the Saltire Society, he has also been Chairman of the Scottish Arts Council. He is a Fellow of the Royal Society of Edinburgh, and author of several books on current affairs and Scottish history.

RLS – A Living Experience in my Upbringing and Adult World

DR CATHY RATCLIFF

I WAS 16 when my mother discovered that RLS had lived in our house. We'd lived there since I was two and, until my mother made this discovery, people thought that he had lived at the current No. 1 Inverleith Terrace. When my mother looked at archives to find out the history of our house, she found that our house used to be No. 1, and former residents included the Stevensons. Thus, Robert Louis Stevenson lived in our house from age three to age six. After we found out, my mother corresponded with some of his fans in San Francisco – one of them even coming twice to Edinburgh to take photos of our house in just the right light to show how it would have looked when Leerie the Lamplighter came to light the gaslights in our street.

I don't know how many American fans came to see our house, but one came when only my brother and I were in, and we showed him the cherry tree in our garden that RLS had known – while knowing full well that my mother had planted it! Another wrote an article for *The Scots Magazine*, in which I was surprised to read that our house still rang with the patter of children's feet. As I am the youngest in our family, and my 16-year-old self had proudly sported my platform boots when that visitor came, I was bemused by the phrase. Another pointed out to us how the door handle and locks in RLS's night nursery on the top floor were different from those in all other rooms and speculated that this could be evidence of the lock needing to be changed after the young RLS had locked himself in his bedroom in a fit of temper.

So, since teenage years, I have known that ours is a very special house. Fifty-three years after we moved in, my mother, partner and I still live here, and it is still largely unchanged from the time when RLS's parents rented it for three years. As it is now No. 9, it has terraced houses on either side, and so is no longer a damp end-house, a factor which may have worsened RLS's health. The layout of the basement, where the servants lived and cooked, had been slightly changed before we moved in, in that a corridor now runs from front to back, a cupboard is in the place of the previous kitchen's exit into the back garden, and an exterior wall was added at the front to create a bigger new kitchen. But in the three upstairs storeys, the only changes are décor, bathroom and kitchen fittings, carpets and furnishings. It is a magnificent house, with large rooms and high ceilings, and double doors on the first floor which turn the drawing room and main bedroom into one grand room.

It was an exciting house to grow up in, the staircases lending themselves well to makeshift chutes as we four children pulled each other down on quilts, screaming at the speed; and the wine cellar in the basement being our tunnel, useful for scaring friends who believed us when we told them that there were dead bats hanging in it.

I don't know if the RLS connection made me read more RLS than I would have otherwise – I did read *Kidnapped*, *Catriona*, *Treasure Island* and *Dr Jekyll and Mr Hyde* as a child. But then I also read a bit of Scott, Burns and plenty of Scottish children's fiction. It was later in life that I felt that our home's connection to RLS should make us read his work especially. So I was delighted when *Dr Jekyll and Mr Hyde* was a set text in my daughter's Higher English class in 2013. Shortly afterwards, I read Ian Bell's brilliant biography of RLS, and as a result, when on holiday in California I visited Monterey, only to find that the RLS museum in the house where he stayed was shut that day. Then I read Bell's biography out loud to my mother, followed by *Kidnapped*, *Catriona* and *Treasure Island*. Bell's book gave us a thirst to read RLS's writings on the South Sea Islands, so they are next on our reading list.

It's the inherent quality of RLS's work that has been the biggest stimulant to reading his works, with their atmosphere, engaging stories and thought-provoking histories and tales. I specialised in Russian, and so I'm intrigued at RLS's place in the literature of split personality or doubles, such as James Hogg and Dostoyevsky wrote about. I read *A Child's Garden of Verses* as a child, and to my daughter, and they are so memorable and lovely that it wouldn't matter who had written them – we would still have read them. Many of its verses are etched in my memory now, and I love to quote lines from it with one similarly minded friend. I think that *Kidnapped* and *Catriona* should be set texts in Scottish schools, describing as they do so vividly post-Culloden Scottish society split in two, in relatively recent times. So overall, it is the quality of RLS's writings that has made me read and enjoy them, although recently our family connection to him has added an extra impetus to get to know more about him.

Without particularly thinking about it, we have even continued the writer's tradition in this house. While RLS can surely have written little by the time he left our house at the age of six, we have written some non-fiction tomes in it. My mother, a doctor, wrote our family history, which revolves around the Highlands and north-east of Scotland. My partner wrote *The Poor Had No Lawyers* plus another couple of books on the same topic of landownership and land reform. I wrote a PhD thesis on language and discourse analysis of Russian and Soviet newspaper media. Our daughter has been the artistic one, learning the fiddle and voice in the old RLS house, composing several pieces of music in it, and going on to pursue a career in music.

Most of all, though, we've lived here as an ordinary family. The layout of the house allowed my parents to let various friends and family live in the basement, and more recently allowed three generations of us to live peacefully side by side. And so we've stayed in it far longer than most Edinburgh houses host one family. Knowing that RLS lived in it, we've taken care to make few changes to the house and hope that it will be as well cared for in the future. Whatever happens to this house, thank goodness the City of Edinburgh planning department will not allow fundamental changes to it, due to its listed building status, and because the department does not allow major changes to old staircases, which in this house form an elegant space from ground floor to second floor. The special architecture of the house means that RLS's second home, 9 (formerly 1) Inverleith Terrace, will surely be largely preserved as it is and was.

Aid worker and development discourse analyst, Dr Cathy Ratcliff is the daughter of two doctors, Dr Jamieson and Dr Ratcliff, who bought 9 Inverleith Terrace when their four children were aged two to eight. The young Stevenson's home has been in the family since 1965, and has housed three generations during that time.

For We Are Very Lucky: Recollections of 17 Heriot Row

JOHN MACFIE

For we are very lucky, with a lamp before the door,
And Leerie stops to light it as he lights so many more;
And oh! before you hurry by with ladder and with light;
O Leerie, see a little child and nod to him to-night!

ALMOST ABOVE ALL THINGS, Robert Louis Stevenson's life was marked by movement. His story is peppered with travel, whether as holidaymaker, invalid, walking tourist, adventurer or emigrant in body or mind. It may, then, seem a trifle paradoxical that one who has lived almost fifty years in Louis's childhood home might offer some thoughts about what it has been like to live in the home of our favourite, but restless, author, a writer for whom place was rich, evocative, vivid and living but essentially transient.

What, then, has it been like? My first memory of 17 Heriot Row is of the summer of 1971, the year my parents bought it, and is wholly unconnected to its most famous inhabitant. I was puzzled to find a curious contraption fixed to the wall next to one of the windows in the top floor bedroom, a sort of sling attached to a metal drum, presumably containing rope; I could not fathom why it should be there. It was eventually explained that the previous owner, despite having lost a leg in the Great War, had made his bedroom on the second floor (the third, for our American cousins) undeterred by the fifty-six steps up from ground level. Being a prudent man, though, he had had this device installed as an escape in case of fire: as the flames rose and the smoke billowed, you were supposed to put the sling around you and throw yourself out of the window, trusting the mechanism in the drum to retard your fall. My ten-year-old plea to be allowed to try it out was brusquely denied.

As to the house itself, I cannot better the words of James Pope-Hennessy in his 1974 biography *Robert Louis Stevenson*:

> A paramount feature of the Heriot Row houses, as of the rest of those in the New Town, is the well-designed ironwork which shuts in the area from the street, runs up on each side of the steps to the front doors, and, in the case of Number 17, forms three separate ornamental balconies outside the drawing-room windows, which look down over the street and the gardens from the first floor. Number 17, like the rest of Heriot Row, has an outer and an inner hall, a broad handsome flight of stairs to the first and second floors and, on the dining-room and drawing-room floors, tall elegantly-proportioned windows with astragals, facing due south. The spacious high-ceilinged dining-room, with an alcove in it, is lit by the two windows on the right of the solemn front door. At the back of the dining-room is a smaller, more intimate study, with a view of a narrow strip of walled garden, at the end of which, in the Stevensons' day, stood a privy. This study would have been Thomas Stevenson's own 'den'. Upstairs was his wife's domain – the big L-shaped drawing-room, lit by three tall windows; in the western and central windows, Mrs Stevenson placed 'kangaroo-vines', [fast-growing climbing plants] which she tended with solicitude...
>
> The large bedroom with a dressing-room attached which

lay behind the drawing-room would have been that of Louis's parents. The boy's own quarters were on the floor above, where a fine oval dome made of glass-panes and ornamented with lions' heads lets the light into the staircase well. Louis's day-nursery, in later years his workroom, has two large windows whence, held up in Cummie's arms, he could peer at the gardens on the other side of the Row and, in winter, through bare trees, at Queen Street far over the way. When he could not sleep and had the night horrors, his faithful nurse would hold him up to the window, suggesting that the few lights glimmering in the blackness of Queen Street proved that there were other children, too, who kept awake. Louis' night-nursery, in which Cummie had her bed until he was almost ten years old, was a small room to the east of the day-nursery, and likewise commanding garden and street. The two back rooms on the top floor may have been guest rooms – as Louis grew up Mrs Stevenson would hopefully ask his girl-cousins to stay – or may have been used by the maids, At the bottom of the house is a huge kitchen and other offices. In the Stevensons' day there were no bathrooms but merely hip-baths in the bedrooms. Commodes in bedrooms or closets served the purpose of the modern W.C., and 'night-soil' was collected by carts each morning to be sold to the market-gardeners on the outskirts of Edinburgh for their plots of vegetables.

In the drawing-room at Heriot Row, Maggie Stevenson had her desk placed in the easternmost of the three windows, facing outwards so that she could watch the privileged children of the local residents at play round the pond in the gardens below and could benefit by every gleam of the fitful Edinburgh sun. We may safely assume that Mrs Stevenson's drawing-room was, like her own character, feminine and gay, whereas her husband's ground-floor den would have been book-lined, serious and of a sober colour.

> Up on the third floor the kingdom of Smout, as Louis's parents called him, was doubtless an unorganised confusion of lead soldiers, picture-books (he did not learn to read until he was seven), paint-boxes, coloured chalks, and the intricate cut-out sheets for *Aladdin, The Old Oak Chest, Jack Sheppard, Der Freischütz* and the other pieces to be mounted for those toy theatres that were then called *Skelt's Juvenile Dramas* and which a later, London, generation knew as Pollock's of Hoxton. 'Penny plain and tuppence coloured', these sheets of characters, with other sheets of backdrops and wings, were sold at Mr Smith's shop in a neighbouring side-street, a shop which 'was dark and smelt of Bibles'.

Well, apart from the advent of rather better plumbing, electricity and central heating, this is still a remarkably accurate description of 17 Heriot Row, down to the populous disorder of Smout's old rooms, now infested by my children.

When I first arrived, the house and the Queen Street Gardens opposite became a grand adventure playground for me and my friends. If we looked to the shade of the young Smout at all, it was to drag him over the road with us to play explorers or invaders in the gardens, or indoors to fence our way, musketeer-fashion, from cellar to attic and, later, to imagine ourselves gamblers on a Mississippi steamboat battling it out over the cards. My mother was a keen Stevenson networker and through this I gradually became aware of a steady trickle of Stevensonians through the house. They ranged from the idiosyncratic James Pope-Hennessy, with his impressive load of index-cards covered with facts for his book, housed in rows of shoe-boxes; through the young American post-doctoral researcher and his wife who stayed for some months in our basement while he researched Stevenson in libraries and archives and who, despite the advancing years, remain still the young friends they became then; to the rather bewildered bus-party of tourists my mother once kidnapped for an impromptu tour of the house. She loved to play to the gallery, and the tour bus drivers clubbed together each Christmas to buy her a huge bunch of flowers as a thank-you.

I was particularly impressed by the American gent, armed with a machine that looked like an old-fashioned reel-to-reel tape recorder, with lots of dials and lights and needles, who solemnly pronounced that we were blessed with two ghosts, though he could not tell us if either of them were Louis. Until then, I had thought there was only one, and that female. I also found myself sharing some of Louis's experiences of the house. While my bedroom lacked the 'knickering, flighty, fleering and yet spectral cackle' of gaslight, I could share his connoisseurship of the howling wind around the chimney-pots, and on many a winter afternoon I looked out, with him, through windows spattered with windy raindrops into a darkening world dotted with street-lamps.

As one grows up, perspectives change, and so my conscious companionship with Louis and the house waned through my later school and university years. I do recall, being about the same age that he was then, being struck by the image of the eighteen-year-old Louis emerging from the gloom of a late winter afternoon in his mother's drawing room to be discovered as a writer-in-waiting, the boy who talked in his peculiar, vibrating voice in a manner reminding Mrs Stevenson's guest of the essayist Charles Lamb. Through my early twenties, as student and law apprentice, I was unconsciously Louis's companion in exploration of our 'rortie, wretched, city' and in enjoyment of the companionship and repartee of the Speculative Society – but I was living away from the house, not really part of it. So it was only after I was married, when my wife and I had had our first child and my then widowed mother with great courage handed over the house to us in 1992, that we began to comprehend the house as a family, and be comprehended by it.

Breakfasts, and sometimes other meals, became public performances as the hapless passengers in touring coaches witnessed our successive offspring progress from bottle to spoon-feeding to creating Weetabix art for themselves on the floor – and beyond. Dragons drawn in street chalks on the front step grew tails that snaked along the pavement onto the steps of the neighbouring lawyer's office: what a surreal sight it was to watch the office workers on Monday morning carefully stepping over that tail on their way to work, presumably for fear of draconian consequences. A German-language *Treasure Island* was enacted with puppets using an upturned double-bass as a stage to an audience of rapt Edinburgh primary school children, whose knowledge of German was *nil*, but nevertheless fully comprheneded the drama. The Lord alone knows what tales tour guides regale their guests with about the zoological garden behind our windows. Oft is the time you return laden with groceries to find an enthusiastic Spaniard occupying the steps, regaling an attentive tour party with an animated, and, one hopes, accurate, account of Stevenson. We have even had to retrieve a party of Far Eastern visitors who had penetrated the hall in the time it takes to put the refuse out, who were asking where they could buy tickets. All part of the rich tapestry of life in the Wild Kingdom of Heriot Row, as one of our au-pairs put it.

The detail of Stevenson family life in the house now drew me. Who was here? What servants? I will always have a particular soft spot for Isabella Williamson, who appears in the household as 'servant, unmarried' in the 1861 census and is last seen in the census of 1881 as cook: there is a hint indeed from Louis's letters that she remained with the Stevensons until the home was broken up after Thomas Stevenson's death and Margaret left to join her son in the South Seas. More than twenty, maybe as many as thirty years in the Stevenson *familia*: what she must have seen!

Long-cherished myths sometimes crumbled to dust, as when I discovered that our lamp before the door is certainly not Louis's, being put up only in the 1950s: Leerie's light was a stand-alone on the pavement's edge. Occasionally, we have been commandeered as a film set. Once, memorably, a BBC Schools poetry programme presented by Roger McGough brought an appropriate old lamp borrowed from the city council to be set up outside for filming *The Lamplighter*. Indoors, our son played the sick Smout, feverish in his bed upstairs. Then, for once, a myth was confirmed when I was told by the flat-hatted-and-boilersuited man from the Edinburgh City Lighting Department (keeping an eye on the borrowed lamp) that leeries really did run from lamp to lamp, for fear of their pay being docked if they were slow completing their round.

As our children grew to adolescence I began to look at Louis from a parent's vantage point. I wondered at the tolerance of Thomas and Margaret Stevenson for their boy's antics, and smiled at Louis's fond imaginings that they did not know. The wonderful new Yale University Press edition of Louis's letters has led me on the highways and byways of his life, to endless satisfaction.

As a family, we have opened a new chapter for the house, sharing it with bed-and-breakfast guests from many lands, as well as Stevensonians equally diverse. The cycle has once more come round, and our children are growing up like I did amid a stream of interesting strangers in their home and at their table. If they are spared, I wonder what any of them might write here for the Club's 150th birthday celebrations.

I have spent most of my life in this place – now that makes one feel old just to write it – hefted to my hill, one might say. Louis, however, has been in one way or another, a constant though always evanescent, companion. While, as Milton has it, I have been:

… collecting toys
And trifles for choice matters, worth a sponge,
As children gathering pebbles on the shore

Louis has continued to flit about the world doing what he does best, talking and telling tales, paying us here but fitful visits; though I am glad to say his companionable shade has always been an easy and welcome guest.

Years before I came to this house, an occupant fixed a small additional sign to the brass doorbell at the front door, stating boldly 'PRIVATE HOUSE NOT A MUSEUM'. I am glad that it has proven a singularly ineffective charm against strangers, as we have gained in all sorts of ways from their attentions, solicited and unsolicited. We are, truly, very lucky, with a lamp before the door.

Retired lawyer John Macfie and his family have been custodiers of Stevenson's childhood home at 17 Heriot Row in Edinburgh since 1971. As a family home and a place of literary pilgrimage, it is a lasting bridge for its inhabitants between RLS the man and the world today.

Yonder is Auldhame

CYNTHIA STEPHENS

WHEN WE WERE CHILDREN, we would ride on horseback along the North Sea coast to a farm called Auldhame, where my paternal grandmother lived. *'Yonder is Auldhame, where the London smack went ashore and wreckers cut the rings from ladies' fingers,'* wrote RLS in *Edinburgh: Picturesque Notes*. My grandmother was very keen on Stevenson and would recite his poetry; she made sure we all read at least *A Child's Garden of Verses* and *Treasure Island*.

In my adult life, when I was living outside Scotland, I discovered RLS in my own way; often I would read Stevenson as a reconnection with the Scots language of my youth, hearing in my mind to the old forgotten sounds and trying to connect with lost memories of my own childhood on an East Lothian farm. In 'The Maker to Posterity' RLS wrote:

No bein' fit to write in Greek,
I wrote in Lallan,
Dear to my heart as the peat-reek,
Auld as Tantallon.

The ruins of Tantallon Castle had been one of the sites of our teenage adventures.

In the late 1980s, when I had been overworking for a number of years, I was given as a present Nicholas Rankin's *Dead Man's Chest: Travels after Robert Louis Stevenson*. It was sent from Scotland by my father's sister, my aunt Anne Gray. As I was reading the book over my Christmas break, I realised I had already met the author, but within a completely different context, a Hispanic context in Cambridge. This book rekindled my interest in Stevenson and his connection with my family; this connection, which started as a genetic one, has remained active within Edinburgh literary circles for several generations.

I then discovered that my great-grandmother had written a piece, entitled 'Fresh Side-lights on RLS', for Rosaline Masson's classic book *I Can Remember Robert Louis Stevenson*. My great-grandmother, Mrs Dale, was a cousin of Robert Louis Stevenson, and used to play with him as a child. Her maiden name was Joanna Jesse Smith; her grandfather was the Reverend George Smith of Galston, great-grandfather to RLS. (Robert Burns wrote about Smith in *The Holy Fair*.) Jesse married a farmer, Thomas Dale, and they lived at Scoughall farm near Auldhame. In Masson's book she describes weird scenes when ships were wrecked on the coast beside her home before the lighthouses were built on Fidra and the Bass; dreadful dramas in which crowds of men with lanterns hurry across dark rocks in search of bodies. And she says her husband, my great-grandfather, was 'first officer of a volunteer rocket apparatus'. Two generations later my own father similarly volunteered to save people from drowning on that dangerous but beautiful coast, where we and our cousins had such fun riding on horseback as children.

Jesse continues:

> RLS speaks in *Catriona* of the 'lights of Scoughall' as seen from the Bass Rock; but it can only be from the very top of the island that they can be seen. However, he purposely put 'Tam Dale' in charge of the prisoners there, saying the name

should be associated with those parts; and when I said he need not have made my husband a jailer, the reply was: "Oh, it was two hundred years ago!" Stevenson put the character named after my great-grandfather into this classic story written in Scots within the novel *Catriona*.

Jesse's daughter-in-law was my paternal grandmother, Mary Waugh Dale (née Paterson). Mrs Mary W. Dale was Chairman of the RLS Club from 1956-58, and she was Speaker at the Club Lunch or Dinner, delivering the Principal Toast, in 1962. She knew Stevenson's work well, loved to recite his poetry, and introduced me and my many cousins to him from an early age. RLS became part of our family's culture, and many of my relatives have been members of the RLS Club over the years.

Mary's daughter was my aunt, Mrs Anne C. Gray, and she was appointed Chairman of the RLS Club in the year 2000. In that year, the RLS Club published *The Robert Louis Stevenson 150th Birthday Anniversary Book*, compiled by Karen Steele, with articles by Ernest Mehew, Richard Dury, John Shedden, John Scally, and others. In her 'Chairman's Thoughts', Anne Gray wrote:

> RLS Club was founded in 1920 and the first meeting held in Edinburgh in the North British Station Hotel (now the Balmoral) on 13th November. Edmund Gosse, who had been a close friend of RLS, proposed the toast describing RLS as 'the most beloved author of our time' and added that 'a more striking honour had never before been paid to an author than the formation of a great club, within 70 years of his birth'.

I fell in love with Stevenson's poetry, particularly some in *Songs of Travel*, in which he remembers from the tropics the Edinburgh of his youth, which he knows he will never again be able to visit; and he remembers his old friendships:

The tropics vanish, and meseems that I,
From Halkerside, from topmost Allermuir,
Or steep Caerketton, dreaming gaze again.

'The Tropics Vanish, and Meseems that I', 'To My Old Familiars', 'I Heard the Pulse of the Besieging Sea' – I found these poems very moving and very sad; they fed my own sense of sadness at having left Scotland, which was never something that I had planned. RLS's words drew me to contemplate returning home after three decades away:

The voice of generations dead
Summons me, sitting distant, to arise,
My numerous footsteps nimbly to retrace,
And, all mutation over, stretch me down
In that denoted city of the dead.

In the new millennium I started attending the annual Edinburgh RLS Club lunch regularly, often coming north to spend a weekend with my family, choosing that weekend in particular so as to fit in the gathering. I enjoyed these outings tremendously, and felt the pull of Scotland every time, willing me to return home.

In June 2004, having just shed six years of heavy commuting on the rails and roads of the south, I came north to visit the isles with my family and friends. I went on the RLS Club excursion to 'Robert Louis Stevenson's Earraid', driven to Mull by Catherine Home with Anne and George Gray also in the car. In spite of the multiple ferry trips we took that day, the weekend sticks in my mind as one of the best in my lifetime, with the wind blowing in our hair and the sky blue. Earraid, the little islet which features in *Kidnapped*, can only be reached by walking over at low tide; the welcome by the Findhorn Community could not have been better.

Not long after this I decided to return to live in Scotland, and once here I quickly realised that I did not know my own country as well as I had thought. I decided that every year I would go to new places so as to get to know it better. I did some of that exploring on my own, but some with the help of many RLS Club walking trips, where we visited places that feature in his books. Amongst the people who welcomed me to the RLS Club were Ian Nimmo, Alan Marchbank, and Gillean Somerville-Arjat.

I went 'On the trail of the Appin Murderer', when we visited sites around Appin associated with RLS's *Kidnapped*. My picture is on the front page of the RLS Club News, October 2007, along with my friends Wendy Rimmington and Richard Lungley. I also visited Oban, and walked and picnicked in the Pentland Hills near Edinburgh; and near Maybole in Ayrshire. I walked the coastal route from Cramond Bridge to the Hawes Inn at Queensferry which featured in *Kidnapped*. I visited Old Glencorse Kirk, and Colinton Manse and garden. In 2017 I went on a fantastic boat trip, organised by Rex Homer, from Anstruther to the May Island where we visited the Stevenson lighthouse. These are just a few of the marvellous outdoor adventures I enjoyed with the camaraderie of the Club, exploring some of the many Scottish places that RLS frequented in his youth.

I always enjoyed the many literary events I attended over the years at the Hawes Inn, at the Jekyll and Hyde pub in Edinburgh and at other venues. And I enjoyed the addresses by distinguished speakers at the annual RLS Club lunch. In 2009 the principal address was given by James Robertson, author of *The Fanatic*, a novel set largely on the Bass Rock – a subject close to my own heart, and to some of my 'Old Familiars'.

Cynthia Stephens (née Dale) was born in Edinburgh and studied English and Spanish at Newcastle University. She is a member of the Association of Hispanists of Great Britain and Ireland, and has written about Jorge Luis Borges. At present she is doing literary translation, from her seaside home in Dunbar.

Curating Stevenson

ELAINE GREIG

MY KNOWLEDGE OF RLS – in common with that of many others – was limited to *A Child's Garden of Verses* and *Treasure Island*. I was only introduced to him properly when I became responsible for the literary collections at Lady Stair's House (renamed The Writers' Museum in 1996), where I was curator for 20 years. During this time, I got to know 'my boys' – Burns, Scott, and Stevenson – extremely well. The museum attracted visitors from all over the world, most of whom had their favourite writer, and it was a pleasure to meet a wide variety of people, but it always struck me that, unlike the Burns or Scott enthusiasts, the RLS visitors were often as interested in the man himself as in his works. There was something about RLS, perhaps aided by the era of photography, which appealed to all ages and genders who found his life as intriguing as the stories he created.

The nucleus of the RLS Collection comprises items acquired by Charles John Guthrie, Lord Guthrie, a friend of Stevenson's from student days. On Guthrie's death in 1920, the items came into the care of the City of Edinburgh, before being displayed in RLS's birthplace at 8 Howard Place which had been purchased by the newly formed newly formed RLS Club. The house was devoted to RLS and many other items were acquired over the years. By the early 1960s, when film producer Walt Disney visited the house, RLS had taken a dip in popularity and it was decided to sell the property and give the items into the care of the City of Edinburgh for display at Lady Stair's House. Robin Hill, Assistant City Curator, was given the task of transferring and displaying the collection in the basement area where, although redisplayed several times since, the Stevenson rooms are today.

Robin was a great admirer of all things RLS, with a special interest in his French travels. He and his wife Barbara spent many holidays in France and had a great love of the Cévennes in particular. Robin was a great help to me as, even after he retired, he still came in once a week as a volunteer.

It was Robin who invited me to join the Committee of the RLS Club, being a long-serving member himself. Meetings were in the offices of Skene Edwards on Albyn Place, mainly because the Club Secretary was a partner there but also with the added link to RLS himself – Skenes, in a previous incarnation in Hill Street as Skene Edwards and Bilton, being where RLS did part of his legal training.

A resurgence of interest in RLS grew from the events and publicity organised during 1994, the year of the centenary of his death. I had the privilege of curating a major exhibition at the City Art Centre entitled *RLS: Jekyll or Hyde*? It was an opportunity to bring items from many of the places RLS visited, not least from the Stevenson House in Monterey, California. Kris Quist, curator there, accompanied the crates and I was delighted that I had the task of returning them, as it was a fantastic opportunity to see the collections in Monterey and in St Helena and make contact with other RLS enthusiasts.

The centenary brought many leading RLS scholars to Edinburgh and I clearly remember the pleasure of watching Ernest Mehew, Roger Swearingen, Robin Hill and Nick Rankin crammed into my small office poring over the fascinating and unique albums of photographs, taken by RLS and his family, which document life in the South Seas.

The redisplay of the collections and the renaming of the museum in 1996 allowed us to establish our team of The Writer's Museum Volunteers who were given special responsibility for welcoming visitors to the RLS rooms – a most dedicated and knowledgeable group without whom the rooms would not have been open to the public due to staff shortages.

The Stevenson collection has attracted many visitors over the years and from all parts of the world. A lot of 'weel-kent' faces have been keen to visit, too – ranging from *Neighbours* actor Terence Donovan and US singer, songwriter and musician Emmylou Harris, to the Crown Prince and Princess of Japan!

If I were to pick one object of special interest it would be the gentleman's wardrobe which was in Stevenson's bedroom in 17 Heriot Row. The item was given extra significance as it had been made by the cabinet-maker William Brodie – by day, the respectable Deacon of the Incorporation of Wrights, by night a housebreaker and thief – the inspiration for the exploration of the dual personality in *Strange Case of Dr Jekyll and Mr Hyde*, a theme which fascinated RLS. The wardrobe was given by RLS to his friend W.E. Henley when he left Edinburgh in 1887. It was subsequently purchased by Lord Guthrie and was one of the first items in the Stevenson collection.

Enquiries came from all over the world, often from biographers and publishers looking for photographs to reproduce. Occasionally, these were used in an inventive way. One journalist from *The Scotsman* chose the photograph taken of RLS, Fanny, Nei Takauti and Nan Tok in Butaritari, sitting on the grass with flowers in their hair. Picking up on the hippy look, when the black and white photo appeared in the newspaper, RLS was sporting a very colourful, Sixties-looking psychedelic shirt! I think this is why RLS appeals to the modern audience. He was not a typical Victorian – he would have been at home in the 1920s or 1960s... or now!

Through my work at The Writers' Museum and my involvement

with the RLS Club, I have come to admire Stevenson and enjoy his writings. I also appreciate the appeal which unites like-minded enthusiasts the world over – the RLS 'family'. RLS would be gratified to know that the Club which was founded to foster interest in his life and works is celebrating its centenary. His memory is secure in its hands – long may it continue!

Elaine Greig has lived all her life in Edinburgh, where after graduating she worked as a curator with the City of Edinburgh Museums service for 22 years, mainly at The Writers' Museum with its collection of RLS memorabilia. She maintains her link with RLS by serving on the Robert Louis Stevenson Club Committee.

Not 'Watching the Detectives'

MARTIN WHITE

'JUST COUGH AGAIN,' the doctor said. 'That's a nasty cough you've got there. I'd better up the dosage.'

Nasty cough; bloody cancer more like. Taking an aspirin would be more use.

Dead in weeks. Reduced to husk. Why is it so often the good ones that get taken early?

And she was a good 'un; guile, wit, charm in abundance. A campaigner for stuff – mental health, anything closing down, you name it. I first saw her in action after becoming an accidental Trustee of a local museum in Stevenson's childhood haunt of North Berwick that re-opened after many years of being closed. 'We need an authentic recording of World War I songs for this exhibition.' And £1,000 later we had a scratchy set of 78 recordings produced by some expert who usually works for David Attenborough – never mind that you could get the same off the internet for the price of a rewritable CD.

Some years earlier she'd been one of the driving forces behind the first and only annual RLS Festival at North Berwick. I never saw it but did see some of its aftermath – a video, pictures of children being entertained, of a gala dinner, of an exhibition. It even included the flag borrowed from the Speculative Society that had been on top of his coffin when he was buried in Samoa, along with other precious things. She was a great fan of Stevenson the underdog.

I was a bit baffled by the Museum making no mention of RLS at all. He did seem to be connected to North Berwick. Even allowing for spurious authentic recordings, his omission just didn't add up. I felt drawn by her enthusiasm, even from beyond the grave, to try to do something about it. I was sure that getting RLS the underdog his rightful place was exactly what she would have wanted. I wasn't well placed, but I did have time. My only exposure to Stevenson had been a faint memory of a plaque at the school we both went to. My father had given me *The Coral Island* by R.M. Ballantyne (who also went, as briefly as Stevenson, to the same school) and then *The Adventures of Sherlock Holmes*. *The Coral Island* could easily have led straight on to *Treasure Island*, but instead I followed the scent of Sherlock Holmes ever onwards to Agatha Christie and beyond, to the spurious trail of the detectives that 50 years later was being satisfied by endless repeats of detective series on ITV3.

Finding information about Stevenson proved easy; be it from his books, the biographies, the internet, the National Library, his complete letters, Yale university archives at the Beinecke, complete works on Kindle. The more I dug, the more I found his sparkling descriptions of places he had trampled as a boy. These were ideal materials for me to create an important piece of his life story through a set of interpretive panels. The Museum now has a good exhibition about the young RLS and memories of North Berwick, and like the 'popping rabbits' that RLS saw when he was there long ago, plenty of other elements have popped up since. Many of these have found their way into the www.mrrls.com website for even wider awareness and enjoyment for many others, young or old. And for me, a lot of fun, new contacts, new ideas, enjoyment of other loosely connected authors: Borges, Schwob, Montaigne, Hogg, and more. But most of all, a feeling of doing something much more worthwhile than 'Watching the Detectives'.

Not 'Watching The Detectives'

Martin White curated the RLS exhibition at the museum in North Berwick, East Lothian, and went on to provide the font of all RLS knowledge about that area through his website www.MrRLS.com. He is now aiming to widen its coverage to other parts of the Lothians.

RLS – Scotland's Greatest Writer?
CRAIG ROBERTSON

IN SEPTEMBER 2019, I was tasked with choosing three books to take with me to a desert island, one of those useful islands that come with early warning of shipwreck plus a library in the life raft. The occasion was a panel at the Bloody Scotland crime writing festival in Stirling. I had to debate my selections in a literary wrestling match with fellow authors Caro Ramsay and Abir Mukherjee.

Two of my choices – Flann O'Brien's *The Third Policeman* and James Ellroy's *The Black Dahlia* – were well enough received but did no more than hold their own against stiff competition. I had an ace to play though. With a smug flourish, I laid down *Kidnapped* by one Robert Louis Stevenson and was met with immediate murmurings of appreciation and spontaneous applause from the audience, and grudging curses from the defeated Mukherjee.

I was taken aback by the amount of love in the room for the book. I knew, of course, that it was an enduring favourite, but it had inspired a love of reading in me and subsequently motivated me to write. In my personal association with the novel I think I'd overlooked just how much it had meant to so many others.

Fuelled by the communal enthusiasm, I got carried away. I finished my testimony for *Kidnapped* by declaring Stevenson to be Scotland's greatest ever writer – something I'd had no intention of doing until that point. It could have been a fatal mistake, a point taken too far, but instead, it was a notion that was greeted with loud acclaim and no discernible dissent.

When the panel was over and the adrenalin rush left me, I had time to consider the claim that I'd made in both haste and bravado. Was Stevenson greater than Scott or Burns? Better than Spark or Hogg or Grassic Gibbon? Was he more accomplished than Barrie or Banks, Graham, Tey, Rankin, McIlvanney, McDermid, Mackay Brown, Welsh, Kelman or Gray? Was he better than those considered more literary?

The notion of literary fiction goes to the heart of Stevenson's standing as a writer because, after his death, it became fashionable to dismiss his work as romanticism or diminish it by labelling him an adventure writer for children, or, even worse, a horror writer. Even if there was merit to this, it would conveniently ignore the fact that he created two of the greatest adventure stories ever written as well as arguably the most resonant horror story of all time.

Kidnapped and *Treasure Island* are books for the generations, as thrilling and meaningful today as they ever were. *Strange Case of Dr Jekyll and Mr Hyde* is the definitive work on the duality of man and an intrinsic part of the modern vernacular. That such genre-defining works originated from a single author is remarkable.

I'm not convinced that the charge of romanticism bears too much scrutiny either. *Treasure Island* and *Kidnapped* are celebrations of courage and comradeship but they are also subversive tales of betrayal and torn loyalties. Stevenson never flinched from looking into the recesses of the human psyche, something that gives the lie to the lazy accusations of sentimentalism.

His novels are much darker and more complex than they might first appear – blurred shades of morality, peopled with flawed protagonists and continually poking a stick at the worst we can be. His short story *Markheim*, a precursor of sorts to *Dr Jekyll and Mr Hyde*, is a deliciously brooding tale of murder, introspection and evil.

Indeed, I like to think that if he were writing today, RLS would be a crime writer. All the available evidence points to this most likely being the case. Dark tales; an obsession with the internal battle of good and evil; a cast of imperfect heroes and irresistible villains; exploring the human condition while all the time being entertaining and thrilling. Sounds like a crime novel to me.

He also wasn't afraid to embrace the prospect of making money from his writing and enjoyed phenomenal commercial success as a result. That this made him a target for writers with loftier opinions of themselves said far more about them than him.

Even his critics would concede, if grudgingly, that Stevenson was a great storyteller, but would question if he were a great writer. Invoking the Monty Python logic of the People's Front of Judea – what else did Stevenson do for us? – not only misses the point about a writer's principal task, it also wilfully ignores the sheer quality of the man's prose.

Consider then Stevenson's acknowledged admirers; authors whose own literary status is beyond reproach. His international fan club included Vladimir Nabokov, Bertolt Brecht, Marcel Proust, Ernest Hemingway, Rudyard Kipling, Jack London, and Henry James. It was another devotee, GK Chesterton, who adroitly observed that Stevenson 'always seemed to pick the right word up on the point of his pen'.

Without excellence in prose even the best story is a fireside tale or a five-minute wonder. Stevenson's work endures because of his effortless ability to weave words sparingly yet with precision, passion, craft and sensory description. That's what gave life to his storytelling and created some of the most memorable characters and unforgettable passages in fiction.

The early scene in *Kidnapped* where David Balfour climbs the spiralling, unfinished tower of the House of Shaws 'in the pitch darkness with a beating heart' remains one of the most terrifying things I've ever read. Stevenson's power to hold captive the reader's imagination was peerless.

In my last novel, *The Photographer*, I have characters approach the old Templeton's carpet factory on Glasgow Green, the building foreboding and sinister in the gloom of dusk. I didn't have the words to do the moment justice, so I stole some. One character gazes upon the outlandish Moorish façade and is moved to quote Stevenson to the other: 'Some places speak distinctly. Certain dank gardens cry aloud for a murder; certain old houses demand to be haunted.'

The words, which came from 'A Gossip on Romance', were perfect for the situation. The skill and the poetry were his, the shameless larceny all mine.

For far too long, Stevenson was massively under-appreciated by critics, but I sense that has changed. Perhaps it has simply become impossible to ignore the weight of opinion and the quality of what he left behind. In both his charm and his darkness, in his storytelling and his prose, he is remembered and loved.

Scotland's greatest writer? Quite possibly. Scotland's most loved writer? I'd say most definitely.

Craig Robertson is author of nine crime novels, mostly set in Glasgow. A *Sunday Times* bestseller and international bestseller, he was shortlisted for the Crime Writers Association John Creasey Dagger for his debut novel *Random*, and for the McIlvanney Prize for Scottish Crime Novel of the Year. He is a director of the Bloody Scotland crime writing festival.